the glass collector

anna perera

ALBERT WHITMAN & COMPANY
CHICAGO, ILLINOIS

Library of Congress Cataloging-in-Publication Data

Perera, Anna.
The glass collector / by Anna Perera.
p. cm.
Summary: A fifteen-year-old boy lives amongst the rubbish piles in the
slums of Cairo and collects broken glass while hoping he will find a
future he can believe in.
ISBN 978-0-8075-2948-5 (hardcover)
[1. Poverty—Fiction. 2. Refuse and refuse disposal—Fiction. 3. Cairo
(Egypt)—Fiction.
4. Egypt—Fiction.] I. Title.
PZ7.P42489Gl 2012
[Fic]—dc23
2011022672

For more information about Albert Whitman & Company,
visit our web site at www.albertwhitman.com.

For Mum, my sisters and brother

"It is only with the heart that one can see rightly; what is essential is invisible to the eye."—Antoine de Saint-Exupéry

the glass collector

Chapter One
Aaron

"Cairo treats the dead better than the living."

Aaron is overwhelmed by the truth of what the man says as he pushes past. The words roll into him in a blind-person-seeing kind of way, because the stranger in the dark suit is right—the mummies and old bones in the Egyptian Museum are better cared for than he is. Inside there are plush rooms with air conditioning and marble floors for the sacred dead, while the despised Zabbaleen people are treated like the lowest of the low, left to live like pigs, scrabbling through the city streets for garbage to recycle.

Aaron walks slowly and painfully, trying hard to take the weight off his left knee, which is throbbing badly after a fall this morning from the pony and cart. The toe he jabbed and the elbow he bashed when he landed on the hot, potholed road hurt almost as badly and, for one awful moment, he thinks he'll just sink down on the pavement and give up.

He stops beside a stall selling King Tut replicas and papyrus pictures of blue flying birds, and stretches his leg, which eases the pain a little. If Aaron has broken a bone it'll be too bad. When he gets home the best he can hope for is to sleep despite the pain, because the health clinic isn't open every day. When it's closed the Zabbaleen have to visit the hospital, and Aaron won't go there after hearing his best friend Jacob's stories about patients dying from little things like a nosebleed or an ingrown toenail.

"And sometimes the doctors take one of your kidneys without you knowing," Jacob once told him.

Aaron has no idea where his kidneys are. Are they at the front or the back of his body? Through his dirty green shirt he presses down on the sponges of skin on either side of his navel but finds only soft flesh and a tender spot that wasn't there before. Another bruise from this morning, he decides, as it sparks the old ones to life and his whole body begins to throb more than ever.

He checks for the industrial-strength plastic bag that's safely tucked under his arm, then straightens his back and sighs. If he doesn't get on with clearing the last alley, which is still more than fifteen minutes' walk away at this slow pace, he'll have to find his own way home because his stepbrother Lijah can't be bothered to hang around for him.

With a grubby hand, he wipes hot tears from his face and makes a silent promise to get even. Lijah—the creep, the bully. What did he say to make his stepbrother shove him off the cart and into the path of a passing car this morning, almost killing him? If it hadn't been for the quick reactions of the man in the silver BMW, he'd be dead now.

"You all right?" The man had slammed on the brakes and jumped out of the car to stand over Aaron, who was already on his feet by that time.

Aaron's insides shake at the memory. The man had a nervous face—the vein in his forehead was sticking out and he kept glancing at his jewelled gold watch. He was rich and Aaron regrets leaping up from the road so quickly. He should have stayed where he was, pretended to be hurt, and asked for fifty piastres—at least. Instead he took to his heels to catch up with Lijah, who was ages away by then, not caring if he was dead or alive.

Aaron hadn't noticed the trouble with his knee at first. It was only when he tried to climb back on the cart that it started aching, and his toe began to throb and the pain in his elbow kicked in. All the while Lijah was staring ahead, as if nothing had happened. He was squinting at the road with his hard insect eyes, and when Aaron finally turned to face him Lijah said, "Keep your mouth shut or I'll kill you."

But Aaron wasn't worried by the idle threat. When Lijah was really angry his eyes popped out like bubbles. Only then was it time to run.

Jacob had once said, "The trouble with Lijah is he never dreams."

Aaron sort of knew what his friend meant and had agreed, saying, "Yeah, he's useless." It made sense that Lijah was stupid because he didn't have an imagination.

"He has got a bit of a brain, though," Jacob went on, backtracking, cushioning his comment.

"But it's up his backside," Aaron told him, "so it doesn't count."

Aaron smiles at the memory of Jacob laughing, his Adam's apple jackhammering in his throat. At least his friend understood something of what he was going through, of how tough life could be. These people around him on the streets of Cairo now, they have no idea.

Aaron glances at the sky to catch his breath. The closer he gets to the main road, the more it seems as if every car horn in the city is honking at once and the curling exhaust fumes are out to gas him to death. A blue tourist coach, with the pyramids of Giza painted on the side, moves alongside him as he limps past a burger bar, and when he looks up he sees a middle-aged woman staring down at him. She eyes him with a cool expression and he knows what she's thinking. He's seen that look a million times before. She's wondering if he's an innocent street kid or a homeless refugee, ex-mental patient, or some other kind of reject.

She probably thinks he's stupid and can't read or add.

She doesn't know that there's a primary school in Mokattam, where he lives, and that the clever kids can continue with their education elsewhere while the rest have to leave at the age of eleven to collect and recycle waste. She doesn't know Aaron wanted to stay on but had to help his mother instead.

Aaron stares back at the woman—at the slow way she

flicks her fair hair behind her ears. He stops dead in his tracks to watch the coach overtake him.

"I know who you are, lady, but you don't know anything about me," he mutters.

The coach pushes on and Aaron starts limping again as a sudden burst of exhaust fumes intensifies the feeling that his knee is about to give way.

This part of the city is always busy and, when he finally reaches the main road, he heads for the only safe spot to cross, which is a distance from the backed-up cars queuing to get on the ramp. Aaron gazes at the road as the traffic echoes around him. He could be standing on a thousand streets in Cairo, with the same four lanes of taxis, cars, and buses hurrying to nowhere, the same blank faces between him and the dark alley opposite. He checks that the plastic bag is still under his arm and the sudden movement aggravates the pain in his elbow.

He screws up his face in agony. But at least the bag's still there. A couple of weeks ago he'd dropped it without noticing and Hosi, his stepfather, went crazy when he came home with one less bag of garbage.

"Those bags cost money, you idiot," he yelled.

"Someone stole it from me," Aaron tried to explain. But it was no use; Hosi screamed anyway.

Staring out at the dirty traffic, Aaron's fury moves from the picture in his head of Hosi yelling, to the cars, then to the businessman beside him, who's puffing on a cigarette and tapping his scuffed-up leather shoes. Maybe he should pick another place to cross the street. By now Lijah has probably given up and gone back to Mokattam without him. While part of Aaron hopes Lijah will turn up, another part is too tired and in too much pain to care anymore.

Aaron turns his attention to the crowd gathering behind him. Emerald-green light shimmers off their dark clothes, sequins reflecting in the sun's rays. It's normal in Cairo—this city of magic and ancient mysteries—for rich and poor to stand side by side, to share the same doorways and buildings, the same streets, without ever really seeing each other. The congestion is building and Aaron's thin body aches with the impulse to hit out at something. Something big. Something that looks and feels like Lijah would be great. What would the priest back in Mokattam say to that, Aaron wonders. *Say a prayer? Ask for forgiveness?*

He turns to look at a woman in a blue headscarf. She's smiling down at her little boy as if she loves him more than anything in the world. As if he's the only kid who was ever born. The little boy clutches his mother's hand tightly. Aaron's mind travels back to when he was younger, because the woman looks a bit like his mother. Except she's dressed in a new galabeya, while his mother wore dirty rags every day of her life but one.

The woman smiles and Aaron is suddenly floored by the memory of the day his mother married nasty Hosi. For a second he brings up the picture of her wedding day—the only time she was able to rent a pretty dress. It was cream with lace at the hem and gold edging, and she looked like someone else in it. Someone he didn't know. Someone younger. It was hard to look away from her in that dress, dancing and smiling at Hosi, white ribbons swinging from her hair to her eyes. Aaron saw clearly then that she loved her new husband more than she loved him, her own son. That was the day she ruined his life. And when she died she left Aaron with a stone in his heart. A stone he's kept hard by returning to the picture of her on her wedding day, again and again.

But now she's dead, and he's stuck with Hosi and two stepbrothers. Stuck with a family he hates and it's all her fault. Lijah's her fault.

Lijah. How Aaron detests that name.

The sun burns into Aaron as if on purpose. Deliberately hurting him while he still waits for a gap in the traffic. The businessman steps on his cigarette and pats sweat from his neck, while the woman runs a red-nailed hand through her son's hair, pulling him closer to her.

The crowd pulses with irritation.

Everyone stops breathing for a moment when a black-and-white taxi screeches to a halt behind a yellow bus, but the gap's not big enough for anyone to get through. *Come on.* There's just one more alley to clear, if he can reach it. Another filthy alley in a city of tourists and people who'll never know him or how and where he lives. Yet Aaron has touched their dead skin cells on sauce bottles, tins, and old socks. He's wiped lipstick prints off wine glasses and tried on their old shoes. He can imagine their whole lives from the way they crush white plastic cups until they crack and split.

Sometimes he can feel them. Feel their breath on his neck.

Close by, the traffic on the ramp has come to a complete stop. Automatically, Aaron reaches to check for the folded

7

bag under his arm again, then glances at the tall hotel on the opposite side of the road. With its plain brown windows and discreet entrance, it radiates peace and quiet. He's never been through the dark revolving glass doors, and he probably never will, but the sight of them cools him for a moment as he imagines the air conditioning inside.

Aaron rubs the sting of exhaust fumes from his eyes—then blinks. Instantly his life stops. He blinks again, hardly believing what he sees. What is that? That—something—a woman—flashing on the hotel doors? A beautiful face on the dark glass, lighting up, then moving, now staring out at him. It's making him feel as if he's being lifted from his body and taken to heaven.

The traffic disappears as separate pieces—a face, a wing, a headscarf—float past him with a power so strong he can't look away. It's her, Mary, and it feels as if she's wrapping her arms around him as he gazes in awe at her soft face. But he knows that hotel well. He knows those dark swinging glass doors. There's nothing etched on the glass. No marks. Nothing. But her ghostly face floats from the door again and a powerful feeling that she's real, she exists, she's part of this life, part of him, overtakes Aaron and he falters.

The Virgin Mary, Queen of Heaven, is here in Cairo, on the glass doors of the Imperial Hotel.

And only he knows.

How can he explain what he's seeing? Who would believe him? He hardly believes it himself, and at the same time he also knows he's seeing something that doesn't really exist. Maybe the pain is affecting his mind. He never thought she was real—

just a story, an old story—until now. Shocked and confused, he thinks it's as if another version of himself is looking at a different world. A world that's changing shape right in front of his eyes. Her appearance must be a message. But what? And why him? He's nobody. He doesn't go to church. He never listens to the priest. Being constantly told what to believe, how to live, who to follow—all that gets on his nerves.

A shrieking truck shoots by, blocking his sight for a second. The sudden draught shaves his sore knee and he steps back, forcing his bare feet against the edge of the pavement. Aaron tries to make the vision disappear from his mind. *Go away!* It scares him.

He ignores the strange appearance of Mary by looking down at the oil-stained pavement. When he dares to glance back at the doors, expecting her face to have gone, he's shocked to see she's still there, staring out at him. Something—and it feels soft—just touched his heart. Even the sight of his ugly feet and the pockmarked pavement can't rub out the gentleness of her face. It just can't. The same feeling of being lifted from his body and taken far away returns, but stronger than before. Almost as odd is the sudden pang of hunger that gurgles a strange "yes" to what his eyes are telling him. And, when Aaron looks back at the doors, the beautiful, bright lights are even more amazing than he first thought. She's more perfect than ever.

Somewhere at the back of his mind are a thousand pictures just like the one he's gazing at: paintings, drawings, postcards, mosaics, statues, and carvings all exactly like this. Beautiful, strong, and powerful pictures of the Virgin Mary with her head to one side. They're everywhere and always she looks lovingly down, leaning gently, a scarf falling from her head to the sleeping baby in her arms. Staring at her, Aaron forgets his aches and pains.

For the first time since his mother died, Aaron feels loved, special, chosen.

Chapter Two
Lijah

Through Aaron's head flash the Nile, the Four Seasons, the Sheraton, the Marriott, the Hyatt—the poshest, most expensive hotels in Cairo. Surely those hotels are the right places for miracles to occur, not the silly old Imperial, which is only a three-star, and without any concrete security barriers or sniffing dogs to check for bombs. You can't even see the River Nile from there.

Aaron is aware of a feverish feeling that makes itself known by covering him in a prickly sweat. It's as if the sun's rays have reduced him to an unbearable-to-touch mass of flickering cinders. He turns slowly and looks at the crowd waiting to cross the road: women, children, businessmen. They wait with glazed, anxious faces. Sunken eyes. Nobody's staring at the vision on the opposite side of the road. No one can see it except him. The Virgin Mary is gazing straight at Aaron as if she's waiting for him, him alone, and it feels as if a thousand heavens are opening their golden gates. Just for him. But now and then, when something special comes to you, it's hard to believe it's really meant for you . . . Only saints see angels and God and Mary. Don't they? Is she showing him the light or telling him off because he has decided to get Lijah back once and for all? Or perhaps this vision is a sign to keep going because the world is coming to an end, which it will any day soon, according to Lijah.

Aaron trembles. The sounds of the city echo around him. The sun, sky, people, cars, buses, and taxis change shape as he gazes at her face. The filthy gutter beneath his feet is still there. Nothing's really changed but everything feels different. Less solid. Less real. Lighter. And when he looks at the hotel doors the outline of her form, painted in pastel lights, is the most beautiful thing he's ever seen, and it feels as if she's welcoming him as the colors change from pale yellow to a lost, un-pin-down-able red.

"Why?" Aaron whispers. *Why has the Mother of God come to me—a Zabbaleen whom everyone hates? No one will believe me. Miracles don't really happen, do they?*

He wants to point and scream, but he's a Zabbaleen and if he makes a fuss the police might come and carry him off. He knows the women in their headscarves behind him and the businessmen and the children and that old lady with the big yellow teeth and the tourists won't understand that what he's just seen is real.

As the molten cars screech past, the small flame inside

him grows. He's in a strange state of happiness and no longer feels like himself, or a Zabbaleen. But is Mary, Mother of God, trying to tell him to be a better person and pray more? Well, that won't work, because Aaron never prays, but still he itches for the chance to run to her, though now there's too much traffic in the way. Then, when he glances again—no—she's gone. The world turns solid and dull. The colors have disappeared. Where? How can that be? Maybe Mary didn't want anyone else to see her?

Come back.

The road closes in until a guy elbows him in the neck. Wobbling dangerously, he's forced to grab someone's arm. Trying to regain his balance, Aaron crashes into a small man who smells of fresh laundry. The guy quickly shrugs him off. Drenched in sweat, Aaron steadies himself, but now the vision has gone he feels heavy and stifled. Disappointed. Left behind and unloved.

If Lijah came round the corner on the pony and cart right now and said, "That's it for today," Aaron would forgive him for this morning; he's so eager to get away from here and home to Mokattam. But for this to happen, the bag under Aaron's arm will have to be filled and tied fast, and at this rate the sun will be going down before he gets across the road.

In the road, cars suddenly stop. One car in front has braked hard to avoid a flea-bitten dog that appears desperate to get killed. The dog wags its tail and wanders off, leaving behind brakes jamming, horns blaring.

It's the moment Aaron's been waiting for. With a quick leap, he grabs a red elastic band from the gutter and slips it on his wrist before diving between the slowing cars. He plunges awkwardly through the sound of horns, cackling radios and yelling drivers. He can see the dog a few paces ahead. Everyone dashes past him now as a man in uniform takes the center of the road, holds up a hand, and nods the traffic to stop.

Aaron ducks away from the screeching, chaotic cars, but the stench of exhaust fumes follows him when he reaches the dark silence of the alley beside the hotel.

His eyes take a second to adjust to the blackness and he catches his breath. A foul chemical smell greets him as he scans the piles of rubbish. A smell that suggests detergents have recently been sprayed here to disguise the filth.

There's tons of stuff here, more than he's seen in ages. Glass glints from piles of rotting noodles, chicken carcasses, paper serviettes, plastic containers, newspapers, tea bags, stale bread, and threadbare blue towels.

There's twice the usual amount of wine bottles, beer bottles, and broken glasses here, which means there was a big event at the hotel yesterday. Aaron's heart sinks at the thought of cramming so much stuff into the last bag.

A sick feeling rises in his throat, as if water that's gone down the wrong way is coming back up. Aaron blinks the rubbish away and eyes a small blue chair lying on its side. Great. But then he looks again: It has only three legs, the seat's split, and the side is cracked. It's no use to him. He rarely finds anything good in this hotel alley. The workers who tip out the rubbish take first pickings.

There may not be a vision of Mary here to help him but there is a way of touching broken glass, a way of picking up the sharp lids and bottles so you don't cut yourself, and Aaron's an expert. There's a slip of light glancing from a green bottle and for a while he forgets himself. It's no longer glass, not solid or smooth or real but just a feeling—a tickling feeling, like a feather landing in the palm of his hand.

He knows stuff about glass that no one else knows and he's only fifteen. Plus he knows other stuff too; stuff about what happens to light when you hold glass up to the sunshine on the horizon. How you can shape dreams out of red and purple reflections. How a certain shade of blue glass can make you feel peaceful. Yeah, that's right, peaceful inside and all over, when he . . . How can he explain? It's a bit like the feeling he gets when he stares at water—any water—but especially the waters of the Nile, which aren't even blue in this city anymore.

Aaron sniffs before unfolding the warm, thick plastic bag, swiftly slapping it on his thigh and shaking it out until it fills with air. Then, despite his aching elbow, and with a deftness that only a glass collector knows, he begins to pluck out green stems, smashed jars, pale curving triangles, wine and soda bottles that glint like giant pearls from within the stinking rice, bread crusts, and plastic spoons.

With the skill of a master pianist, Aaron waggles his fingers to pluck even the smallest bits of glass from the collapsing rubbish. It's second nature, this fast, easy scooping, because the glass feels soft as gum and his touch is so light, the sharp edges barely skim his leathery skin.

Aaron lets go of the wriggling tail of a disappearing rat and steps back to wipe his filthy hands on his filthy jeans. Rats are the worst part of the job and they're out in force today. Perhaps it's a good thing he's no longer hungry, and anyway there aren't any remains of pastries tempting him to eat. The rats have had the lot. It's just as well, because many times he's been ill after eating scraps from this waste pile.

He's supposed to clear everything, but there's so much glass today, he can fill the whole bag with it and leave the rest of the garbage until next time. Yellow rice and red sauce stick fast to his grubby jeans, arms, and rolled-up, faded green shirt as he grabs at the glass. Thinking foul things about Lijah keeps him moving. Then, as if by magic, the moment Aaron tightens gray twine around the rim of the bag, he hears, "Whoa." The pony responds by neighing weakly and Aaron can just make out Lijah's shape blocking the light at the end of the alley. With a swift tug, Aaron plants the bag on his back and, shaking himself straight to gather his strength, hobbles out to join his stepbrother.

The noisy traffic and piercing sunshine hit Aaron with full force as he swings the bag on to the cart, which is already crammed with bursting sacks. The glass tinkles and shatters further as it lands. Lijah doesn't look around as Aaron tries several times to clamber up to join him. Of course he doesn't mention what happened this morning. There's no point in talking to Lijah about anything, but especially not at the end of the working day before he's had anything to eat. Instead they sit in silence.

As they perch side by side on the pony and cart, taking the

waste home for recycling, a large grin breaks out on Aaron's handsome face whenever he pictures Lijah dead. He knows it's wrong to wish that on anyone, but he can't help himself.

The cars and taxis stream past, hardly noticing them. On they plod with a soft *clip-clop* that only they can hear, and inside Aaron's head is a picture of himself taking a bottle of poison to his own lips and pretending it's delicious so that Lijah becomes desperate to try it. So desperate that in the end he grabs the bottle and swallows the whole thing in one go, like he did with that carton of chocolate milk Aaron found in the doorway of the leather shop. Only the chocolate was safe to drink. It would be so easy to get hold of poison from one of the medical waste boxes waiting to be sorted at the other side of Mokattam. There are so many bottles of half-finished medicines there, his friend Jacob wouldn't mind him taking one instead of emptying the dregs down the drain as usual.

Yes, getting Lijah to drink poison would work nicely. The idea of him finishing himself off through his own stupidity is Aaron's best yet. What could be easier? Aaron could honestly say he tried to stop him from drinking out of the bottle but Lijah had taken no notice of him. Like always.

It might just work.

Another big smile is about to break out on Aaron's face when the flea-bitten dog he saw earlier jumps in front of a badly dented black-and-white taxi. In slow motion Aaron watches the taxi screech to a halt. The dog's feeble body crumples from the impact, splaying on his side.

"NO!" Without a thought, Aaron leaps from the cart, dodging a beaten-up brown car to get to him.

"Come back, you idiot!" Lijah yells.

Swiftly, Aaron falls to his knees to cradle the dog's battered face in his arms. Luckily, he's not badly hurt. The dog coughs with a gooey tongue and big teeth and wags his tail. Aaron helps him up, rubbing his hands quickly over his skinny, hot body to check for wounds. Then, leaning in to caress a ragged ear with the side of his face, he whispers, "Keep off the road. Stay on the pavement."

The dog bounces up, in the same way that Aaron had done this morning, without thinking. With an arm around his damp, hairy neck, Aaron gently guides him to safety while the taxi driver spits with anger.

"You're not going to live long if you do stupid things like that," Lijah crows when Aaron climbs back on the cart.

"Good," Aaron says, and today he means it.

Chapter Three
Shareen

The usual sounds of the foundry ring out to tell them they're almost in Mokattam. The second shift of collectors, who start at midday and return at seven in the evening, left here an hour ago. Different families work different hours, but seven hours a day, every day of the year, the Zabbaleen are always on the streets of Cairo, picking up trash to recycle.

Aaron and Lijah are struggling to stay awake as the pony turns toward the rows of glassless, roofless brick tenements that lead to the center of the village. This is Cairo's dirty secret: a hidden village built into the side of an abandoned limestone quarry at the foot of the Mokattam Mountain.

The noise of traffic dies away when they reach the oldest part of the village and pass under a high arch with dusty pillars leading to the tunnel of shops and stalls at the entrance to Mokattam. There are no visitors' cars today. No crackling radios or TVs. The silence is the thing that Aaron likes about Mokattam—that, and the low brick wall beyond the church where he sits to look out at the pigeon coops on the buildings that stretch into the distance.

The pony slows to a thirsty walk, head down, gray ears flopping forward. Turning into the alley with its overhanging tiles and dark doorways feels like turning into an underground canyon. Bags of garbage are piled high beside crumbling concrete walls and giant wooden doorways with Coptic crosses and faded pictures of Jesus.

The pony moves slowly past the wooden sign of St. George and more shops—a foundry, shoe mender, greengrocer, barber, all with crosses over the doors. Plodding on past stalls that sell stickers of Mary, statues of the Holy Family, clocks, clay lamps, and candle holders.

"Praise be to heaven," a man says, and Aaron glances at the scraggy orange beetle above his head that his friend Jacob spray-painted on the wall last week when everyone was asleep.

The village doesn't look too bad, but by the time the pony reaches the end of the first row of shops and stalls, a forest of tumbling plastic bags and rivers of rotting, stinking filth greet them. Alley after alley of desperate hovels stretch out in every direction. This is where the men and boys bring home the day's garbage and where the women and children shuffle through it for plastic, metal, glass, rags, paper: anything that can be sold for recycling. Some families stack the bags neatly against the walls, to make room for the next pile of rubbish to be sorted. Others haphazardly throw sacks on top of each other anyhow, before sitting on the uncleared remains of chicken bones, potato chip packets, broken toasters, and magazines, which spread from the houses to the street.

As the pony clops around the last corner, eight-year-old Abe dives out from a dark gully with a gray ball in his hand. His eyes light up when he spots Aaron.

"I've been waiting. Where have you been?"

"We're behind. Have to sort this first." Aaron waves at the bags of garbage bundled high on the cart. "I'll come when I'm done. Where's your friend Simon?"

"He's not back yet." Abe smiles. "Hurry up!"

Lijah doesn't bother to acknowledge him. Abe is considered weird for knowing everything there is to know about jellyfish. His mother keeps a black potbellied pig called Marris that she takes to church on a piece of string. No man will marry her because she won't get rid of the pig. Perhaps that's why she keeps it. Abe's her only child and they struggle to survive.

"Think of the bacon they could get from that stupid pig," Lijah says. "What a waste."

The pony comes to an abrupt halt outside a two-story concrete building that's covered in dirt. The middle of the downstairs room has no fourth wall and is open to the street. Backed up against the walls are the bags that have already been sorted, ready for the merchant Faisal to collect. He comes every thirteen to fifteen days and, with at least four to go until he arrives, the smell's overwhelming.

"You're late!"

Hosi appears from upstairs, a tin cup smelling of strong

21

coffee in his bony hand. Eyes on the bags, Aaron's stepfather counts them to check if they've done the whole round and not skipped off for an hour somewhere.

"It's his fault we're late." Lijah punches Aaron on the shoulder.

"Ow! That hurt!" Aaron twists carefully down from the cart to protect his knee. "I hate you, Lijah!"

"Yeah?" Lijah snarls, not daring to punch him again while he's working. That would annoy Hosi, who insists the work's done quickly and without interference because he wants it over with in the shortest possible time.

Aaron pulls at bags, hurling them at the three sides of the building as if he's throwing them at Lijah. The stabbing pain in his elbow isn't enough to deaden the hatred inside and he continues in a fury until everything's unloaded. With one bag already full of glass from the alley beside the Imperial Hotel, Aaron's saved himself some work, but with sixteen bags spread out waiting to be sorted, a hollow feeling rises from the pit of his stomach.

Lijah leads the pony it to the yard for a much-needed drink. The moment he's gone, Aaron's eldest stepbrother, Youssa, appears. He's a sad creature who smells of beer and loves to sleep. He never goes out on the cart and spends his mornings helping one of the Zabbaleen to brew a local beer that's sold by the cup to the desperate. With a whittled-down body and dead eyes, he nods at each of the fresh bags as if trying to count them. He usually does the minimom amount of work and then disappears back to his mat upstairs. Sometimes he doesn't even eat the food Hosi prepares for the family. He's not worth bothering with as far as Aaron's concerned. Luckily, he's quite harmless though, drunk or not. "At least it's not drugs," Hosi always says.

As Aaron drags the first bag to the middle of the room and unties the twine, he becomes aware of yelling from the building next door.

It's Shareen making a fuss about something. She's a radioactive force who drives everyone crazy with her need for attention, and her screeching now digs metal spikes into Aaron's brain. At just sixteen, Shareen reimagines her life as a movie crammed with prize-winning scenes. With luscious, long, curly black hair, little hands and dainty feet, a tiny waist, and a pointy, oval face, she's small and pretty, but her personality is larger than life. She can scream louder than anyone in Mokattam and even her father runs for the hills when she loses her temper. The only things that Aaron and Shareen have in common is the fact that both their mothers died when they were eleven and that she lives with her aging father in the same two-story, windowless slum as he does.

Aaron tries hard to ignore the racket but can't help swearing under his breath as he lugs bags to the middle of the room and empties trash out at their feet. It's the same routine every day.

Immediately, as they begin separating the garbage, Lijah gets into a fury. Sorting plastic is his job, and his heart pounds at the thought of the measly fifty piastres Faisal the merchant will pay for a kilo of it. Boiling with anger because the price will be marked up five times that when the merchant sells it to the manufacturer of blankets and other goods.

Paper and cardboard are Hosi's job and he goes into a trance when he's sorting. He is bent over with age and his hands have so many lumps and bumps they look like the paws of a goblin. Metal is Youssa's, but there's rarely anything more than tin cans to be found, so his job is just a minor nuisance in a life of nuisances. He moves in slow motion, with a wet mouth that is always half open. Glass is Aaron's responsibility here and he works hard. With clinks and rustles, sighs, and expert hands, he picks glass from the heap of garbage and flings it into a huge, empty bag behind him. Fierce eyes scan the decreasing pile for the items they want. Everyone bends and reaches, deeper and deeper, elbow-deep in filth and debris that smell like a sewer.

As the bags are sorted, noodles, tea leaves, soiled nappies, computer cables, and paper fly everywhere, hitting walls, jeans, and arms. The clink of glass, clatter of metal, rustle of paper and plastic ring out like scurrying vermin. Once done, all that's left is the rotting food, meat carcasses, and rags. Between them, in silence, they gather up the rags for the last bag before kicking the food remains to the center of the floor to send the rats running.

Being the lowliest member of the family, Aaron has the job of finishing the day's work by scrambling to pick up the last of the congealed mess—fish skins, sticky rice, bones, meat, and vegetables—and take it to the pigs at the other end of Mokattam. Sometimes he borrows Shareen's wheelbarrow. Sometimes they walk to the pig enclosure together if Shareen has nothing else to do. Sometimes, though, Shareen won't lend the wheelbarrow unless he pays her, so Aaron has to fill more bags and haul them there on his back.

Though Aaron can reasonably predict what Lijah will do next—Youssa too, and even miserable Hosi—it's impossible to know how Shareen will react to a request to use her wheelbarrow. The sound of her idly moving a wooden spoon around a tin saucepan tells Aaron this isn't a good time to ask. But he's reluctant to wait. He'd rather get the food to the pigs now and eat his own meal later than the other way around, because then he can avoid eating with his stepfamily. Cocking an ear to the sounds coming from next door, Aaron realizes that at least Shareen's no longer screaming.

———————

Gazing at her reflection in the mottled mirror on the wall, Shareen grabs a hank of damp, sticky hair from her neck and twists it into a bun before cooling herself by leaning back and letting it go. She pulls aside the cheap patterned green cloth that divides the room in two. On the floor are her mat and a pillowcase printed with a picture of a curvy belly dancer. She glances briefly at a poster of the Cairo International Stadium pinned on a box that serves as a table and, taking a precious tissue from a small packet, wipes her forehead.

The moment she returns to stir the rice through a mess of steam, her thoughts switch from wondering what it must be like to be cheered by thousands for kicking a ball into the air to her dream of becoming the prettiest bride in the history of Mokattam. Whenever she flashes up a picture of herself dressed in gold shoes, a silk white dress, her luscious hair braided with red ribbons, it's as if a ten-ton weight has suddenly been lifted from her head.

"Do you want to burn the potatoes?" Mahir, her father, leans over her, head tilted sideways from the steam.

"What?"

Shareen catches sight of his sticky-out ears and thin neck in the mirror and drops the spoon. Opening the oven, she swiftly picks up black potatoes with her bare hands, flicking them to the lap of her galabeya. Soon the meal of sweet potatoes, rice, and pale lentils from yesterday is served on metal plates.

As always, they take the food from the tiny upstairs cooking and living space down the concrete steps to sit in the doorway and eat while watching garbage being cleared and ferried around by their neighbors.

Next door she can hear Aaron aimlessly scraping the last of the food remains into the center of the open room.

"We have a decision to make," her father says, biting into the black crusty potato as if it's an apple and sending fluttering burned flakes over his chin.

Shareen knows what he's going to say and doesn't want to hear it ever again. At the same time she's pleased to see Aaron hovering nearby, trying to guess what mood she's in. It's a dance they do every day: The pros and cons of wheelbarrow lending—helping, ignoring, delaying, refusing—go back and forth between them with each sideways look.

"Time's running out," Mahir says.

"No, it isn't. Don't make things up!" Shareen hits back.

"Daughters shouldn't argue."

"Fathers shouldn't whine." Always one step ahead,

Shareen pinches rice into a ball with her fingers and deposits it on her tongue. "You can't talk about it until you buy me some sandals . . ."

"Where will I get money for those?" Her father frowns suddenly as the conversation veers away from his intended path. "What am I to do with a daughter like you?"

"Buy her more stuff," Shareen snaps back immediately.

Next door, Aaron turns away to pretend he's not listening.

"What with?" Her father sighs. "If you want things, then marry Daniel like I asked. He makes good money from the walking sticks he carves in the craft center."

It was all going quite well until that moment, but at the mention of the wizened, toothless Daniel, Shareen bangs her metal plate on the concrete step and jumps up, thrashing her arms about and hurling her long black hair from side to side.

"I WON'T MARRY DANIEL!"

"She's got the Devil in her again," Youssa shouts, and thunders downstairs to watch.

Lijah appears from nowhere. The whole street falls silent. That's Shareen.

Finishing the last mouthful of lentils, Mahir taps his plate on his knee before standing up to stretch his stiff limbs. Without blinking or showing any emotion whatsoever, he calmly wanders off down the lane, plate in hand, to visit Daniel, the man in question. Leaving Shareen to quieten down with everyone watching each stamp of her dainty little foot.

Aaron's fascinated and annoyed at the same time, until she turns to face him.

"And you . . ."

"Me?" Aaron raises his eyebrows. "What have I done?"

"You," she says again.

"Yeah?"

"You can shut up about the wheelbarrow!"

She tilts her head, pointing a finger at his chest. There are people here who can shrink Aaron to the size of a pea just by looking at him, but only Shareen can make him feel smaller than a pinhead.

"I didn't say anything!"

"Well, don't, then!"

Turning away, Aaron begins calculating how many bags are needed to clear the heap of food in the middle of the floor. Now the drama has finished, Lijah and Youssa disappear. Aaron glances over his shoulder at her. Not that he likes her, though he's about the only boy who doesn't. Even Jacob fantasizes that she's his, apparently.

The sound of rustling breaks out as people return to sorting garbage.

Shifting the food slop is so much easier with the wheelbarrow and now the fact that Shareen won't lend it means Aaron will have to load more bags and carry them one by one to the other end of Mokattam to the pig enclosure. If Lijah was allowed to leave the pony outside he could use the cart instead, but there are rules to obey here and keeping ponies out of the alleys and away from the cooking pots is an important one.

With a tired heart, Aaron begins scooping cupped handfuls of unrecognizable yellow and brown stinking glob into the plastic bags. He fills two to the brim before the smell overwhelms him and he's forced to stop for a second. Again he becomes aware of the pain in his elbow, which is now too old and constant to make him wince much, while his throbbing knee is hurting more than ever and distracting him. He tries bending it right back and moans softly.

Trust Shareen to lose it today, when he really needs the wheelbarrow. That's her all over—nothing but trouble.

Chapter Four
Abe

Before long Abe is beside him again with the soccer ball under his arm. He seems more anxious than ever for Aaron to come and play.

"What happened to your knee?"

"Lijah pushed me off the cart. I banged it on the road."

Aaron gives him a sad smile as Abe sets the soccer ball in a safe place to one side and starts to help with the food.

"It's OK," Abe reassures him. "We can play tomorrow."

"Yeah, sure."

"Are we taking this swill to the new place?" Abe asks.

"Yeah."

Aaron frowns at the memory of the Zabbaleen's problems last month, when government officials ordered the slaughter of all the pigs in Cairo as a precaution against an outbreak of swine flu. A procession of four cars and vans arrived in Mokattam to carry out the order, but they hadn't reckoned on the importance of the pigs to the community and the resistance they would encounter.

"They say it was you, Abe, who threw a brick at the van's window and smashed it."

"Nah, it wasn't me. There were loads of us crowding them," the small boy replies.

"The government said they'd pay after slaughtering the pigs, but everyone knows that's a lie. The priest says they'll be back to carry out the order. Anyway, what can we do with the rotting food if we don't have pigs?"

"Maybe goats would be OK?" Aaron says.

They stand back to wipe their arms on their jeans and eye the four bags they've filled. The smell is sickening.

"Simon's going to buy a jellyfish on the Internet," Abe says, his face lighting up with excitement, which makes Aaron smile as he drags a stinking bag into the limestone-dusted lane. Simon's one of the oldest and cockiest kids in Mokattam and Aaron's never understood why Abe wants him as his best friend.

"Where's Simon going to put the jellyfish?"

"I don't know." Abe frowns.

"You need a credit card to buy stuff on the Internet," Aaron warns.

"He's going to get one from somewhere." Abe almost trips on the bag as he positions himself to swing the slop on his back to allow him to head down the alley. "You'll see."

"Simon's never going to get a jellyfish on the Internet, or

be a famous soccer player and play for an English team."

"But he promised," Abe says.

"Yeah, but he won't."

Leading the way down several alleys to the pig shacks with Abe trailing behind, Aaron passes families lounging on the ground, feet out, resting after the morning's work and eating spicy noodles from plates on their laps.

When they arrive at the shacks, two sandy and three black pigs are sprawled under the crumbling, wooden shelters, which are held together with nails and wire. Shelters that are too small and broken to keep the sun from the animals' skin. The pigs are spread out in different enclosures throughout Mokattam, and the hotels and tourists of Cairo would go without pork, bacon, and sausages if it weren't for the Zabbaleen's pig-rearing.

"No one's filled the water up." Aaron bristles at the sight of the empty trough.

"I'll do it!"

Abe drops the bag and races for the limp, bent hose hanging from the tap. Swinging it around his neck, he twists the screeching tap until water starts to flow down his blue shorts and bony legs before stretching the hose to fill up the rusty trough. Aaron empties the waste from the bags into a heap beside the fence.

These pigs belong to four different families, but they leave their care to whomever is the last to dump rotten food here. The deal is that everyone fills the water trough, though. It's never been empty before, so something's gone wrong. Aaron frowns, then breaks into a smile, taking pleasure in watching the smallest pig snuffle his way through the overflowing water. As Aaron and Abe turn to leave, Shareen appears, pushing the creaking wheelbarrow.

"There you are again."

"What are you doing here?" Abe asks. "You're too late. We've finished."

"I wasn't talking to you." Shareen drops the barrow with a thud. "I've been looking all over for Aaron."

"We've emptied the food now." Aaron gazes in awe as she runs a dainty bare foot over the barrow's front wheel to display her new toenail varnish. The red color—dark and rich, the same shade as plums—shocks him. The thought occurs to him that after all her yelling and her father walking off in a huff, she'd calmly sat down to paint her toenails, then come to find him as an excuse to walk through the village and show them off.

"How do you get that stuff off your toes?" Abe asks, goggle-eyed.

"You don't."

Shareen twists her ankle up and down and from side to side, to give them a better view of her delicate foot from every angle, while throwing in quick flicks of her shiny black hair. All of this has the desired effect of hypnotizing Aaron and Abe, firmly rooting them to the spot, open-mouthed.

"You just paint over it when it chips. Malia's done ten layers so far, but her toes don't look good anymore. You can overdo things, you know."

Aaron and Abe respond to her pouty smile with a sneaking awareness that girls—any girls—can ambush their thoughts and feelings just by waggling red-painted toes. Luckily, Aaron comes to his senses and grabs Abe by the shoulder.

"Let's hope the football's still where you left it."

He strides ahead, arm resting on Abe's shoulder, leaving Shareen to straggle behind, clutching the handles of the barrow high in the air to allow for the best view of her feet as she trots along.

"Jellyfish were alive before dinosaurs," Abe announces.

"How do you know that? You weren't there then," Shareen shouts crossly.

"Leave him alone," Aaron warns. "He knows everything there is to know about jellyfish."

"Yes, shut up." Abe turns to glance at her. "For six hundred and fifty million years there have been jellyfish on earth, with tentacles longer than a soccer field."

"You expect people to believe that?" Shareen laughs, but her mind drifts off to imagine a huge, slippery jellyfish lolling in front of the goalposts of the International Stadium, hundreds of tentacles reaching across a sea of green.

"Have you had anything to eat today?" Aaron asks Abe.

"Not yet."

"Follow me. There should be some bread left."

Without another word they cut through an alley as the beautiful sound of the call to prayer echoes over the city. Eyes to the sky, Shareen follows behind, with a jellyfish fight playing in her head. They carefully avoid disturbing the heaps of stinking bags packed tight against the walls of the open-sided buildings and head toward the last lane on the left, where Aaron lives. By the time they reach home Shareen has vanished, after stopping to talk to a friend.

Aaron lets go of Abe's shoulder when they spot the soccer ball resting on the same spot on the stained concrete floor where he left it earlier. Abe runs to kick it into the air, but suddenly Lijah's there and belts it with the flat of his arm. The ball shoots to the ceiling, bouncing back with a thump. They scramble to catch it, but Lijah knocks Abe out of the way, grabs the ball with one hand, and tackles Aaron to the floor, kicking him in the side for good measure the second he's down. Lijah has only one method of communicating: his fists and feet.

Aaron curls into a ball to protect himself, but Lijah loses interest and walks off with the ball under his arm, smiling happily.

"Hey! Hey!" Abe shouts.

"Don't worry." Aaron picks himself up. "He only wants it because you're with me. He hates soccer."

But Abe's close to tears. Lijah's taken the only thing he owns.

"I promise you'll get it back."

Doing his best to reassure Abe, Aaron leads the way up the filthy concrete stairs to the muggy room where his family eats, lives, and sleeps. In a corner cupboard is a hole in the floor—the toilet. Four curling mats are thrown against three walls. A small gas stove dominates a tiny area full of bent pots and pans crusted with baked-on food. There's a blackened bucket and tap beside it and two threadbare towels on a nail. Soiled sweatshirts sit on top of a straggle of dirty jeans. Another bucket, a large metal box, a picture of Jesus on the cross, and an apple core are under the small open space that serves as a window.

Aaron drags the metal box out to the middle of the floor and edges off the lid with his fingernails. A whiff of stale herbs and sweet spices fills the air as it clatters to the concrete floor. Half-empty screw-top jars of paprika, coriander seeds, black peppercorns, and green cardamom pods roll from side to side, clonking against the sides of the tin. Paper bags of rice, lentils, falafels, three fat tomatoes, and a bottle of chilli sauce take up the corner spaces, along with a bunch of hibiscus leaves, a stack of flatbreads, and a box of eggs.

Abe gazes in amazement at the contents.

"How come you've got so much food?"

"It's Monday. Hosi buys everything for the week today. It will all be gone by Wednesday at the latest. Here."

In a flash he hands Abe bread, a tomato, two crumbling falafel and the bottle of chili sauce, then sits on the floor beside him to picnic.

"Wait a minute."

Aaron leans over to replace the lid on the box so he can drop his food on top before awkwardly getting up to turn on the tap and wash his hands, as the priest said they must before eating. But the dirt is too ingrained for the water to make much difference to the color of his skin, and the scrap of soap stuck to the sink is dirtier than he is.

Aaron shoves his mouth under the sparkling, warm water, gulping quickly before patting a dirty towel with dripping fingers. Abe's too busy pushing bread into his mouth to follow suit and is almost finished before Aaron starts. Three minutes later they're on their feet, wiping crumbs from their jeans, and Aaron smiles.

"You wanna sit on the wall, then?" he asks.

"What about my soccer ball?" Abe can't believe Aaron's forgotten about it already.

"Lijah's always hanging around near the church."

Aaron tries bending his knee once or twice before putting his weight on his left foot. It doesn't feel too bad, but the side where Lijah kicked him is tender to the touch. He tries not to think again about how much he'd like to kill Lijah.

"Don't worry," he says. "We'll find him. Do you know who I saw today?"

"No. Who?"

Flies track their footsteps as they leave the dark room and head into the harsh, airless heat of the afternoon.

"Mary, Mother of God." Aaron smiles nervously.

"The picture that Jacob's cousin Karim has stuck on the back of his cart? I saw it too. What's the point of putting it there? Someone's going to steal it, aren't they? I'd sell it if it were mine. Where did he find it anyway?"

Aaron was going to tell Abe the whole story of the vision he saw on the swinging glass doors of the Imperial Hotel, but the boy's questions make him feel suddenly tired. Torn between lying and brushing him off, he decides to keep quiet and just shrugs.

Once they leave the stinking alleys behind, the sweet scent of jacaranda descends. They walk arm in arm beside the cream quarry walls, which are decorated with religious scenes. Joseph, Mary, and Jesus are carved into the limestone to show the Holy Family arriving in Egypt after their journey from Palestine.

The vista of an uphill winding path, empty of filth, opens up like a magic walkway with small bushes and trees. The route to the church has an oasis-like feeling of peace and harmony. Its beauty is in stark contrast to the hellhole they've left behind and never fails to make Aaron smile ruefully.

Aaron notices Michael, the church's shy sculptor and artist, up a ladder with a handkerchief on his head, carving a new shape into the high wall with a hammer and chisel.

Aaron glances to the right at the vast church with its curved stone benches, enough to seat fifteen thousand people. Literally hollowed into the mountain, the church is the beating heart of Mokattam and sets the moral code for everything that happens here. *Do good and avoid evil. Don't steal. Don't harm. Don't lie.* The seats form a semicircle leading down to an altar that is carved on either side with scenes from the Bible.

Aaron and Abe watch Michael chip away, their eyes roaming over his creation to fill in the gaps in their minds. They conjure up hands and feet for the figure he's unveiling from the wall, and for a second Aaron wonders if he has the nerve to tell Michael about the vision of Mary he saw this morning. But Michael's too engrossed in his work to notice them.

It's a while before Michael shakes the dust from his hands and pauses to gaze at the marks he's made. By then Aaron has completed a huge Madonna for him in his head.

"Are you doing a carving of Mother Mary?" Aaron asks.

"Not this time." Dropping the tools in the flap of his dungarees, Michael turns to them and smiles.

"No?" Aaron's disappointed.

"Joseph?" Abe asks.

Moving quickly down the ladder, Michael lowers his eyes to the ground and walks quietly away.

"Doesn't say much, does he?" Abe sighs when he's gone.

"He once told me he dreams the whole thing first. That was ages ago," says Aaron proudly. "Come on."

They walk past flowering trees and a small stone table and benches where children are playing, and head toward the low wall beyond the church where they always sit. For the first time today, Aaron notices his knee isn't throbbing as much and for a moment wonders if a second miracle has occurred. But as soon as he sits down there's a bone-crunching noise and the pain starts up again. He's about to roll up his jeans to examine the damage when Abe yells, pointing wildly.

"There's a new one. Look! Over there."

Aaron squints, shading his eyes from the sun with one arm. Far below the low wall at the outer perimeter of the church, pigeons flutter across tenement rooftops that stretch to the horizon. But before Aaron can make out what Abe is talking about, a dark shadow appears beside him.

It's Lijah and his eyes are popping out like bubbles.

Chapter Five
Omar

Even straining his neck and leaning back against the wall, there's no way Aaron can avoid the fist that lands on the side of his head like the blow of a hammer.

He lets out a cry, covering his face with his arms in a panic, but Lijah's blood's up and he grins as he lands punch after punch until Abe yells, "Leave him alone, you bully," and kicks Lijah's shins.

The distraction gives them the time they need. Aaron grabs Abe and together they run from the wall, veering away from the open walkway in front of the church and the high limestone carvings and statues. Thundering past the playing children, they quickly leave behind the sweet smells of the flowering bushes and race down the hill. They run through the alleys toward the buildings where all the neighbors know their names and won't hesitate to shout at Lijah if they see him hitting his stepbrother.

Sweat drips from Aaron's forehead as he comes to a stop in front of his house. He gasps for breath, smiling at Abe, suddenly aware that although his knee's throbbing, it's not as bad as it should be after so much exertion. If he'd spent a moment wondering about the state of his injuries, he wouldn't have dared to run so hard and fast, which makes his smile even wider. Plus he's vaguely pleased that Lijah punched him, because he's learned that Abe, the kid he took for granted, is a lot braver than he thought, although he's worried for him all the same.

"Abe," Aaron says between gasps, "you're going to get it from Lijah now."

"Don't care." Abe flicks a fly from his face with a dirty, broken fingernail. "If I tell the priest Lijah's hurting a kid my age, he'll be in big trouble."

Aaron nods. "Yeah, that's right."

Abe charges into the stinking, open room, bags stuck to the walls like huge, dead bats.

"What's Lijah done with my football?"

"Come out tomorrow on the cart," Aaron offers. "I promise you by the time we get to the first pick-up—the perfume shop—Lijah will have finished you off or he'll be laughing so much at your nerve in coming that he'll tell you what he's done with the soccer ball."

"You think?" Abe comes back outside, presses his arm to his nose, and wipes it, revealing the small blue tattoo of a cross on his wrist that he was given at birth to show he's a

Coptic Christian like Aaron. "Hope you're right."

It's a fact that Lijah can't be trusted, but for some reason Abe has never been afraid of him.

Aaron can't help looking forward to the sight of Lijah's face when Abe jumps on the cart tomorrow morning. He's an innocent, gentle-looking kid with big, soft eyes who likes a good fight, though he rarely gets the chance to have one. Abe can win over most people in Mokattam just by smiling or talking about jellyfish, but there's one person who's on to him—his mother—and it's her screeching voice that breaks the silence between them now.

"Marris, come back!"

Turning quickly, Abe sees her wild black galabeya bouncing with air, slapping her as she dashes after the potbellied pig that's snorting and charging down the lane.

"See ya tomorrow," Abe shouts, running after her.

Aaron can hear Shareen singing to herself next door. Her voice feels close as he climbs upstairs to his mat. Only Youssa's here now, asleep on the grubby floor and probably drunk. Arms wide, feet out, a scratching noise rattles in his throat. It sounds like he's having trouble breathing. Falling in a crumpled heap of exhaustion with his fingers in his ears, Aaron closes his eyes before he hits the floor.

Aaron dreams he visits his mother. She looks different. He looks different. Her life has changed. She's in a plush room, surrounded by smiling women he doesn't know, and she tells them this is her son. They seem pleased he's come and ask him questions about his life, which he finds hard to explain. But whatever he says doesn't matter. They smile anyway.

The rising sun spreads a sudden burst of golden light over Mokattam, illuminating the dark shapes of children uncurling from the floor to face another day. Buzzing flies circle Aaron's head as he opens his eyes. Instantly he remembers the dream, which felt so real. With the sound of water drizzling from a distant tap and the clop and creak of ponies and carts making their way out of the village to begin work, Aaron wishes he could return to the dream.

He glances over at Youssa, who's making the same scratchy noises as he breathes and is still lying in the position he was in last night—on his back, arms wide, feet out. Hosi is facing the wall, snoring and hugging his knees. Lijah's beside him, head buried in his chest. For a moment the smell of sweating bodies overpowers the smell of garbage downstairs, which adds to the pinched-in feeling of waking up in the wrong place. Only the thought of seeing Rachel when he goes to fetch the pony stops Aaron from wanting to vomit.

Lijah's always the last to struggle up after a deep sleep. He takes his time coming round while Aaron's up and away from everything he hates, running through the dark lanes to the pony yard, with Rachel's oval face and almond-shaped eyes at the front of his mind. A slow simmer of excitement starting up inside.

Each day, by the time he arrives, Rachel has watered and fed four ponies with a spread of hay, equally divided between their feed bins. This is work she's done since she was eight and now, aged fifteen, she sometimes sits by the fence until the bins are empty and the sun's half waving from the horizon before she runs home to help her stepmother with breakfast.

Starting the day with the hope that Rachel might smile at him isn't a good idea, Aaron decides when he reaches the last corner. When she's not here, like today, his heart sinks and the rest of the day feels emptier than usual. Even though he's thought up a way to explain the lack of money in his pocket to pay her this week, it doesn't help him feel better. Rachel never complains when this happens, but the light in her eyes dulls and he knows she's disappointed, which makes him feel like a gutter snake.

The yard is always clean and newly swept. To say Rachel loves the ponies is an understatement. Unlike the nearest pigpen, which is dirty and bereft of anyone's real attention, the pony yard is full of hope, with its wire and wooden fences, straight nails, and metal poles, and the large ramshackle shelter. And it's all down to Rachel. The ponies regularly have their hooves picked out and every week she pinches the flesh on their ribs to make sure they're eating enough. Fresh water's always waiting on their return from the hot, dusty streets and many of the Zabbaleen say she understands ponies and they understand her because she's a bit of a pony herself.

It's true, Aaron thinks, that the way Rachel turns her head and stares with soft, deep eyes, plus the gentle whimper she makes when she moves around the yard, and then the sudden skips she does when she thinks no one's watching are all pony-like.

He decides to get to the yard earlier tomorrow. As he rides the cart back to collect Lijah, the low sun on the back of his neck, he sees Abe waiting for him.

Lijah's suddenly behind the cart. Aaron's and Abe's eyes meet for a second before the boys turn to face him. "And what are you doing here, kiddo?" Lijah asks.

"He wants his soccer ball."

"Give me a hundred piastres and you can have the ball now." Lijah grins. "I'm saving up to get married."

"But it's mine," says Abe. "Why should I pay to get it back?"

"Because you want it and I've got it!" A look of contempt crosses Lijah's face as he dares Abe to lose his temper. "And I *am* getting married."

Abe's sudden silence draws a few people from the neighboring houses. Sensing that a fight's about to break out, they wipe the sleep from their eyes and gather round, amazed that Lijah's picking on a kid now.

But no one had counted on Shareen coming up from behind to land a swift kick on the back of Lijah's leg, toppling him into the cart, where he almost smashes his head. It forces Aaron to quickly jerk back the strings to stop the pony from bolting into Cairo.

"Give him his soccer ball, you creep," Shareen yells at the top of her voice, her eyes blazing.

A wave of laughter ripples through the crowd as Lijah reclaims his manhood by struggling to straighten up and then marches off. Shareen follows him, hammering the back of his Old Navy shirt with her fists, screaming, "Where is it?"

Two minutes later she's returned, punching the gray football in the air. She throws it to Abe, who runs off kicking it from knee to knee.

"Lijah's waiting at the arch," Shareen tells Aaron. "I don't envy you."

"Thanks a lot." Aaron sighs. A graphic picture of being beaten to a pulp pops up in Aaron's mind. He's going to have to pay for Shareen's moment of triumph.

"I'll come with you if you like." Head to one side, Shareen eyes him cutely, adding a quick pout to prevent him from thinking for too long.

"Shouldn't you be at the weaving center?" Aaron's wondering why she wants to spend the day on the cart.

"I don't have to go in today. Anyway, I need to go into town." Shareen nods.

"What for?" Aaron asks suspiciously.

"Mind your own business."

Soon Aaron and Shareen are on the cart, sitting side by side as it creaks through the oldest part of Mokattam, where the smell of burned milk fights to overpower the stench of rotting vegetables.

Aaron glances at Lijah, who's standing in the distance, waiting by the arch that leads out of the village, and by the look on Lijah's face he's not happy that Shareen's on the cart. Girls aren't supposed to go out on the cart, but he knows better than to argue with her. She pokes her tongue out at him for good measure as she climbs into the back to make way for him.

Lijah has clearly decided it's best not to get tangled up with her temper again today and grabs the reins.

The noise of the city increases along with the fog of exhaust fumes and the heat of the sun as it slides up through the cloudless sky.

As the pony plods along beside slow-moving taxis and cars, pigeons flutter toward the silvery high-rises in the distance. The city of ancient mysteries opens up with the sudden appearance of statues with the heads of falcons and lion-headed goddesses with sun discs for hats.

Before too long, the cart comes to a stop in front of Omar's Perfume Emporium. Despite the ache in the pit of his stomach, Aaron recalls the night when the moon was large and low in the sky and his mother returned home to Mokattam and told him about Omar and the shop. She passed Aaron a stick of perfume to sniff. It smelled of a whole bush of roses. She described the glass bottles on the shelves and the relaxing atmosphere of the shop and . . . the next day she died.

Aaron glances at the wide, gold-tinted window beside the wooden doors and the narrow glass shelves heaped with bottles of every color and shape, some covered in delicate copper-colored nets. It's so beautiful, Shareen's eyes race across the window and crammed shelves. She's like a child who's stepped out of a cave and into a palace.

Afraid Shareen will forget where she is, jump down, and try to race inside, Aaron turns from the front of the cart to touch her shoulder and remind her: "You can't go in there. It's not open yet."

Then a car screeches past, making Lijah impatient, and he cries, "Get going, both of you!"

His sharp instruction force Shareen to uncurl herself from the cart and slip to the pavement. Aaron grabs a few of the folded bags and leaps down, then watches Lijah lead the pony along the edge of the busy road and disappear into the traffic. He'll circle the area while Aaron fills the bags, returning from time to time to collect them.

Lijah knows every secret nook and cranny in Cairo where he can tie up the pony and pass the time with a card game or tea and cigarettes with one of the refugees or street orphans. If he were to wait outside the perfume shop while Aaron worked, the police or Omar himself would soon force him to move on. The sight of filthy, dumb-looking Lijah sitting on a moldy cart held together with splints, string, and rust and attached to a feeble pony would do Omar's business no good at all.

"I'll help you."

Shareen follows Aaron down a long brick alley that is empty apart from four cardboard boxes. It's Aaron's favorite alley because the only smell here is of exotic perfumes.

"I don't need any help!"

He's eager to lose Shareen before he starts and seeing her standing there, arms behind her back, looking needy, annoys him. This is the only part of his work that he enjoys and having someone else here—especially her—is spoiling the whole thing.

He's thinking it's too early to spy on Omar selling his perfumes. Shareen searches for a reason to prevent Aaron from getting rid of her. "I needed to escape because Daniel was coming to the house after breakfast to give me a betrothal present."

"What? Now we'll get blamed for stopping that." Aaron shakes his head.

"You can't follow me around all morning. I'm working."

"I won't get in the way."

But she's already in the way and they both know it. When Aaron punches the top one of the four cardboard boxes lined up under the side window of the perfume shop, it tinkles with the sound of shattered glass.

"What's in there?" Shareen flashes a sweet smile.

Aaron flips open the box to show her. "Every day Omar throws out what the glass-blowers brings if it's not perfect. Any small crack in a bottle and it's dumped. If he thinks a stopper is a bad fit and needs an extra twist, he flings it back in the box where it came from."

"What a waste!" Shareen sighs.

"Some of the women can't cope with this shop at all," Aaron continues. "At least once a day one of them faints from shock, because the smells are really strong. The glass gets to them too. Omar hypnotizes them. They don't know what to do."

He's enjoying talking about Omar and he pauses dramatically.

"You're making it up," Shareen sneers. "Women don't faint because of a perfume."

"They do." Actually, it had only happened once, but Shareen's so startled Aaron decides not to tell her that. "*Some smells bring back difficult memories and glass is a mirror that shows you who you are,*" Aaron quotes, and flutters his hands like a magician who knows more than he's saying.

"That's stupid!" Shareen's not having it. "How do you know all this?"

Aaron points to the small open window in the wall above

the boxes. "I just wait here and listen."

Shareen looks at him with envy. She wouldn't mind hanging around here every day, listening to Omar.

"I stand like this . . ." Aaron flattens himself against the wall. Palms flat on the cool stone. "First, I go quiet inside. Then I don't hear the traffic, just footsteps, voices, the cash thingy, the door and that. Once there was a car accident right out front but Omar went on talking about how the pharaohs communicated with the gods. Sometimes Lijah doesn't come back for ages and when he does it's like I'm lost, just listening."

"Lost?" Shareen asks. She blinks and steps closer.

Stories and words that Aaron didn't know were inside his head spill out as he exaggerates wildly. "Sharing the scent of ancient oils and their magic is the way a perfumer kneels to serve his god."

"What god?" Shareen's jaw drops even farther.

"That's what he says, 'my god.' 'Come. Come. Sit down." Aaron imitates Omar ushering a woman to a cushioned corner bench before turning to his assistant, Bilal. "The first glory—go."

Shareen raises her eyebrows.

"That's what Omar calls the first faint—I mean swoon— of the day, and once, when I was staring through the open front door, I saw the assistant come in with a gold tray of tea in tiny pink cups with flowers on them." Aaron takes a deep breath before conjuring up the next bit of the story. "Mint tea!"

"How tiny were the cups?" Shareen asks.

"About this big."

Holding two fingers a thimble-length apart, Aaron can't help straightening his arm to add to the miniature, ladylike size of the bone china cups.

Shareen tries hard not to look put-out, but by the time he's finished telling her about Omar she's overflowing with jealousy, not just because of the rich lady shoppers and their cups but because of the exciting life he's been leading. Girls don't go out on the carts and she's never wanted to before, until now. She had no idea Aaron was having so much fun.

Chapter Six
The Pony

Blowing open his plastic bag while feeling puffed up by the effect he's had on Shareen, Aaron turns his attention to the contents of the crammed boxes. He focuses on the task of spotting and deciding which of the discarded bottles to take. Before tossing the chosen ones in the bag, Aaron checks each of them to satisfy his curiosity as to why they've been rejected. Carefully touching the first cracked, greenish bottle, which has three rows of golden metal weave around the stem, he spots a small dent in the base, which means the bottle, when filled with perfume, could roll from a shelf.

The moment his rough fingers land on the cool, smoothly blown glass, a feeling of satisfaction spreads over him. Aaron likes working out how Omar thinks. Imagining himself touching the bottles as deftly as the perfumer while noticing that this ones's wonky, that one's uneven, the glass is too thin here, or the surface cracks are too visible there. And all the time, slivers of light from the green glass turn yellow, then gold, then green again as the color blends and melts into the winks of sunshine coming from the edges of the alley.

That's the thing about glass, Aaron thinks. Even when it's old and chipped, it's somehow clean. The light leaves nothing for anyone to clear up.

The noise of zooming traffic fades and the sound of shattering glass increases as bottle after bottle lands in the plastic bag. With the sudden overpowering whiff of strange blossoms that might once have been used to bring the dead back to life, Aaron becomes lost to the world. Despite the push to do as much as possible in the least amount of time, he lingers over a heart-shaped bottle with an amber-colored stem.

"Give me that!"

Shareen's hands briefly touch his when she grabs the bottle. Aaron looks up blankly. He'd forgotten she was there. The surprising touch of her soft skin was as hot and sharp as a wasp sting. Not since before his mother fell ill has he been touched by a girl—or in fact by anyone who doesn't want to hit him. He stares at her, but she's caressing the bottle with love-starved eyes. She wants to own it.

"See . . . ?" Shareen asks.

Aaron lowers his gaze to the bottle. Yes, the glass-blower has left a mark on the rim, but it's a small one and hardly noticeable. Omar's getting fussier about which bottles he decides are worthless. Just as Aaron's surprised that Shareen noticed the blemish before he did, he's angry with himself for overreacting to her brief touch.

Suddenly a taxi screeches to a halt, letting out a stench of exhaust fumes. A tall, broad-shouldered figure leaps from the car to peer down the alley. Aaron can't quite make out the face but from the way he's standing—elbows out, hands on his smart navy galabeya—he's certain it's Omar himself.

"Quick!" Caught red-handed, Aaron swings the half-full bag over his shoulder.

Shareen grabs the pile of folded bags from the floor and shoves them under her arm. In her rush, she knocks over the unsorted boxes, which crash to the ground with a rattle of breaking glass as Omar gallops toward them. She glances back to see a smile as treacherous as quicksand on his face as he jumps over broken glass, his hands out to catch her.

The sight of the alley walls disintegrates as a shaft of dazzling sunlight hits Omar's contact lenses, blinding him, forcing him to pause and refocus. By the time he blinks a few times, Shareen and Aaron have gone.

They move like gazelles, the wide street juddering and thumping along with their hearts as they run. Dashing into an adjoining street, with huge grins pasted all over their faces, they dart between schoolchildren and push past shoppers. Their rasping breaths and pounding feet drown out the sound of the rhythmic clink of glass drifting from the bouncing bag on Aaron's back. Even the traffic appears to fall silent the second they stop beside a snack kiosk several roads away.

Drained of energy while trembling with laughter, Aaron can hardly take in the sight of Shareen beside him. In a sweat, cramped up and hugging the thick squares of folded bags to her waist, she looks at Aaron and giggles with sheer excitement.

"I'll have to go back and get the rest," Aaron says, swinging the bag of glass to the pavement. His knee throbs as he looks back the way they came. "When Omar's gone. No problem."

"Are you serious? That guy's a crazy man."

"He's not crazy, he's clever, and he chases me at least once a week," Aaron explains. "It's a sort of game we play."

"Has he ever caught you?" she gasps.

"No. That's why he keeps doing it—I suppose."

Sweat pours from Aaron as he swings the bag on his back again. At the same moment, a broad-shouldered man steps in front of him, shocking him into losing his grip. The bag crashes to the ground as Omar's black eyes bear down on him.

"Come back to the shop. I want to talk to you."

Omar's stern voice and firm gaze let Aaron know he's got him now and there's nothing more to say. He trembles as he nods an agreement. Meanwhile, out of the corner of his eye, he sees Shareen bolting down the street.

———————

There's a space at the far end of the perfume shop that is used for coffee breaks and storage. It smells and looks like a newly dug cave, complete with bare walls. Shovels and buckets that the builders have been using to dig below ground, to make space to store more vats of oils, are on one side. Leaning back against the uneven wall, on a stack of breeze blocks, Aaron wonders if there's a hidden burial chamber nearby, the sensation of being in a passage leading to a tomb is so strong.

Omar has left him here to attend to something and, as time goes by, Aaron can't help worrying about Shareen being alone on the street waiting for Lijah. Also, Lijah might just go crazy when she tells him what happened.

He can see that close by, behind the door and waiting to be shelved, there's a collection of rose-colored glass bottles that are filled with dark oil.

Aaron's heart beats faster and sweat sprouts like dew from his body. He's scared, but the excitement of finally owning one of these perfect perfume bottles proves irresistible. His expert fingers race over the tiny bottles and a few seconds later two are inside the wide pockets of his jeans.

Aaron fondles the bottles in his pocket while eyeing those still on the floor. There are so many he doubts Omar will notice that two are missing. Suddenly he looks up, biting his lip in terror at the sound of quick footsteps coming toward him. As the small door opens, he is aware of a strong smell of cedar wood before he sees Omar in a smart navy galabeya. For some reason the man's lavish leather sandals, studded with gold, prove what Aaron already knows: that Omar's an important man. He sways for a moment, with his hands behind his back, before opening his mouth to speak.

"Now listen." His hand out to prevent Aaron from

escaping, Omar sighs. "This shop—our family business—we can trace back to the beginning of time. Since the pharaohs, there's been perfume here."

Aaron raises his eyebrows. How does he know that?

"Our task," Omar goes on, "is to continue the practice of making the world more beautiful by spreading the power of these sacred oils, which are beyond the experience of humanity as we know it. You understand?"

"Yes," Aaron says, pretending. What does that mean? He tries not to bat an eyelid, suffocated by the overpowering smell of cedar wood, unsure of where Omar's going with this speech. A speech that has little to do with him stealing rejected bottles.

"The oils we use are distilled in the same way they have always been. They are part of Egypt, just as the cells in your body are part of you. In abundance these blossoms have grown along the banks of the river and been picked at the perfect time of the moon's cycle through the heavens. The glass-blowers who create the bottles come from the same old families too. We're connected by creating beauty. Adding to, not subtracting from, the world we live in."

Omar stops to gaze directly into Aaron's eyes. A powerful gaze that Aaron can hold only for a few seconds before looking away, embarrassed.

"You see what I'm saying?" Omar asks again.

This time Aaron doesn't answer. Head down, eyes on the earth floor, he has the sensation of headlights burning into his forehead. Shocked by the even sound of Omar's breathing and the depth of feeling behind his words, Aaron feels suddenly weak. This could go on for hours and Lijah will be in a temper, waiting outside.

Like Omar, Aaron loves glass and light and the colors that shine so brilliantly they're like something from another world. He wants to hear all of this, but when is he going to tell him off for stealing the bottles from the alley?

"You think that when you hold something in your hands, take it home, and put it in your house, that it's yours? Nothing on this earth belongs to you. You come with nothing. You leave with nothing. Things are just veils. Barriers to prevent you from seeing what's real."

In a fever, queasy and weak, leaning back closer to the gritty bumps of breeze block, Aaron can't think properly. His mind spins from pictures of the bags of rubbish outside, to Lijah, and to the bottles in his pocket. Then to policemen with guns—Omar's obviously waiting for them to come and take him away.

"You've gone green. Are you all right?" Omar whispers. He opens the door sharply. "Bring hibiscus tea with honey," he calls to running footsteps.

By the time Aaron gathers the courage to look up, a decorative round tin tray with a small gold china cup—not a pink one!—floats past his face as the assistant hands it to Omar. The unlikely combination of being caught red-handed and then being given tea to make him feel better unnerves Aaron.

"Drink this and go," Omar says. "But next time, think about what you're doing and whether you're adding or taking away from your own soul when you steal my glass."

The moment Aaron realizes he's been given a strange telling-off and nothing more, he unfolds his thin body, grabs the small cup with a rough, dirty hand, and gulps down the sweet tea. It's sickly sweet and makes him gag.

He puts the china cup down with a clatter, grabs the bag of glass, and darts past Omar. With a single leap, he's through the small door, racing past the glittering shelves. Barging through the big black doors, he bursts into the crowded streets of Cairo, with its honking cars and dazzling sunshine, and crashes straight into the side of the cart.

"Quick," he gasps. "There's a maniac after me."

Lijah takes off with Aaron's legs still dangling over the side of the cart, but the traffic is so dense the pony is soon trapped between two buses, like a slice of bread in a toaster. Before long they stop. Aaron glances back at the shop, expecting to see Omar and the assistant staring after them down the street, but the shop door is closed tight. He glances at Lijah, who gazes straight ahead at the traffic with a heavy, dumb expression.

In the back, Shareen leans toward Aaron and whispers, "What happened?"

Aaron shakes his head. "Nothing."

Annoyed by his lack of an answer, Shareen pouts at the passing cars.

There are two hotel alleys to clear before they can return to Mokattam and, as the pony lowers his head to plod down the busy street, Aaron notices that he's wobbling slightly as he walks. Pulling the load plus the three of them in this sticky heat is taking its toll on the pony's thin body and now there's a slight limp in his back leg.

"Did you give him any water?" Aaron asks.

A flicker of irritation passes over Lijah's face as he tightens the reins, taking pleasure in forcing the pony to go from a slow walk to an uneasy, fast trot down the middle of the street. The pony stumbles more than once, as if trying to get rid of the cart, and attempts to turn into the traffic instead of the pavement when they come to a stop outside the next hotel.

Aaron hurtles from the cart to the alley in a desperate bid to find water to quench the pony's thirst. With a *look at me* swing of her shiny hair, Shareen comes to life as she leaps down, hoping to find something expensive that a rich guest has accidentally thrown out.

Nearby, a talkative group of tourists spill from the hotel doors. One of the middle-aged men looks Shareen up and down as she runs toward the alley, eyeing her graceful steps and long, luscious hair and ignoring her filthy hands and feet and dusty, threadbare galabeya. Shareen pauses, catches his look and tilts her head to one side, which embarrasses him and his huge wife.

This alley's cramped and smells of old meat. Aaron fumbles through the rapidly decomposing rubbish like a madman, scrabbling for plastic bottles that might contain a drop of water. Sticky marmalade jars, cracked glass candle holders, burnt oven dishes, and a split juicer are flung to one side as he grabs at warm, blue plastic buried in the mountain of filth. Bottle after bottle is ignored until he spots the dregs of jewel-like water swimming in pale, dented plastic.

Shareen watches Aaron with a vague respect as he dashes

back to the street and pours the last drops into the pony's reaching, gasping mouth.

"Omar must have said something," she whines when he returns.

"Shut it!" Aaron turns on her. "Help me! The pony might die."

Once Shareen understands the danger of the situation, she sets to work. They pick their way through trash, searching for bottles of water like a well-ordered team. Aaron takes one side of the alley, Shareen the other, but anxiety spreads as they discover that most of the plastic bottles are empty, dry as bones. In a fury they bounce them at the walls and as time wears on become more and more frightened the pony's going to drop dead in the street from dehydration.

After a while they stop for a second and silently agree to bag the broken glass, jars, and burned dishes. Shareen squints at the light at the edge of the alley to check on the pony's hanging neck and moving mouth. Lijah suddenly twists from the sun and stares back, untroubled by the pony's fate or their distress.

"He doesn't care," Shareen cries, tugging frizzy hair from her damp neck and swallowing hard. She realizes she's as thirsty as the pony and hasn't had a drink since before they left Mokattam this morning.

"Hey! We missed this . . ." Aaron smiles as he twists off the cap. "Some idiot's only had a few sips."

"Can I just . . . ?" Grabbing at the bottle, she knocks it out of his hand, and the plastic hits the edge of a broken laptop before Aaron can catch it. But by then only a few mouthfuls of water remain.

Shareen leans flat against the alley wall. Will he lash out at her? She's never seen him lose his temper but suspects he might now.

"There's a bit left," Aaron says calmly while taking off.

A moment later, when he lifts the almost-empty bottle to the pony's mouth, Shareen starts to wonder what would have to happen to make Aaron show his anger. Everyone in Mokattam says that since his mother died he hides his feelings to protect himself. As they clear the rest of the alley and continue down the street toward the main highway, Shareen decides she agrees.

The few drops of water revive the pony enough for it to plod slowly toward the second-to-last hotel for some respite while Aaron works. Once this alley has been cleared, instead of heading to the Imperial Hotel, Lijah turns to Shareen, who's curled up on a bag, half asleep in the back.

"Get off! The pony has to rest."

"I'm tired. I've had enough," she grumbles.

"Shareen, come on," Aaron says.

Not wanting to provoke Lijah any further when his eyes are popping like that, Aaron's at the side of the cart in record time, waiting for her to get down. The high-voltage sound of a police siren helps catapult her to the street. The cart swiftly pulls over, along with honking cars and taxis.

Everyone swings around to witness a convoy of police cars heading in their direction. Instinctively Aaron shoves his hands in his pockets, ready at any second to jettison the stolen bottles of perfume, but the police cars sweep past in clouds of dust, surrounding a black Audi, which is safely cocooned in the middle of the huge escort.

Shareen screws up her eyes toward the sun to catch sight of the passengers of the Audi as it speeds past, but the glossy black windows hide them. She wonders what it would feel like to be in the air-conditioned car instead of out here on the hot pavement. Crossing the busy street, she's tired and fed up, but she can't help smiling with delight when the Audi and its police convoy come around the roundabout to a sudden halt outside the dark, swinging doors beside them. She's frozen by a rush of excitement when a young, good-looking man in a smart suit gets out of the back of the car, glances at her for a second, and jumps into the seat next to the chauffeur. He almost smiled.

Then the cavalcade continues on its way.

In the alley, as she helps Aaron by holding out the plastic bag for him to throw in beer and wine bottles, she imagines the man from the hotel is the son of a sheikh who's fallen in love with her—a poor Zabbaleen girl. Imagining holding his hand and sitting beside him on the black leather seat as the car shoots away, she can't help blushing when she thinks about what might have happened if he'd stopped to speak to her.

While Shareen invents, Aaron reflects. Swinging the clanking bags on the cart with hands stinking of beer, he pushes hair from his face to glance back at the glass doors of the Imperial Hotel. The smoky doors revolve as guests enter and leave the hotel, but the Virgin Mary is nowhere to be seen today. For a second his mind goes blank. A small voice inside his head doubts he ever saw her in the first place and his world shrinks with the thought that this road, these cars, that wide sky are all there really is to this hard, lonely life.

Back on the cart as they skirt the edge of the city, Aaron starts monitoring his stepbrother's breathing. A couple of times it seems as if Lijah might push him into the road again, so staying alert is always on his mind. By the time the silence of Mokattam settles on them like old sheets, Lijah has calmed down, Shareen is a princess in love with a man she saw for only ten seconds, and Aaron's lost in a vision he saw on the Imperial Hotel's glass doors.

Once the chaos of the main road is left behind, the pony begins to stagger, gasping heavily and barely able to move in a straight line. Aaron and Shareen get down and walk slowly beside the cart as they enter the village. Aaron pats the pony's drooping neck and hot ears, trying to calm himself by studying the tiny arrows of glass on the dusty ground that glitter in the sun.

Stumbling farther past a man bashing a broken cupboard to bits with a hammer, Aaron doesn't notice the pony's right knee buckling until the cart comes to a sharp stop. There's a flapping sound, mixed with a strained creaking from the cart, as the pony sinks to the ground.

Aaron quickly unhooks the shaft and the bags topple, thumping and rolling off the sides as the pony shudders. Shareen jumps clear of the crashing bags in time to stand over Aaron as he leans in and cups the pony's clamped mouth in his hands. Shareen watches the pony grunt a last breath and flop to the ground before scooting home as if her life depends on it.

The reins loose in his hands, Lijah can't believe his eyes. A pony is a precious animal that can't easily be replaced, and the fear on his face reflects what they and everyone watching is thinking: That family's finished now.

Chapter Seven
Concrete Walls

The lane is jammed with people climbing over filth and crossing themselves as they gather and mutter in singsong voices over the corpse of the dead pony. Eyeball to eyeball, they shake their heads as Aaron and Lijah wearily lug the fallen bags out of their way to unload what's left on the cart.

As the sun beats down on the pony's thin, bony shape, a doom-laden feeling settles over everyone watching. To lose a pony is too terrible for words. But by the time the stepbrothers fling the last bags at the walls of a nearby building, people's interest finally peters out. There's work to be done and they begin to wander off.

An eerie silence falls until the sound of wheels, echoing like a rickety train, starts up in the distance, getting louder as it heads toward them. Soon Shareen theatrically bursts into view, as if coming onto a stage, pushing the wheelbarrow with elbows akimbo.

"You can pay me later." Unpredictable as ever, Shareen touches Aaron's arm with the wheelbarrow's smooth, metal handle.

"Thanks," he says, and means it. "After we've figured out what to do with the pony, you might want to help us carry the bags home in the wheelbarrow."

Like a princess, she looks down her nose at him. "You'll be lucky."

Aaron notices her glowing skin, the strands of gleaming, curly hair plastered to her neck as she swirls her eyes from him, to Lijah, then to the pony and friends in the thinning crowd. Humming with satisfaction, she hugs herself at the sight of so much unexpected drama. But sadly her center-stage moment is cut short when the Mebaj brothers" cart turns into the lane. The Mebaj family don't swear, curse or drink. They're the opposite of Aaron's family.

Just before they reach the crowd, the elder brother pulls the reins and they rattle to a stop.

"What's going on?" He can't imagine what's behind the sad faces walking toward them. All he can see is Lijah, Aaron, and Shareen in the distance.

"Go back," Abe warns, appearing from a side alley. "There's something not very nice in the way."

The Mebaj brothers climb down to push through, curling their lips like pirates at the sight of the pony stretched out in the middle of the path. With only twelve months between them, the brothers act more like twins, and when one pulls a face, the other says what they're both thinking: "Get the pony on the wheelbarrow!"

The idea's too much for Aaron. It's not going to work. Staring at the pony's limp body, at the skin and bones swarming with flies, he can't bear to touch it. In a temper, Lijah wrenches the barrow's handles from Aaron and roughly guides it alongside the corpse. The animal looks ridiculously huge compared to the size of the barrow, which is less than a third of its length. It's a stupid situation. One or two kids laugh and issue instructions about the best way forward. But there's only one way to do this. With a superhuman effort, Lijah begins to swing the pony's hind legs in the air.

"What are you waiting for?" he yells at Aaron.

Having no choice in the matter, Aaron bends over the horse's chunky mouth and touches the hard skull.

"Not the head, you idiot," Lijah screams. "Your end."

Aaron drops the head with a thump and grabs the warm body. With a quick shuffle, he reaches under the furry skin and, swallowing his feelings of revulsion, grunts as he tries to lift the pony from the ground. It's heavier than he thought and he staggers awkwardly until Simon lends a hand by grabbing the front legs and twisting them to the sky. Swinging the corpse between them, they groan as they drop it on the creaking wheelbarrow. Most of the pony is over the sides: legs stretched out at an angle, jaw on the ground. Only by carrying the back legs in his arms, with Abe holding the head up by its ears, is Lijah able to manuever the wheelbarrow and drag the pony all the way to the yard at the edge of the village.

By the time the evening light fades and the sun goes down

in Mokattam, the pony has been delivered to the butcher, the bags have been wheeled home, and the rubbish has been separated into recyclable piles. The necessary work has been completed, but one awful meeting remains. Hosi was out this afternoon at the bone-fixer's house, having two teeth pulled because he can't afford a trip to the dentist. Only when his anger's been faced will Aaron and Lijah get a morsel to eat and a few hours' peace. Hopefully, Aaron will get the chance later to run and tell Rachel why the pony hasn't returned to the yard. She's on his mind, and the thought that someone else might tell her what's happened makes him feel so desperate his pulse starts racing.

While checking for the now-familiar bumps of the perfume bottles hidden in his pockets, Aaron gazes down the lane. Shareen and her father are nowhere to be seen. Abe and a few of the kids kick a ball at a concrete wall while Lijah sits, half asleep, picking his nails and breathing in the smells of other people's dinners. Abe lets the ball bounce from the wall and roll away at the sight of the thin, stooped figure coming toward him.

A shiver of expectation suddenly brings everyone alive. The gossiping stops as they watch Hosi getting closer. Mouth open, hands clasped in agony to the side of his jaw, he's on fire, and by the look on his face, he already knows what's happened to the pony.

"How are we going to live? How? How?" Dribbles of blood leak from Hosi's stained teeth and gums.

Although the past hour has been spent in peace, with hardly a word between Aaron and Lijah, a return to their usual hostility breaks out the moment Hosi arrives.

"Ask Shareen if you don't believe me. I tried to get water for the pony. Lijah should have got it, but he went off and left the pony to die of thirst," Aaron says.

Hosi's expression changes from fury at both of them to narrow-eyed hatred for his son. Lijah squirms at the force of his gaze. But learning the truth of the matter doesn't mean Aaron's off the hook and Hosi slowly turns to face him with the same venomous expression.

For the first time in Aaron's experience, Hosi believes him and not Lijah, but it doesn't make any difference. He clips Aaron on the side of the head. Cowering, rubbing his ear, Aaron ducks and gazes up at Hosi, shocked. His stepfather's lips are quivering and he looks like a baby about to burst into tears. With red eyes and a puffy, swollen face, he's shaking so hard Aaron wonders if he might collapse. If Aaron didn't feel the same horror and fear as Hosi, he might for once have hit him back.

Aaron shoots down the stairs and runs off down the lane. There's a lack of restraint in the way he runs; in the way his feet slap the ground before he fists the air to work off some of the fury eating away at his insides. As he races around each corner in the growing darkness, past every pile of rubbish and stinking slum, he searches for Rachel. She's the only person in Mokattam who can ease the horror of the pony's death. And Aaron has a present for her—an expensive present.

When Aaron reaches the yard, he's out of breath and the smell of dung mixed with hay brings on a sneezing fit. A storm of sneezes that threatens to drown out the growing commotion approaching from nearby. It's a group of girls, bunched up, crowded around one another, laughing and joking. The girl in the middle is Shareen.

Oh no. Not now. With two girls hanging on her shoulders and several others whispering in her ears, Shareen isn't trying to impress them. She's the natural leader and the group has no choice but to follow her when she comes to a sudden stop in front of Aaron.

She's clearly wondering if he's a suitable victim for a pushing-around session. Shareen slowly eyes her mates while Aaron scans the group for Rachel. She's not there. He glances over the fence at the three ponies munching hay and wonders if she's up at the church.

"No one's ever going to marry *you*, Aaron," Shareen starts.

A giggling ripple spreads through the girls.

Constance, who has a scar on her lip and gray-green eyes, clasps her stomach in preparation for a side-splitting laugh while they move in on him.

"Not like Shareen," a gawky girl adds.

"You've never kissed anyone, have you, Aaron? You're too scared, aren't you?" Shareen says. "Oooh, never been kissed and nearly sixteen."

"I have!" Aaron blushes, surrounded by mischievous faces as the girls shove each other to get closer still.

"My brother got married at fourteen," the gawky girl adds.

With the fence and feeding ponies behind him, there's nowhere for Aaron to escape to, unless he crashes through the girls' linked arms. They know he won't dare do that, because touching them would bring howls of complaints from everyone in the community and, of course, they'd run and tell the priest immediately. Aaron's their unwilling hostage and if *they* push or touch him, that's different because they're just mucking about, and what would they want from him anyway? Aaron suddenly places his hands behind his back to show them he's not intimidated in the least, but he swallows too slowly, giving them a reason to continue.

"Who did you kiss, then?" Shareen asks.

"I'm not saying." Aaron adds a vague, sideways grin, as if recalling someone special.

"I know who it was!"

Everyone turns to Malia as she wipes her nose with the sleeve of her galabeya.

"Go on, then, Malia . . . Tell us," another girl begs.

"It was Rachel."

Shareen nods.

"NO!" Aaron's horrified by the mention of her name.

"Found out. Found out," they chant.

"Bet you gave her a Coca-Cola to get her to kiss you." Shareen widens her eyes. It's the ultimate trick to goad him into losing his temper, but Aaron knows her too well. She's worse in a pack and, when he refuses to take the bait, she changes tack, secretly disappointed.

"Let's go and ask Rachel."

"How stupid," Aaron fumes. "Go on, then."

"We will," Shareen says, laughing for the first time.

"Yeah, well . . . 'bye." Aaron tries hard to come up with

something else he can say to stop her from embarrassing Rachel. But the truth is written all over his crumpled, anxious face.

It takes two seconds for Shareen to say what every-one's thinking.

"Aaron loves Rachel," she announces, with an edge of irritation in her voice.

His feelings for Rachel have been hinted at before and now they're out in the open there's little Aaron can do but die a small death and hope for a quick, painless escape, which is sadly thwarted by the sound of their hilarious giggling. Now they think he's pathetic and in love, the rumours will spread like wildfire through Mokattam and he'll never be able to give Rachel the bottles of perfume or look her in the eye again. Shareen was put here to drive him crazy and Aaron vows never to forgive her for this. Then another idea twinkles to life from the flicker of irritation that crossed Shareen's face earlier.

"Let's face it . . ." Aaron picks his ego back up. "Rachel's the prettiest girl in Mokattam. All the boys are a bit in love with her. Not just me. The other day Jacob said Rachel's beautiful on the inside too."

Outright fury flashes across Shareen's face faster than a guided missile.

"Well, no one's asked Rachel to marry her, have they?" She stoops to pick up a stone, examining it for a moment before suddenly flinging it at her target: the feed bin. The stone pings loudly. "Unlike . . . me," she adds firmly.

"Who'd marry Rachel?" Constance grabs a smaller stone, aims for the feed bin and misses. "Well, maybe Sami would!"

Everyone laughs. No one likes Sami from the second-hand electrical shop because he says unkind things about people. Aaron has even seen him refusing to help his own mother carry home a huge bag of flour: "It's not that heavy," Sami had said.

"She would never marry him," Aaron says, then sighs.

But no one is listening to him now. They're too busy competing to hit the target—scaring the ponies into stumbling backward from the pinging noises, ears pricked for further signs of danger. Now that the girls are pretending to have lost interest in Aaron, he grabs the chance to slip past them and creep away.

A shiver of relief runs through him as he reaches the pale, wide, dusty walkway leading to the church, and just when he begins to feel safe again, he spots his best friend. Jacob, the kid with the curliest hair and most clownlike face in Mokattam, is racing toward him with his head in his hands, muttering to himself.

"What happened?" Aaron grabs him by the shoulders.

Jacob's in shock, trembling, stuttering wildly. Immediately, Aaron spots the problem before Jacob opens his mouth to answer. Sticking out slightly from his arm, directly beside the edge of his elbow bone, is the point of an old-fashioned needle. Without thinking, using two fingers, Aaron tries to tweak the brittle tip from Jacob's smooth flesh.

"OW! You're not supposed to touch it." Jacob flinches as if he's been bitten by a snake. The curve of his arm is covered in scratches and red marks. "I was going to look for someone with tweezers to pull it out," he says. "Those needles were covered in blood. AIDS, hepat . . . ize, the lot. I'm going to die and so are you now."

"Nothing gets through this skin." Splaying his ridged fingers high in the air, Aaron almost blocks out the sunlight from Jacob's eyes, his hands are so big.

"I fell on loads of used needles," Jacob explains. "They're not supposed to put syringes in the bags. They should burn the used stuff, but they don't anymore. I'm dead, aren't I?" His clownlike face droops and his lower lip sticks out as if he's about to cry.

It's a nasty moment. Plenty of kids in the hospital-waste clearing area of Mokattam have died of fatal diseases. Everyone feels sorry for them. These families are so far down the pecking order that hardly anyone questions the details of the horrible work they do, or asks why so many suffer illnesses that could easily be avoided if the hospitals disposed of the clinical waste in the proper way. Medical-wasting is a job that gives Aaron nightmares. His hands go clammy just imagining the constant fear that Jacob and his family live with.

"No. No, Jacob . . ." Aaron starts, but then forgets what he was going to say. He's unable to take in the full horror of Jacob's pleading eyes because there she is—Rachel—coming down the wide path, dressed in a blue galabeya, calmly frowning, as if trying to remember something important. His eyes are fixed on the vision that's almost upon them. The last thing he wants to happen is for Rachel to run into Shareen and her mates.

It's not until Rachel waves at them that Aaron regains some control of his wandering mind. "See, Jacob, someone . . . who was it? Well, anyway, someone told me that most of those syringes are, are . . . yeah, they're used to stir the . . . the . . . red wine they give to the rich patients—whenever they run out of, er . . . spoons. Not all syringes are dangerous."

"Eh?" Jacob's more flustered by this mad explanation than he was by imagining an early death.

"Honestly, I wouldn't worry if I were you." Aaron slaps him on the back. "Hi, Rachel. Where you going?"

"To the church to say a prayer for your pony." Rachel gazes past Aaron in that self-contained way that scares him. Does she blame him? "He was my favorite—your pony."

Aaron follows her gaze.

"Why do you want to pray for his pony?" Jacob's baffled. "It's not sick, is it? Aaron? Is it?"

The dusty path seems to shrink and the distant towering hills push down on Aaron like a huge giant as he nods and watches the alarm creeping over Jacob's face.

"Yeah. The pony died."

"That's a disaster," Jacob says. "You've had it now."

"I know," Aaron says.

Jacob shakes his head. "I'm going to find someone to help me."

"Want me to come with you?"

Aaron is only asking to be friendly. He doesn't want to go. Doesn't want to leave Rachel here either. *Go on your own. On your own*, he silently prays.

"It's OK." Jacob grins. "Looks like you want to talk to

her." He makes a swift exit in the direction of the old part of the village.

"Do you want me to pray for the pony?" Rachel asks.

Aaron sighs. "What's the point? It's not going to bring the pony back, is it?"

Suddenly lights twinkle from the interior of the church, as if to say *you're wrong*, and he shivers.

"But praying will help it get to heaven," Rachel says, and smiles.

"How do you know that?" Aaron mutters.

"Everyone knows."

"Well, I don't. Here, you might as well have this."

Aaron fishes a perfume bottle from his pocket and thrusts it at her. His fantasies about how he was going to present it to her disappear in an instant.

The dark liquid slides around the rose-colored glass as she widens her eyes. "Where did you get this?" she asks, staring at the bottle but not taking it.

She isn't impressed. She's never impressed by anything he says or does. He might as well not have bothered.

"I found it on the street. Do you want it or not?"

Aaron's trying to act unsurprised by her cool reaction, but the force of his heart thumping against his chest gives him away. He starts to tremble unnaturally. Even his hand's quivering.

"Well?"

In silence they look into each other's eyes and the power there reels them together somehow. Linking something deep and unseen. When their eyes fall away, the sense of loss makes them instinctively glance back, but now, slightly afraid, their eyes slide over each other, as if neither of them dares spark that powerful feeling again.

Without a word, Rachel turns on her heel and walks hurriedly toward the church, leaving Aaron standing in the lengthening shadows of the low perimeter wall with sensations he can't account for.

Did she feel what I just felt? Why didn't she take the perfume? I didn't get the chance to explain. Why did she walk off without saying anything? I was being nice, wasn't I?

Time, space, gravity, the stars above, girls, Mokattam, the dead pony—it feels as if none of them really exist. Placing the perfume bottle back in his pocket, Aaron heads down the wide walkway, past the bright, open cavern of the church, which is empty, apart from three old women sweeping and cleaning the altar. Rachel isn't there. She's not praying for the pony.

Where did she go?

Aaron eyes the deep darkness beyond the low wall. A moonless sky envelops the distant tenements. Beams of yellow light from the glassless windows stand out like sheets of yellow paper stuck to a huge blackboard, which he stares and stares at. When, one by one, the lights go out, Aaron turns his attention to the hard earth beneath his feet, searching for a good place to hide the perfumes.

He considers the corner where the brick wall joins the high limestone. It's worth a try and he starts digging into the ground with his fingers. A side pit opens to reveal a concrete hole in the foundations the size of a small bowl. Thumbs firm against the bottom of the glass, intent on remembering the exact place, Aaron carefully pushes both bottles into the gap. It's the perfect place. He covers them with cakes of soil, which he carefully pats down.

On the way home, Aaron pictures the bottles buried underground, safe and secure like hidden jewels curled up in a secret burrow. His burrow. That night he falls into a deep, sweet sleep—a sleep that not even the smell of his moth-eaten mat or the sound of Hosi's snoring can disturb.

Chapter Eight
Saharan Sandstorm

The next days and nights pass by in much the same way until on Friday morning Aaron opens his eyes to the surprise of a film of sand on his body, hair, and hands. The wind from the Sahara has gathered up limestone from the abandoned quarry and the yellow desert sand has turned dusty white. The mat, floor, stove, walls, sink, food box, and old clothes have been brightened and look brand new. Even the empty cup and crushed cigarette packet beside Youssa's elbow are sculpted in sand. If Aaron hadn't gone to sleep with his face in the crook of his arm, his eyelashes would be covered in the same pale grit. Luckily, the whistling sound of the Saharan sandstorm didn't wake Aaron and cause him to change position when it blew through in the night.

Listening to the noises coming from next door, Aaron can

make out the swoops of a bristle brush that Shareen's using to clear the sand. The same *sweep*, *sweep* rhythm can be heard in every corner of Mokattam as women and children shake out the effects of the desert winds. Then Lijah's and Hosi's voices start up outside as the stink of garbage fills his nose. The memory of that wonderful feeling he shared with Rachel returns as Aaron stretches his arms. It's enough to make his life worth living, with or without the pony and despite the fact that Shareen and her friends are trying to wreck his chances with Rachel.

"Big John is richer than anyone in Mokattam," Hosi grumbles. His voice outside grows louder. "Tell him we're starving."

"What difference will it make? He won't give me any more free bread or tomatoes," Lijah says.

"For heaven's sake, what are we supposed to do? Get that useless idiot off his mat. Tell him to go down to the market and ask for the bad fish, the bruised bananas, and a handful of flour. Tell him to search the bins for something to eat," Hosi shouts.

The moment the mad activity of the lane reaches fever pitch, with the sound of ponies, rattling carts, and banging pans, Aaron forces himself to sit up. When he hears Lijah bounding up the concrete steps he jumps to his feet, quickly shakes himself free of sand, and runs to the tap to wash his face and hands and grab a few mouthfuls of water. He stifles the dread of another hopeless scrounging expedition to the city.

Aaron smears his mouth with a damp wrist and slowly

turns around, sensing Lijah waiting angrily behind him. By the look of him, it's clear he'd love to take out his frustrations on Aaron, but Hosi is outside listening. Not that he's concerned about his son's bullying, but he's impatient to eat and won't be happy if Lijah delays that.

They exchange cool glances.

As Lijah reaches for the dusty, blackened saucepan on the stove, which still contains a cupful of the green juice left over from the boiled *ful* beans they ate last night, the danger passes. Aaron had found the beans, still in their bag, at the doorway to the souk, and they'd eaten them along with the last of the soft tomatoes. It was the worst meal they'd had since the pony died. There are still up to two days to go before the merchant comes to collect and pay for the bags of sorted trash, and after that there's no hope of any more money coming in.

Lijah greedily slurps the green juice, even though there's sand floating in it. He's pleased that Aaron will have to walk the streets without even this tiny portion of sour liquid to keep him going. At the smell of it, saliva fills Aaron's mouth, and his stomach lurches as he watches Lijah licking his lips.

"Tough luck," Lijah says, before dropping the pan on the stove with a clank and swaggering off, scratching his head as if to prove he's got better things on his mind than food. The moment he's gone, Aaron can't help glancing at the saucepan to make sure it's empty. It's pathetic, he knows. The rough, black pan contains nothing but windblown grit. There'll be nothing there at the end of the day either if he doesn't find more than a bag of beans today.

Without any real hope, Aaron lifts the lid of the food box,

where a corner of moldy bread that's been there for weeks sits beside the same bunch of hibiscus leaves.

A groaning sound from the corner of the room startles Aaron as he clicks the lid of the box shut. Stirring from a deep sleep, Youssa blinks at the whitewashed, dusty room, scarcely believing he's awake and not dreaming. He blinks at the burst of sunshine coming through the hole in the wall and suddenly realizes where he is.

"Yay!" Waving a dusty hand, Youssa turns over and goes back to sleep.

The smell of his beery breath fills the room as Aaron crosses the dusty floor, stupidly trying not to tread in Lijah's footprints. It works until he gets to the bottom of the stairs and trips, making him angry, as if he's touched the creep.

Unhappy at the thought of more heat and dust and unkind people who pretend not to see him when he holds out a hand for money, there's a sharp pain growing inside him. Hunger. All the time he's searching for an unopened packet of something to bring back for the stepfamily, the smell of hot falafel sandwiches from the street vendors will be driving him crazy. Worse still, he'll be trying to resist the temptation to crash into the stall, grab some spicy falafel and run for it. Last time the vendor caught him, he pulled his hair, then kicked him on the backside. The day ahead holds little appeal, but there might be time to visit the perfume shop and drown in the flickering colors of the bottles in the window.

When Aaron reaches the lane leading out of the village, he sees a familiar sight. "Hey! Wait a minute. Hey!" A flurry of dust smothers him as he shouts to the Mebaj brothers, Joseph and Luke, when their cart turns into the lane. The brothers look disturbed to see him trying to hitch a lift from them.

"Please! We've got nothing left to eat," Aaron begs.

Joseph, the kindest brother with the big sticky-out ears, pulls on the reins, slowing down with a sudden creaking noise. Aaron exaggerates his begging face, emptying his dust-filled pockets to show there's nothing else there. The brothers finally relent and nod Aaron to clamber on.

"Thanks," Aaron says, and grins. His luck's in at last. Yesterday, when he shouted out, they didn't bother to stop and he walked all the way to the main road before getting a lift with Simon, the older kid whom Abe wants as his best friend.

Clip-clopping along the wide highway into town, Aaron watches the Mebaj brothers' strong pony endlessly twitching sand from its ears. Aaron feels sorry for it and is sad for his pony, which died of thirst. He shoves against the edge of the cart as if to push the hurt away. With his elbow on the rough, splintered wood, he stares at the mass of seething cars ahead. Why couldn't his mother have married ugly old Mebaj? At least he has money. And the family has goats and chickens too.

Leaning forward, Aaron eyes the leather straps on the brothers' big, fine watches. Their family are doing well in Mokattam thanks to the eldest sister, nicknamed Nefertiti because of her good looks. She married a wealthy Zabbaleen who owns the barber's shop, four pigs, and a truck with huge silver wheels.

Aaron glances at the younger brother, Luke. His neat hair hangs straight and loose like pieces of curtain. He's slightly better-looking than Joseph and for a second Aaron wonders if he wouldn't be a better match for Rachel. The brothers are more respected, richer, and come from a nicer family than he does. Aaron ends up thinking he might as well give up on Rachel while Joseph and Luke live in Mokattam.

He can't help wondering how his life would have been if his great-uncle hadn't left his small village and no-good farm in Upper Egypt to search for work in Cairo. The rest of the family followed soon after. Suddenly a putrid whiff of gasoline floods into the back of his nose, making Aaron suddenly angry at the unknown great-uncle who joined the Wahiya, the people who came to the city to get rid of the rubbish. In school, they said it was when the Zarraba, who bred pigs and fed them on the waste, began working with the Wahiya that they became known as the Zabbaleen.

If only his great-uncle had stayed where he was, Aaron wouldn't be here today. He longs to see the small mud house that his family left behind on the banks of the Nile, with mango, fig, lemon, and orange trees within hand's reach. He longs to catch fish from the river and take a donkey to the well with two buckets on a stick balanced on its back. In his mind, there are only hills, a broad blue sky, and the smell of blossoms beyond the mud house. No plastic, cardboard, diapers, and rotting food ever meet his eyes.

The cart hits a bump in the road and Aaron's thrown off balance, wobbling from side to side until the wheels putter on to another stretch of smooth tarmac. He glances at a round man arranging glass pyramids on a stall outside the mirror shop. Light glitters from the sunstruck mirrors and the pyramids twinkle like stars. He once overheard Omar say that the ancient Egyptians believed human beings would eventually become gods.

That's the thing about Cairo, Aaron thinks. *The magic's everywhere.* When the first visitors came here years ago they would kiss the ground to give thanks. Perhaps he'd miss it if he lived in a village by the banks of the Nile.

Once they reach the new shopping center with locked metal shutters, the brothers turn to see if he's ready to get down. It's written all over their faces that they'll be glad to get rid of him. Aaron barely smiles and jumps off the cart before it stops. He mutters his thanks for the ride as he takes off into the crowds.

The first alley smells foul. He can see combs, knife handles, broken latticework, and tin cans mixed in among disgusting piles of food remains and heaps of plastic bottles. A brief scan of the mess tells Aaron there's nothing to eat here. After a swift kick of a cracked white jug, he returns to the road and walks along, pretending he's not interested in the stack of fat oranges a street vendor is polishing with his sleeve. But then Aaron's practiced hand swings an orange from the stall and into his pocket.

Once Aaron is out of sight, the juice soaks his lips and the stringy flesh catches in his teeth as he bites and sucks like a wild animal. Never did an orange taste better. Never did he steal one as fat and sweet. Now the day looks good instead of hopeless.

Three hours later, Aaron has scoured several alleys and the Indian, Turkish, and Lebanese restaurants for something to eat, picking up a packet of spearmint chewing gum, two fresh meatballs, and a bag of brown-sugar cubes. It's not much and he's already eaten the meatballs and sugar cubes. Now he's enjoying the gum as he heads toward the square, chewing and popping it with his tongue.

Getting closer to the fizzy-drink stand at the crossing, Aaron eyes the cool box on the pavement that's filled with ice and shiny tins. His mouth waters as he slows down to allow a group of English tourists to reach for the special coin purses they keep hidden in their pockets. There's a perfect moment that always comes when Aaron knows how to get what he wants. This time it comes when one of the women changes her mind about the can she's chosen and the vendor turns to smile at her friend, who also changes her mind. In the split second of laughter that follows, Aaron ducks, grabs a Pepsi from the box, and races across the road. Splinters of ice bounce from his hand like in a TV commercial. The grin on his face is wider than the length of the can by the time he reaches the other side. He can't drink it quickly enough. But, out of breath, the first gulp fizzes up and down his nose like a million ants. He gulps, caught in a frenzy of swallowing and choking.

His stealing session picks up when he spots a white plastic shopping bag on the ground beside two mothers with strollers chatting on the street. Scented oils smother Aaron as he sneaks up on them. To distract anyone watching, he points to a fancy white car with one hand, while using the other to quickly lift the bag from the ground and hurry away. It's not until after he's dashed across the main road and down another street that, heart thumping, he stops to look back and catch his breath.

No one's coming, so it's safe to lean against a wall and grope inside the bag.

There's a heavy white cardboard box, a packet of oat biscuits, a jar of marmalade, a packet of cigarettes, and a newspaper. Not a bad haul. Sinking to his knees with the box, Aaron eagerly pulls it apart, hoping to find rubies or gold. Instead, layers of crackling pink tissue paper reveal an iced sugar cake with the name *Amira* written in pink swirls.

Aaron pinches his nose with disgust, feeling a bit sick. He's suddenly guilty at the thought of ruining a little girl's birthday, but then decides that if the mother was rich enough to have this cake made, she can easily afford to buy another one. Along with the oat biscuits, cigarettes, and jam, he has something to show for his morning's work. But it's not enough and he's out of ideas.

The crowds are building up. The sound of tinny music from the nearby crummy café tempts him to sit for a moment and listen. Maybe look at the paper for a while? But this part of the city is dodgy and he's scared the bag will be stolen by one of the street kids who work the area.

A man in rough jeans and a black shirt drifts over from the café. With gray skin, dead eyes, and lanky brown hair, he looks like a smoker. It's worth a chance. Aaron darts in front of him. Holding the plastic bag tight, he offers the man the expensive cigarettes.

"You can have these half-price. Interested?"

"Yeah?" The man grins with ugly tobacco-stained teeth. "Cheers, mate." He empties coins from his pocket and exchanges them for the packet. "Got any more?"

Aaron shakes his head. "Maybe tomorrow."

The man nods and walks away.

Aaron sighs. He can go home. Now he has enough money to buy rice, beans, and perhaps a few slices of liver that Hosi loves. Along with the cake, biscuits, and jam, that's more than enough. The family will be satisfied. Plus, soon the Mebaj brothers' cart will pass by the *shisha* bar near the perfume shop and if he's lucky he'll get a ride home.

Deciding he's done for the day, Aaron heads to his favorite place: Omar's shop. And with that decision, everything ugly and difficult is left behind for a while. He's free to dream now and a globe of spiraling colors forms in his mind. Smiling to himself, Aaron doesn't at first notice the Mebaj brothers' cart stop at the traffic lights a few feet away. It's only when Joseph calls out, "Aaron, hurry up!" that he sees them.

He runs and the lights change to green the instant he swings his legs over the wooden side. White bag tucked under his arm, he carefully pushes the garbage bags to one side and sits down, feeling pleased but fed up at the same time.

"Just had a call on my cell," Joseph shouts over the car horns blasting away in the background. "We're going back early."

"What for?" Aaron yells.

"Shareen and old Daniel got engaged!" Luke screams.

"He's sixty. She's sixteen. It's disgusting!" Aaron says, wondering why she's given in to her father when she swore she wouldn't. Perhaps she got tired of arguing with him and just shut up. Or maybe she wanted to get away from him and Daniel was the only option.

"I know it's disgusting . . . But he's got money coming out of his ears. It'll be a real feast." Luke turns and laughs, but his laugh is false. Too long and tight to convince Aaron it's real. Maybe he's jealous . . . He must be.

"It shouldn't be allowed!" Joseph agrees.

"Is she taking the wheelbarrow with her?" Aaron asks.

"Dunno. Maybe she'll sell it."

A veiled woman slips through the traffic, unseen. Several cars screech to a halt. She pauses, dark eyes flashing, then rushes to the safety of the pavement. Her near-miss stops the cart in its tracks, the jolt as abrupt as Aaron's surprise at the news of Shareen's engagement.

It'll be the end of her life. Like it was for my mother, he thinks as he traces the pattern of a knife in what's left of the sand scattered between the garbage bags. He's been here before, in a situation where everything's wrong but he can't do anything about it. For some reason, Aaron quite likes the thought of rescuing her. It might impress Rachel and make him look like more of a man to everyone in Mokattam. But since when did Shareen ever listen to him? "Leave her to it," that's what Aaron's mother would have said. But his thoughts are interrupted when he spots something interesting through a gap in the crowds.

"Pull up! Wait just a minute! Stop!" he shouts as they approach the perfume shop.

Luke is so taken aback by the sudden command that he pulls on the reins and the pony clops to a halt. Aaron leaps from the cart with the plastic bag of goodies tight against his chest and runs back a few steps to the richly lit perfume shop.

There's a small parcel in the doorway, stamped and ready for posting.

The last time Aaron saw a parcel here he didn't take it and he has regretted it ever since. Guilt churns his stomach for a second at the thought of Omar scratching his head and wondering where the parcel went, but he soon squashes it by reminding himself how poor he is, while Omar's so rich. Ducking into the huge black doorway, he is briefly aware of the multilayered scents that waft over him, then he grabs the parcel, stuffs it into his plastic bag, and runs to catch up with the cart.

The cart's in the distance now, approaching the roundabout, and without it Mokattam is a long walk home. The pony's being made to almost trot, the brothers are so desperate to lose Aaron after his erratic behavior. "You creeps," Aaron mutters. The white bag bounces by his side, but his luck's in and a bendy bus pulls in front of the cart, forcing it to slow down just as Aaron reaches the back wheels. As he jumps up he crashes into one of the heavy bags, which tumbles on to the street.

"You idiot!" Joseph hisses, angry at the sight of Aaron's happy face.

In a second they're both down and trying to avoid the screeching cars. Between them they manage to throw the bag back. It thuds as it lands on the heap and at that very moment Aaron spots a policeman hurrying toward them. There's no time to argue as Aaron leaps on the cart, though Joseph would like nothing more than to leave him here forever.

Packed tight and safely hidden from view between the

bags of garbage, Aaron rips Omar's package apart. Inside is a folded receipt for four bottles of lavender oil and lovely sparkling violet bottles that are decorated with sprigs of leaves with slim gold edges. Aaron holds one up to the sun and for a second the light sends a wide blue heaven over his dusty, dirty arms before he quickly stuffs the bottles tight in his pockets and wedges the receipt and brown paper between the bags—they're recyclable. He won't recycle these bottles. The glass is new; it's clean. And when the bottles are used up they will still be beautiful.

That's what's great about glass, Aaron remembers. *It's always clean somehow. The light leaves nothing to clear up.*

He's sitting in garbage, looking at garbage—scrunched-up paper tissues on the road, dirty paper cups with plastic lids, blue straws in a doorway. By the railing there's a curling newspaper and crushed cigarette packets. Everywhere he looks there are tin cans, polystyrene packaging, stray cardboard, white plastic, clear plastic, broken things, useless things, forgotten things. Debris. Rubbish. Trash. Junk. It's endless . . .

Chapter Nine
Engagement

By the time the pony clops to a thirsty stop outside the Mebaj home and they start unloading the cart, everyone's surprised by the silence. There's no singing coming from the church choir, celebrating the announcement of Shareen's engagement. No laughing and giggling from the pack of women who are sitting, peeling vegetables on the street. Worst of all for Aaron, there's no smell of roasting chicken or pork coming from the direction of her home. No banners or strips of colored paper have been strung across the shops, stalls, between the houses, or anywhere in Mokattam. And Jacob hasn't been out spray-painting their names on the crumbling walls.

Obviously something's not right.

Aaron gives Joseph a suspicious look as he jumps off the cart, swinging his white plastic bag. He's got it wrong. No party's in progress, but even though there's no smell of food, his mouth's watering just the same. Instead, he is greeted by the same tired picture of families fiddling with broken keyboards, bits of engine, and empty plastic bottles while they wait for the carts to return with the garbage.

"Hey, Aaron!"

Shareen spots him as he turns the corner for home. She is dressed in an old blue galabeya and her hair is hanging loose, unkempt and unwashed, and her toenails have only a few flakes of red varnish left. She doesn't look much like the happy bride-to-be. In fact she looks angrier than ever. Aaron picks up a touch of jealousy in the way she eyes him for signs of an interesting morning while she's been stuck here.

"Are you getting rid of the wheelbarrow?" Aaron asks.

He approaches her slowly to prevent the bottles in his pockets from clinking together. He's desperate to dump the bag and hide the perfumes.

"What? Who cares what happens to the wheelbarrow?" she says. "I'm getting married to Daniel."

"I was just wondering, that's all." Aaron sighs. "Where's the feast, then?"

"Why rush? I want a silk dress, my hair done, ribbons and that. He has to buy me a proper ring. Why should I jump when he says jump? I'm not going to." She twiddles her hair with her fingers and purses her mouth, determined to be awkward and not give in. "The party's on Saturday if you want to know."

"Don't do it!" The words spill out before Aaron can stop them. "You'll regret it. My mom did. Look what happened to her."

"Are you in love with me too?" Shareen isn't surprised by his outburst. "Well?"

A band tightens round his chest. He wants to run away. *Love you? Are you crazy?*

"I was just saying I don't understand, that's all. He's old and he lies. He hasn't got as much money as people think. Jacob told me."

"Jacob? What does he know?"

Aaron can see this conversation is pointless and now Shareen's annoying him.

She reads his mind and glances at the white plastic bag. "What's in there?"

Aaron is just lifting the bag to show her when Daniel, with a toothless snarl, creeps up to startle her from behind— but Aaron's eyes give him away and Shareen twists round.

"Go away!" She slams a fist on his shoulder.

"Don't speak to your love like that," Daniel warns.

"You're not my love," Shareen shouts.

Daniel's face changes from anger to joy. "I was going to give you the money for a new dress. It's just as well I didn't. I'll buy something for myself instead." Then, turning to Aaron, he smiles and says, "Keep away from her, boy. She's mine."

"Don't be stupid," Aaron says crossly. "You don't own her."

"Give me the money," Shareen begs. "Daniel. Daniel. P-please."

Now Daniel has what he wants: her undivided attention.

Aaron escapes. Their sharp words follow him home, taking up all the space in his head until the thought hits him that Rachel would never behave like that. Never.

Three minutes later, with heels in the dust and crouched over tin plates piled with rice and pieces of rich-smelling liver, there are satisfied chewing and swallowing sounds coming from Hosi, Youssa, Lijah, and Aaron as they cram food into their mouths. The flies buzzing around them are no competition for the speed of their fingers. Then there are cake and biscuits with marmalade to come.

It's almost too much for their stomachs to bear but they manage it, and snake-tongued Lijah gets to lick the remains of white and pink icing from the corners and lid of the cardboard cake box.

No one notices the odd clink made by the bottles in Aaron's pockets and, having changed into one of Hosi's ragged white shirts, the bulges are safely hidden from view. When it's evening, he'll hide the bottles in the cavity under the low wall. But first he wants to see Jacob and find out if he's going to die from the needle that was stuck in his arm or if they've taken his kidney without telling him. Aaron wishes he'd had time to see him in the last few days and regrets not looking for him.

With the sun high above him and the clatter of garbage being sorted nearby, Aaron settles back to read the newspaper. Too soon his eyelids turn heavy from gazing at the pages and, weighed down from eating too much too quickly, he's tempted to take a nap. Youssa's snoring beside him, leaning against a bag. Aaron fancies drifting off as well, but what about Lijah? He's pacing up and down. Uh-oh. Anything can set him off when he's slapping the wall like that. Jumping up from the warm concrete floor is a mistake, though. The bottles clink suddenly in Aaron's pocket. Lijah turns and stares, but Aaron's too quick for him. A hand on the perfumes, he dives past him, jumping over a dead rat and a bent coffee pot, and into the lane.

Aaron rushes past Shareen, who's now on her knees doing her best to clip her father's warped yellow toenails while her friends Constance and Malia pull horrified faces.

"Keep still. I'm not going to cut you," Shareen says sharply.

"You did last time," her father complains.

Rather you than me, Aaron thinks, burrowing a dark, slimy passage through heaps of bags and exhausted women. He wonders, as he slips past young kids swiping each other with computer leads, whether Shareen will be expected to cut Daniel's toenails when she marries him. He'd hate to have to do that. The picture sticks in his mind as he hurries down never-ending alleys to the path which leads to the medical-waste clearers' area.

Hot and tired, Aaron arrives at the darkest corner of Mokattam with the sound of cooing pigeons in his ears. There's no one around apart from an old lady sitting in a doorway. Aaron glances up at the tenements reaching for the sky. At the top are bare concrete floors littered with pigeon coops. When a roof covers a building, taxes have to be paid, so none are ever put on. He remembers being told that Jacob's was one of the first to go up, twenty years ago, to house the growing Zabbaleen population. It's a stained, red-brick slum in the sky. Aaron glances at the newer buildings that surround it. Faded, limp clothes hang from washing lines strung between the walls, while inside the rooms rubbish strays from every corner.

Aaron's in time to see Jacob coming home from the pigpens with an empty plastic bag under one arm. Even the hospital waste contains food litter: rice, beans, potato peelings, and sometimes burned bread. Always pleased to see him, Jacob gives a huge grin even though he looks a bit spaced out.

"Still alive, then?"

"The health-clinic nurse gave me a vaccination just in case." Jacob rolls his eyes and rubs his arm at the memory of the tweezers plucking out the broken needle. "It was horrible. I'm never going to that place again. Did you hear about Shareen and Daniel? What's wrong with her brain?"

"She doesn't know what she's doing," Aaron explains. "She hates him."

"Everyone hates him. He shouts you down if you disagree with him. Did you see the bruise on her neck?"

"No. Does he hit her?" Aaron's shocked to hear it, but there's something else that's bothering him. Jacob's on edge. He's twitching. His eyes are darting all over the place.

"I saw him squeeze her neck with two fingers when she spilled his tea this morning," Jacob says, then gazes at the sky, his feet, the next building, the sky again.

"Did he hurt her?" Aaron asks, wondering if the vaccination has made Jacob's eyes ache.

"I don't know!" Jacob scratches his curly hair in an odd, slow way, as if he can't quite get to his scalp, where the problem is. "I've still got that nearly full bottle of poison I told you about. Do you want to sell it to her?" Then he laughs and his big yellow teeth pop out of his mouth, making him look more like himself.

"She could mix it with chili sauce or black coffee," suggests Aaron. "He wouldn't be able to tell."

"I could hold Daniel's nose and chin while you pour it down his throat?" Jacob grins. "Hey, maybe it would be better if she marries him first, because if he *has* got some money, she can keep it." Jacob starts twitching again.

"Maybe give some to us," Aaron says hopefully.

Suddenly the old lady opposite starts wagging a finger and cursing as she struggles out of the doorway and hobbles away.

"Who's she?" Aaron asks.

"Fatima," Jacob replies. "Fatima with the Filthy Mouth— that's what they call her 'round here. Her husband and his brother died last year of that horrible disease. You know, the one I might have? They used to clear the private hospitals. They all sling stuff out that's not allowed."

"Hepatitis?" Aaron wonders what the symptoms are. Maybe that's why Jacob is twitching.

"Yeah. Fatima went a bit crazy after that." A wave of fear crosses Jacob's face. "Do you want to sit on the wall?"

"Maybe later," Aaron says.

He is watching a sagging cart with two teenage boys on it come to a halt. Instantly the boys begin unloading bags crammed with boxes. Boxes marked on all sides with the words "Bio-Hazardous Waste."

"What does that mean?" Aaron asks.

"It's dangerous, I guess." Jacob sighs.

"Why don't they burn it if it's dangerous?"

"You should see those hospital incinerators." Jacob's eyes fly every which way. "They're so old, they're nearly busted. Sometimes they break down. There's never a spare one. They don't have room to store everything and they don't want to pay the special companies to take the dangerous stuff away when we'll do it instead."

"What's in there, then?"

Aaron hasn't ever wanted to hang around in this area when the carts return. He covers his nose at the overpowering smell of old bandages, blood, and disinfectant that turns his stomach. A young girl, no more than eight years old, appears from the side of the building, holding her mother's hand. She is followed by two girls of about eleven and twelve, dressed in rags. The teenage boys nod at their mother and sisters briefly and then head inside for water while Aaron and Jacob watch the mother and girls start to break open the boxes to reveal broken plaster of Paris, cracked beakers, tubes, blood bags, and syringes. They pour the lot on to the street before sorting them into piles.

"Their home's on the ninth floor," Jacob whispers, and Aaron immediately understands that the families who live high up have to work here first before carrying the sorted bags upstairs for safekeeping.

Needles, scalpels, knives, and all sorts of other sharp things clatter from plastic, puncture-proof containers. Soon the path resembles a hospital that's just been bombed.

The only things missing are the dead bodies and walking wounded. Aaron watches in horror as small, innocent hands pick up used plastic syringes and throw them into a pile for recycling. The youngest girl smiles at him as if she's playing with dolls, not death, and the smell and silence of the afternoon heat press down on Aaron and Jacob like a cloud of sulphur as they walk away.

"Hey! I've been looking for you," a voice shouts. From the end of the lane, Abe breaks away from three of his friends the moment he spots Aaron. "Want a game?"

Aaron catches the ball and for a few minutes they kick it back and forth. But it's a half-hearted game. Aaron sees Lijah talking to Shareen in the distance.

"Everyone's after her now," Jacob says with a clown-like grin.

It turns out that Shareen's still the most desired girl in Mokattam and, because she's engaged, even Lijah's moving in. Aaron's sickened by the way he just pretended to touch her arm accidentally. What's more horrible is the fact that she's obviously enjoying the attention, and when Aaron sees Simon rush to join in with Lijah's teasing, he can't help moving closer to listen. Jacob and Abe go with him.

"Are you excited about the wedding?" Lijah smirks.

"I don't know," Shareen says, giggling.

"Daniel goes to sleep at seven o'clock every night," Simon tells her.

"Nah, it's six, you idiot," Lijah says. "I'd be worried about keeping your marriage together if I were you."

"Get lost," Shareen warns.

Simon bursts out laughing. "You're too late, Lijah."

"What are you doing here?" Lijah says to Abe.

"Nothing," Abe replies, kicking the ball at Simon.

Simon catches it and watches Lijah expectantly. A threatening atmosphere descends until Simon throws the ball back and an impromptu match breaks out, with kids appearing from the lane to join in on their way home from school for lunch.

Shareen is clearly crushed by the sudden lack of interest in her and, arms folded, slumps on the ground to watch, anxious for the stupid kicking to stop. At first she thinks Lijah just wants to show off, but the longer the game goes on, the more she sees he's enjoying himself, even though he says he hates soccer.

The only way that Shareen can cheer herself up is by imagining her forthcoming party. She'll have her hair in silky-smooth curls that fall over her eyes and earrings. With dainty shoes and a bright red dress, she'll be the prettiest girl there. The engagement party has given her something to look forward to and, though she doesn't have a dress or shoes yet, Malia has promised to do her hair and makeup. She's having a party and that's all that matters.

By the time Aaron and Jacob reach the open, clean, beautiful lane leading to the limestone carvings and statues surrounding the church, the ponies and carts have all returned from the first trip of the day.

"When I see tons of cartons, newspaper, corrugated boxes

and stuff, you know what I think?" Jacob suddenly pipes up.

"What?" Aaron asks.

Jacob blinks wildly. "That it's stupid. They turn all the paper into tissues and people throw them away and then we pick them up again."

"I know."

As Aaron settles on the warm brick wall and looks back through a haze of heat at the buildings, he imagines what Cairo would be like if, overnight, the Zabbaleen didn't exist. The city would soon drown in garbage crawling with rats and every kind of vermin. Stray dogs and cats would tear into the bags to eat maggoty meat and drag food across the roads. Disease would spread through every home and the tourists would stop coming. The city would soon collapse into ruin without them.

It's too hot to talk and Aaron doesn't have the energy to do much but sit here and dream. After imagining the destruction of Cairo, he conjures up a picture of himself working in—or, even better, owning—a perfume shop.

Beside him Jacob prays to find other work—something that doesn't involve medical waste. He'd be quite happy sorting paper for one of the wealthier Zabbaleen families who don't like getting their hands dirty by touching the rubbish they've collected. Anything would be better than wondering if a terrible disease is eating your insides.

"Someone said there's a new company in the city taking people on to collect printer trimmings from offices to sell for recycling. Do you think they'd have us?" he asks.

"Nah. Easy jobs like that go quickly."

Aaron glances at Jacob, who doesn't usually sit here for long. Naturally restless, he normally jumps up from the wall after a few minutes to wander round Mokattam, eyes down, looking for lost coins or anything else of interest, then returning half an hour later to tell Aaron what he's found. Right now, Aaron sees he's calmed down slightly. His eyes are half-closed instead of whizzing everywhere and he's stopped twitching. Even so, he wishes he'd go.

Aaron's busy staring at the cracked mounds of earth in the corner where the perfume bottles are hidden and wants to see if there's room to bury the four in his pockets. He doesn't dare tell Jacob about them in case he tells the priest they're stolen. Walls have ears in Mokattam.

Tiny beads of sweat break out on Aaron's forehead the longer Jacob sits there.

When Michael, the shy artist, nods to them, patting limestone dust from his jeans as he passes by, Jacob calls out to him, "Are you coming to Shareen's engagement party?" He can't resist asking, even though he knows Michael never does anything but sculpt figures from halfway up a ladder.

"No. No." Michael dismisses the question with a tired wave of his hand, as if the party is the last thing on his mind.

Aaron suddenly realizes he doesn't know anything about Michael. Whether he has a wife. Where he lives. Things he's never asked. But sometimes not knowing things feels good. Not knowing anything about him makes Michael seem more interesting.

Two minutes later, Jacob's on his feet, walking in circles. He needs to get moving. He's been sitting for too long.

"Catch you later," he says, and runs off.

At last he's alone. Aaron twists from the wall to the corner in a single movement, letting an arm slip to touch the bumpy ground. He glances at the open space beside the church. There's no one there. Aaron quickly scoops out the earth until the feel of a deep crevice, then smooth glass tells him the bottles are still there. Peering into the small space, he thinks there might be room for a few more and pushes the first two back to make space for the new ones. Soon he'll have enough to open his own perfume shop. He'll be rich like Omar.

A sudden breeze ruffles the flowering bushes nearby. Aaron glances at the empty concrete benches and table, then at the frescoes on the limestone walls to either side of the church. For a moment it feels as if someone's watching him. Someone who knows he's a thief. The pale outline of a carving in the wall of Mary, Mother of God, stares back and Aaron shivers at the idea she saw him.

It's then that he spots Shareen sitting in one of the open-air concrete pews, quietly crying her heart out, dabbing her eyes with a blue sleeve. Has she been here the whole time? He quickly covers the bottles with soil and walks over to the church, where she's bent forward, leaning on her knees.

"Aren't you supposed to be happy?" he asks.

"Would you be happy if you were going to your own engagement party in a second-hand dress?" she snarls.

What am I supposed to say to that?

"No, see . . . You don't care," Shareen sobs. "No one cares."

Aaron silently agrees and, glancing back over his shoulder, guesses she didn't see him burying the bottles or she would have mentioned it.

"I was sitting on the wall. How long have you been here?"

"I've been here since Daniel said that Seham—remember her? She was at school with us and got married last month. Seham wants to sell me her old engagement dress. Have you seen it? It's *brown*."

Glaring at him with blotchy eyes, she makes Aaron feel uncomfortable. He fidgets. Shareen's got nothing better to do than sit around here feeling sorry for herself, while he has to avoid being punched and kicked by Lijah before scavenging the place for food, with no thanks from anyone. If he walks away she'll accuse him of being mean, but if he stays she'll find a way to make him even angrier. Whatever he does, he can't win, and if he's the tiniest bit shifty she'll cotton on to the fact that he's done something he shouldn't have.

"Jacob had a vaccination after a needle got stuck in his arm," Aaron says.

"And? And?" Shareen sniffs.

Suddenly it occurs to Aaron that she treats him like a heavy-duty garbage bag: somewhere safe to chuck her rubbish when there's no one else around.

"Nothing," he replies flatly. "See ya, then."

He walks away. Behind him, he can hear the intake of several breaths that prove she's amazed he's just ignored her. Then she's on her feet, following him down the wide walkway.

"My grandfather once had a flour mill," she calls as Aaron quickens his step.

Ignoring her feels good, like the time he walked away from Lijah in the city center and turned down an alley he'd never been to before and came across a street parade with belly dancers, drums, and fiery torches. It felt as if he'd stumbled into a new world that was just waiting for him to arrive. But the moment the high walls and clean paths leading to the church are left behind, Aaron's forced to slow down to sidestep the never-ending streams of garbage, and Shareen catches up. She hasn't finished with him yet and folds her arms tight as she bolts past to stand in his way.

Aaron pauses to look at her. She seems more determined than ever to get his attention. The smell of filth settles between them as she eyes him with a new curiosity. Aaron's happy about something and it puts her off balance. Immediately, she goes into attack mode.

"Rachel said you killed the pony."

Chapter Ten
Hiding Place

A few minutes after five in the morning Aaron has persuaded the Mebaj brothers to give him another lift and he's back on the cart, clopping into town with the sound of the morning call to prayer in his ears. It's just getting light and the cart's loaded with empty plastic bags but they're not Aaron's. The Mebajs don't have room for his stepfamily's garbage so his hands are empty as they rumble along the street, with blue-and-white tourist buses and cars building up on both sides.

Aaron's mind returns to Shareen and what she said about Rachel. He hadn't answered her. Hadn't looked at her. Just walked away as if his body was moving forward on its own, her words circling him like snakes. And later, when he went to the yard, all he saw of Rachel was her disappearing home with a friend.

Not until Aaron's off the cart and racing along the steaming streets of Cairo does his anger with Shareen start to die away. Hurtling across roads and down long streets leading to the city center, all the while he's looking for anything out of the ordinary. Those café shutters aren't fully down. The beggar doesn't have his dog with him this morning. There's a new white jacket in the window of the clothing store. On every street there's a known face with a known past, yet Aaron doubts any of them have ever noticed him.

In his mind's eye he can see himself rushing past a fountain, a convent, a dye factory, several shops and offices, hurrying to the one place that can make him feel better. Once upon a time they used to throw trash in the Nile. Old TVs, ovens, sacks of building rubble, even swords. It's against the law to pollute the Nile, but many times Aaron has seen bags being flung there under cover of darkness.

On every corner is a new kiosk selling useless trinkets. It's garbage that people will soon throw away and Aaron despises the waste. Despises the need for this endless stuff that clutters up every street. Between the buildings, to one side of him, he glimpses the Nile. Arriving at the perfume shop, Aaron breathes in the smell of warm wood from the locked black doors. Hands on the delicate carvings, he presses his nose to the rough door and a faint whiff of paint leaks from the grains of wood. Letting go, he stands back to look at the shelves of bottles glowing from the windows on either side.

"There are at least twelve dimensions," he once heard Omar say. "It's possible to enter another world by feeling your way into it."

109

Aaron can easily feel himself into the glass. He's been doing it for years. He takes a few deep breaths and every cell in his body seems to flow through the glass and across the raised points, nail-thin, the crevices, gentle ridges and achingly round, smooth stoppers. He can feel the pale yellow glass turn white and the pink take on a bluish hue.

All the tiny details—black dots in the middle of the glass petals, ivy on the necks of the bottles—jump out like living plants, prickly, sharp, and soft. His fingers tingle at the shapes on the surface of the glass. At the same time, when he's focusing hard, what's real alters. After being part of the glass for a while, he can tell when a bottle has been coated twice with a slightly different shade to make it shimmer. Sometimes the colors, especially the ruby reds, are dense at the base and fade to white at the top of the bottle.

When Aaron is lost in his dreams, everything falls away. The screeching traffic and boom of overhead planes disappear, along with the smell of fumes. He realizes that he felt the same way when he saw the vision of Mary on the doors of the Imperial Hotel and again when he looked into Rachel's almond eyes.

Love.

Love is all he ever wants to feel.

Perhaps there are people who always feel it. Perhaps Omar, with his deep, calm voice, always feels like this. The possibility stays with Aaron until he slips into the alley beside the shop. The cool darkness rolls over his head like a veil and a smell of dead birds fills the air. Beside the wall is an empty, ripped-apart cardboard box, which makes Aaron think someone's already been here, searching for rejected bottles. This alley is *his* territory. In a temper he kicks the handle of the side door, which springs open with a sudden click.

Aaron shivers and looks around him. In the block of sunlight at one end of the alley, he can see people passing by on the street, hurrying to work. No one glances his way. Silent and still, he stands watching and waiting, one hand flat on the cool, chalky wall. There's never anyone at the shop before eight in the morning and it's just after six. Someone's forgotten to lock the door.

Aaron's thoughts come thick and fast. He's rooted to the spot, but with no sound coming from inside he slowly pushes the door wide open with a fist. Creaking loudly, it sounds and feels like an old church door. A rich red tasseled mat comes into view on the polished tiled floor inside.

Immediately Aaron wonders how much the mat's worth and reminds himself to take that or another one on the way out. A strong smell of incense greets him, making him feel invincible as he steps inside. The traffic sounds fade to silence. High up on the wall is a painting of Horus, the God of War. Aaron glances at the falcon head for a second, then to the door leading to the back room where he spoke to Omar, before turning from the corridor to the shop floor.

There's a hissing noise coming from an overhead pipe. Being inside the shop feels strange. Aaron wanders from corner to corner. The plastic bag under his arm makes a small crackling sound when he bends down to touch the red cushions on the benches. Eyeing the expensive rugs and brass lamps, he realizes he could fit quite a lot of stuff in the bag, but he is distracted by hundreds of twinkling bottles lined up beautifully along the shelves. He's torn between stealing them or the rugs and lamps.

The most expensive perfumes on the middle shelves are in gilt-edged glass. Aaron picks one up and turns it over. There are tiny engraved numbers on the base to identify the glass-blower and his company. Aaron pops the bottle in his pocket, along with two more with gold net wrapped around the rose-colored glass. When his pockets are bulging, he unplugs the brass lamp from the wall and drops it in the bag, then rolls up a silvery-gray rug and stuffs it on top. He's about to reach for a small brass incense burner when he hears footsteps.

"Did you leave the side door open?" someone says in a sharp, loud voice.

Aaron races for the wooden door. It's locked tight. In a panic, he swings the bag over his shoulder and, heart thumping, flies into the corridor, where two men in builders' overalls flinch in shock. Startled out of their wits, they press tight against the walls as he thunders past and out of the door.

"He's just a kid," one of them says.

With bottles clanking in his pockets and the brass lamp rattling in the bag like a door knocker, Aaron breaks out in sweat all over and soon the spot on his back where the rug heats his skin through the plastic is sopping wet. Taxis and brown bendy buses stream past carrying workers. Coffee and *shisha* bars are opening their doors and people are flinging last night's rubbish in the street. Having stolen so much, Aaron keeps on running until he reaches Tahrir Square, the home of the Egyptian Museum. The gates are locked. The wooden box on the right where the tourists queue for tour guides is shuttered tight. The courtyard is empty.

Aaron pauses at the locked gates. He's been in the museum three times. Twice with the Mokattam school when he was very young, and once when a tourist took pity on him and bought him a ticket. Each time he stepped inside he was shocked by the amount of stuff there and by the fact that there was a man in every room just watching the visitors to make sure they didn't touch anything. Aaron shakes his head at the idea of such a lucky, easy job as he hurries past the high black railings and down a side road toward a shop that sells things he hopes the owner will want to buy from him.

Aaron drops his bag outside the shop window, which is crammed with racks of cartouches, silver ankhs, turquoise scarabs, rings, old books, framed prints, and bright scarves. A smell of coriander drifts from the restaurant next door as Aaron peers through layers of souvenirs at rugs dangling from the ceiling and pierced brass lamps with white tickets stuck to their sides. Try as he might, he can't make out the prices and is about to give up when the owner arrives in a smart black suit, swinging a bunch of rattling keys.

"Don't beg outside my shop," he says firmly but with a kind smile.

"I wasn't." Aaron's pleased to see him. "I've got things you'll want to buy."

Ripping open the plastic bag, Aaron drags out the silvery-gray rug and the brass lamp with its tangled lead.

"Where did you get them from?" The owner nods. "And don't lie. I can see who you are by the quarry dust on your skin."

The dust always gives him away.

"My grandmother needs to sell them," he lies.

Omar's words flood into his mind as he speaks: "Think about what you're doing and whether you're adding or taking away from your own soul when you steal my glass." Leaning into the shadow of the doorway, out of nowhere, the thought comes to Aaron that he'd now rather take these things back than sell them to this man.

The bottles feel heavier than life itself in his pockets and all the energy drains from him, as if someone's pulled a plug from his spine. He doesn't want to be this greedy, desperate person who steals, lies, and begs. The person he is isn't someone he wants to be. Aaron can see his own reflection in the man's eyes. What he's missing is a feeling that rugs, lamps, houses, cars, gold, and diamonds can't make up for.

Rachel wouldn't want him if she knew what he was really like. With the glare of the rising sun blasting his face like bullets from a gun, Aaron admits, "I stole them," and swings the bag onto his shoulder.

"OK, so I'll give you a hundred and fifty piastres."

It's not a great fortune. It's not to be sniffed at either, but Aaron isn't moved by the thought of that amount of money.

"Nah. No thanks."

Aaron turns away from the shadowy doorway. For the first time in his life, he knows what to do and it eclipses the need to make money from selling stolen goods. Walking back toward the museum, his steps are lighter, even though he's sure God's laughing in his ear. But the truth of that doesn't bother him as he crosses the road and heads back to the perfume shop. Something deep inside him lifts and the thought racing around his head is that now—yes, now—Rachel has a reason to be proud of him. Omar will be pleased too that he's going to give back the stolen stuff.

There's nobody inside the shop except the tall, thin assistant, who's shuffling papers beside the cash register. Going a ghostly shade of white, he stares at Aaron, scared he's going to get clobbered with the bag. As he moves a step back, his round glasses slide down his nose. It takes a second for Aaron to drop the awkward-shaped bag and empty it on the polished tiles.

"Get out! Get out!" the assistant cries, springing to life. He grabs Aaron by the scruff of the neck and tosses him out of the shop. "Don't come back or I'll call the police."

Aaron has no choice but to run for it as a small crowd gathers to see what's going on. A woman pushing a sick man in a wheelchair gives him a filthy look as he charges past, with the sound of bottles clinking away in his pockets. *The perfumes . . . He didn't get the chance to give the perfumes back.*

———

Schoolkids in navy uniforms swiftly cross the road in front of him as he weaves through their polite stares toward the safety of the alleys on Sadat Street. Their neat clothes and shiny skin bring a sudden freshness to the dirty street as Aaron puffs to a stop beside a souvenir stand. A rack of stuffed cloth camels greets him. Chewing on a piece of flatbread, the suspicious owner pokes his head between them and narrows his eyes.

"Do you want to buy some perfume?" Aaron takes one of the gold-netted rose bottles from his pocket and offers it to him.

The man takes the bottle and sniffs the stopper. "My wife has many perfumes."

"And your girlfriend?" Aaron has seen this man chatting up every woman in Cairo. "What about her?"

"Ha-ha." He can't stop laughing, but the flattery has worked and he digs in his pocket for a couple of notes.

"It's worth more." Aaron reaches for the bottle.

"OK. OK." The man's face collapses as he hands him another note.

Now there's enough money for Aaron to fill his face with a shawarma kebab and buy some for the family.

He heads for a pavement café. With the smell of roasting meat, onions, spices, peppers, and lemons drifting from the ovens, Aaron leans against the wall to eat his kebab. A plastic bag of meat-filled pitas sits at his feet. Yes, he thinks, he should have given the perfumes back too, but then he wouldn't be eating this delicious kebab, would he? And he was going to give them to the shop assistant, but he didn't let him, so his conscience is clear, which makes the kebab taste even better . . . for a moment. Despite Aaron's best efforts, though, there's a nagging feeling inside that he shouldn't have five bottles of expensive oils in his pockets. Where's he going to hide them? There's no room left in the hole in the corner beside the wall. Perhaps he should try to sell them to passersby?

Wiping fatty kebab juices from his lips, Aaron takes the other rose-colored bottle from his pocket. He sniffs the rich scent, which is now mixed with the strong smell of onions on his fingers. To get rid of the onion smell, he rubs his hand on his dusty jeans and thrusts the bottle at a veiled woman with beautiful eyes.

"Very cheap price."

She shakes her head and hurries past. An hour later Aaron's still leaning against the prickly wall, offering the same bottle to everyone in his path, but by now the rose bottle is covered in grease stains from his filthy hands and looks cheap and nasty, despite the gold netting.

Clutching the plastic bag of kebabs, Aaron's relieved to get a lift home to Mokattam on the Mebaj brothers' cart. As he gazes at the dozens of desperate families clearing and sorting garbage, even the foul smell of rotting vegetables and rat-infested hovels is a tonic after the stress of trying to sell perfume on the hot, noisy streets of Cairo. Seeing all those people rushing everywhere has given him a headache. At least it's quiet in Mokattam. Quiet until Shareen starts screaming.

"Stop it. Go away!" Slumped on a pile of paper, she's yelling at Lijah, who's leaning over her with a cheeky grin on his face.

"Come off it. Everyone knows you'd rather be with me than with Daniel."

Lijah presses his face closer to Shareen and cracks up laughing when she elbows him in the stomach.

"Try again," he squeaks, doubled up. "That didn't hurt."

"Tell him to leave me alone," Shareen calls to Joseph as Aaron jumps from the cart, swinging the bag of kebabs. But Joseph grins at his brother and they look at Lijah with an eerie respect as the pony clops past them.

"I've got the best kebabs," Aaron says, hoping the food will tempt Lijah to stop tormenting Shareen.

"Have you got a spare one for me?" Abe appears from behind, kicking his ball in the air.

"You can have half of mine," Aaron whispers. "I've already had a whole one." He rips a meat-dripping pita in two and hands the larger half to Abe, who grabs it with both hands.

"Get your mother to kill that pig and you'll have plenty to eat. Why does she keep it?" Lijah asks, turning to Abe.

Suddenly someone shouts, "He's here," and a feeling of expectation flashes across Aaron's face. A few seconds later the lane's crammed with desperate men, women, and children, gathering to watch the merchant rumble his huge truck over the unmade path like a minesweeper. The owner of two factories, Faisal makes a fortune from selling recycled material.

Aaron doesn't stay to watch the haggling that's about to take place as the merchant moans and groans his fat way into paying the smallest amount he can for the paper, metal, and glass they've sweated to collect and sort. The sound of arguing follows Aaron as he slips away from Abe and the stepfamily and dashes through the crowd, down the lane toward the church. Everyone he meets is heading the other way to see what the merchant's paying out, so by the time he reaches the wide walkway it's empty.

The faint smell of flowers takes over as Aaron sits on the brick wall to rest under the wide sky and blasting sunshine, happy to watch the pigeons. Happy to be near the blossoming bushes, clean paths, and high frescoes on the limestone walls. Away from the chaos, filth, and decay of the nearby hovels. It's so quiet, it feels as if the world has ended. He'd like to curl up and fall asleep here, but before too long people will start walking this way after selling their trash to go to church and give thanks, and he must decide what to do with the stolen bottles. He could dig another hole, several holes, but in time someone's bound to notice.

Scooping out the pale earth quickly with his fingers, Aaron rescues all the bottles but one from their small grave and tucks them inside the elastic waist of his jeans. He leaves one of the small rose-colored bottles behind because he likes the idea of someone discovering it in the future and wondering how it got there. The bottles next to his skin are warm and smooth, apart from a few scratchy crumbs of soil, and as he hurries past the church he's glad that Hosi's old shirt hangs almost to his knees. There's one other safe place to bury them—the pigpens.

Struggling up from a long sleep, the smallest pig is curious enough to trot over and nose him, while the rest grunt, blinking flies from their eyes. Aaron resists the urge to jump over the makeshift fence and pet each one, telling them what he's got. With a loud snort, the smallest pig thrusts his wet nose at the sky and drools.

Aaron moves the bottles from the waist of his jeans to his pockets, then fills the water trough and watches the little one drink from it greedily. "A bit of rose oil on your ears is what you need." He whips out a bottle and waves it in the air. "Not

that you don't already smell nice, if you know what I mean."
Although he is tempted to sprinkle a few drops on the prickly
skin and sniff the difference it makes, Aaron realizes that it
would be a waste of perfume, considering the place stinks to
high heaven of steaming dung. And anyway, time's running
out.

Behind the rickety shelter is an upside-down, moldy white
plastic tub that's been there for years. There's no reason for
anyone to come around here, so it's the perfect place to hide
the bottles and easy to lift out chunks of earth and pack the
bottles in tightly. Feeling pleased with himself for choosing
this spot, he stamps the earth flat, then manages to pops the
plastic tub on top before hearing a flapping sound coming
from the fence in front. Aaron peers through a gap in the
shelter and his eyes narrow in fear at the sight of Shareen
running away.

Chapter Eleven
Reputation

Aaron bites his lip. Was Shareen there all the time, watching him? That's what he thought at the church and she hadn't seen a thing. But this feels different. He hesitates. Should he dig up the bottles and take them somewhere else? Then run the risk of being caught red-handed? He could hide and hope she won't grass him up? But he knows she will. She's bound to. Shareen loves drama and telling on him will put her at the center of another good story. Now even the pigs have gone quiet and the sun has dimmed.

Before Aaron has time to decide what to do, Shareen and the priest are upon him. Father Peter is the youngest member of the church and his pale, nervous face is a good cover for his strong-willed nature. Dressed in black robes with a white collar, he's so eager to do what's right that he tends to overdo everything. When he spots Aaron, he crosses himself as if looking at the devil. Meanwhile, Shareen, who's hovering in the background, has a satisfied grin on her face.

"Stealing isn't something we do in Mokattam," Father Peter says. "You must take the bottles back."

"What bottles?" It was worth a try.

"You think no one knows about you, Aaron?" Shareen says.

It's an empty question but one that changes his life for a long time to come. Within minutes the priest and Shareen have dug up all the bottles and a small crowd of people are rushing over to watch the action. At the front are Hosi, Lijah, and Youssa, their faces bursting with fury. Rachel's standing to one side, looking disappointed.

While the priest takes in the situation, Aaron gazes at Rachel. Gazes so hard she turns away, embarrassed.

"They're from Omar's perfume shop," Lijah tells Father Peter, who nods and pockets them in the folds of his black robe.

"I want to talk to you tomorrow," the priest says to Aaron. "Let your conscience be your guide until then."

Conscience? What conscience? Aaron nods but there's a part of him that doesn't care one bit what the priest or almost anyone thinks. It's Rachel's sad, then disappointed glance that's carving a hole in his heart. When Aaron finally looks up, one of the elders catches his gaze. The man's stern eyes are filled with disgust and the same eerie hate is visible in everyone surrounding him. It's then that the seriousness of the situation sinks in and a bubble of fear wells up inside Aaron.

They're waiting for him to react.

In addition to remaining silent, braving their contempt, and trying to hold his ground, an itch breaks out on the back of Aaron's neck that he dares not scratch. It distracts him as he stares into the distance with his hands in his pockets. Not moving is a way of not really being here and though at least twenty people are standing close by and staring at him, it feels as if there's an empty, throbbing space the size of an ocean between him and them.

Not until one of the women shakes her head, as if to say he's a lost cause, does their interest in him finally fade. People begin to mutter and turn away. Aaron quietly sighs, but when the crowd thins to just his stepfamily and Shareen, even he's shocked by what happens next.

"You've cost me my reputation. Stay away from my family," Hosi says. "You don't think about anyone but yourself."

The word *family* falls on Aaron like a heavy weight as he watches Hosi walk away, followed by Youssa, who is sneering at him as if he's a worm. Aaron's heart sinks. They were happy to eat the cake that was obviously stolen. The liver, rice, and kebabs he bought were paid for with stolen goods. Hosi didn't ask how he managed to buy the food. He's only angry because everyone knows about the stolen bottles and he's pretending to be more honest than he actually is. Today is supposed to be a good day. Faisal the merchant has paid for the sorted trash. Everyone has money for food. Aaron took the rug and lamp he stole back to the shop and meant to leave the perfumes there too, and this is his reward. *Thanks, God!*

He's homeless. Despised. Finished. Doomed. All thanks to Shareen.

And Lijah isn't done with him yet. In one sharp move, he turns and spits in Aaron's face.

Aaron crouches as Lijah begins to bust him apart, until Shareen drags Lijah off, hauling him backwards down the path by his shirt, which he enjoys. She's yelling and screaming as if this is all Lijah's fault, not hers, and he's twisting, jumping, ducking, and diving. Still finding time to blow her kisses with his mean lips.

When the sound of her high voice eventually disappears, Aaron uncurls from his crumpled heap on the stinking, hard ground. There's a pain in his shoulder blade, another in his belly, and as he opens his eyes to the state he's in, the same rickety shelter greets him. Instantly, a black hole of self-hatred and bitterness opens up inside. Why didn't he just leave the perfumes where they were—under the wall? Why did he take more? Brushing dirt from his arms and knees, Aaron looks up to see Abe watching him from the pigpen fence, his gray football tucked under his arm.

"You could stay on my floor, but the pig takes up most of the room," Abe jokes.

"It's OK."

A familiar thought flicks through Aaron's mind: He doesn't fit here. Why should he not have a home or somewhere to go like everyone else? He's seen the way real families talk, with the same expressions and instant understanding. People who share blood have a kind of secret language. A language that's been missing since his mother died.

A panting slope of pig appears and begins nuzzling the fence. Aaron's aching all over but if the pigs can grow fat and strong eating congealed crud while living in their own dung, so can he. There's a sharp edge to this thought, but as Aaron heads to the tap to wash his face and hands and soak his feet in the cool water, the nasty pain in his stomach returns. With it the confidence of being able to survive on his own disappears as quickly as it came. He's had it now and he knows it.

Abe points to the oldest pig with the dirtiest snout. "This morning I saw its friend being roasted for Shareen's party tonight."

"Yeah?"

Aaron stares at the old pig with sympathy. The thought of its friend roasting on a spit over a charcoal fire squeezes his heart. The horror of life comes home to him as he imagines the pig's bones picked clean of meat. All that will be left of it in a few hours' time.

In his heart Aaron knows he deserves to be shunned and humiliated. He's broken the basic moral code of their community: "Strive to do your best even in the worst conditions. Don't steal. Don't harm. Don't lie." That's why Rachel hates him now.

As Aaron sinks his head back under the tap, the lack of anywhere to sleep or any idea of what to do now that he can't go glass collecting almost makes his heart stop. He's lost his place in the community. His stepfamily wants nothing to do with him and, though he doesn't like any of them, they're all the family he has. Aaron's fears are so many and so awesome, he laughs—a short, sharp, silly laugh—but after that a deep feeling of shame spreads over him, followed by a shattering hopelessness. Now there's nothing else to lose. He'll never again have to answer to anyone.

With the sound of Abe slapping the soccer ball from hand to hand and water trickling down the short sleeves of his tattered shirt, Aaron lifts his head from the tap, shakes his hair, and steps out of the puddle of water to look at the darkening sky. When he glances back toward Abe he's amazed to see the glowing figure of Rachel in a blue galabeya with a folded warm bread in her hand.

She came back!

Aaron splutters the first thing that comes to mind. "I didn't kill the pony." He can't face mentioning the stolen perfumes.

"Who said you did?" Rachel frowns.

Like a book that keeps falling open on the wrong page, Aaron is suddenly dumbstruck when she hands him the warm bread smelling of cumin and coriander.

"Thanks," he manages to say, aware that on one of the worst days of his life, he's eaten one and a half massive kebabs and now this, and will be filling up with more food at the party—if he's allowed to go.

Aaron's so touched by Rachel's thoughtfulness, his eyes start to water and he turns away to put his face back together.

"I've got to help my father," Rachel says, then walks off as Aaron squints again to look at her. He's missed his moment once more.

"You can have this." Aaron says to Abe.

With nothing to do but wait for the dreaded party to begin, Aaron knows he's in a two-way bind. If he doesn't go it will prove he's not willing to make the effort to change and take part in the community, but if he does he'll be treated as an outcast and ignored by everyone, though he will get the chance to see Rachel again. An hour later Aaron still doesn't know what to do. Sitting on the wall by the church with Abe, he watches the sun slide from the horizon, leaving a blaze of orange streaks behind. Soon a gloomy twilight sets in. Once upon a time Aaron didn't have a clue about twilight, but then he'd overheard Omar tell a customer it's when a door opens up between day and night. When the veil between this world and the other is at its thinnest and spirits are most easily seen. It could be a joke, but even the priest said it was a good time to pray. Perhaps he should pray for an answer to the party question.

Aaron stares into the fading light for a moment, but no spirit appears to talk to him. Perhaps he should just go to the party and try to keep out of everyone's way, then see what happens. Didn't Omar once say that what you intend to do is as important as what you actually do?

Before the darkness takes over, Aaron watches the lengthening shadows and makes up his mind to face the music. He's going to have to one day, so it might as well be tonight, when everyone will be wondering if he's got the guts to come. As a shiver runs down his spine at the thought of the disappointed stares he's going to have to suffer, the overpowering twilight closes in like a thousand demons who are determined to spook him. But instead of strange spirits, it's Abe who surprises him.

"It must be weird being see-through," Abe suddenly pipes up.

"What?"

"Those clear moon jellyfish, how do they feel?" Abe says.

"They're blobs—nothing. They just blob around," Aaron says, sighing.

"But they swim and eat and lock their tentacles together. That's not blobbing. Pretending to be a blob is kind of good anyway, because then tuna and sharks swim right past instead of eating you up."

Aaron nods, standing up to stretch his legs and cock an ear to the sound of music starting in the distance. It's almost night, he's covered in bruises, has nowhere to sleep, no means of earning a living, and they're chatting about jellyfish.

"Fish eat fish eat fish. Can't be tasty, can it?" Abe pipes up.

"No," Aaron agrees, if only to shut him up, although he smiles in the darkness.

The ball bounces from Abe's lap and rolls down the walkway to the wide-open space in front of the church, coming to a stop by the concrete table and benches where two families are chatting. One of the kids has a dragging foot, but he rushes to grab the ball and throw it into the air. The church lights flicker to life as he passes the ball back to Abe, and

Aaron can't hide his irritation as he waits for the boys to stop throwing it around. He doesn't want to arrive at the party on his own, so he has to hang around until Abe's finished playing. With sad eyes, the disabled kid's mother is someone he recognizes. Her daughter was given up at birth; sold to make ends meet. Her black galabeya is as wide as a tent and she sits nervously on the edge of the bench, watching her son try to kick the ball with one working foot and the other lagging behind him.

Nearby, a few of the elders are huddled together, talking quietly. One of them looks at Aaron and frowns. The others dismiss him with a brief glance.

Aaron turns away, embarrassed, and hears one of them say, "If they cull our pigs because of swine flu the heaps of garbage will finish Cairo off before that virus."

"Why kill all the pigs when nobody here has had swine flu?" another man mutters.

They're talking about the pigs, not Aaron, but their anger feels directed at him.

"Come on, Abe," Aaron says, walking off down the dusty path heading toward the community room where the party's taking place.

Although he hates Shareen, he doesn't want her to think she's forced him to stay away. Plus the need to see Rachel is on his mind, giving him the courage and strength to get there.

Like a puppy dog, Abe grabs the ball and runs after him.

———

It's a shame, Aaron thinks, that the community room's

locked at night, because it would make a good sleeping place. Although most celebrations are held outside, with people sitting on faded blankets and cushions laid out on the ground, Shareen has insisted that her party should be inside, which will make Aaron's sudden appearance even harder to disguise.

The nearer Aaron and Abe get to the soulless concrete shed with a single strip light and a broken toilet, the sound of traditional singing becomes clearer. The door's open and the rhythm of voices fills the night air. It's not easy for him to step inside, but the smell of roasting meat is too strong to keep him cowering outside, where a group of men are perched on their haunches in the half-light, drinking, sparking up cigarettes, and studying the shapes on their playing cards.

Aaron sees Daniel slapping a card on the ground with a desperate look on his face. He's more interested in winning the game than being with Shareen, his future wife.

With a quick scan of the bleak concrete room, Aaron sees that Rachel isn't here. A hush quickly spreads from family to family until all eyes are upon him. Only this time, because an engagement celebration is in progress, there's a faint hint of tolerance on their faces.

Aaron shudders. In one corner is an old-fashioned tape deck and a shamefaced Hassan, one of the foundry workers, is suffering the embarrassment of not being able to get it to work. At least it gives the choir in the farthest corner time to sing another traditional song. Opposite the tape deck looks like a safe place for Abe and Aaron to make for as they skirt round several people on their way to the wonky food table, which is being loaded with tubs of beans and slices of pork and chicken. Someone's cut out a red paper heart from a magazine to decorate the faded Formica, and a few plastic roses and ribbons add to the halfhearted celebratory feeling of the room.

Hanging from the wall above the edge of the food table is a picture of the Virgin Mary surrounded by a sparkle of light. Aaron glances at it for a moment. The image makes him slightly less nervous. She feels like a friend and he stands underneath her for protection as his eyes land on Shareen. He tries hard not to make his hatred for her obvious. She is dressed in a faded green-and-blue galabeya with a lotus flower in her back-combed hair. At least she's wearing her own dress and not Seham's brown one, which might be newer but not any prettier. The only new things Shareen has on are a string of black beads and a thin silver bangle. She's almost a head taller than her thin, hungry friends and looks much older. She's smiling sweetly at everyone, but the only really happy person here is her father, who's holding court beside the burner, slicing up meat.

He's happy to get rid her of her, Aaron thinks. *I don't blame him.*

Chapter Twelve
A Wild Stampede

As parties go, it's a bit of a washout. People aren't used to standing around like this. They can't relax and would rather be outside, lolling on blankets and cushions. Aaron doesn't perk up until Rachel finally arrives. She is wearing a gray galabeya, has her hair tied back, and is carrying a gift for Shareen in her arms—a yellow cushion embroidered with the word *love* in red.

Aaron wonders if she sewed it herself.

Try as he might to catch her eye, Rachel ignores him, but knowing she's here improves the party to no end. Instead Aaron catches Sami's eye. His family own the secondhand electrical shop and he's watching Rachel too. Short and stocky, with a tattoo of Jesus on his hand, he's not married and nearly twenty-five. They've all known each other their whole lives, but for the first time Aaron sees that Sami's interest in Rachel is more than friendly.

The thought that Sami might want to marry Rachel sends a shiver down his spine. Sami's unkind to his own mother. How would he treat Rachel if she became his wife?

Scooping a handful of moist beans dipped in a ball of rice from his plate to his mouth, Sami peers back at Aaron, who looks away.

Aaron notices Lijah pushing Jacob out of the door. Jacob's a medical-waster and Lijah prefers to stay as far away from his kind as possible.

Aaron flits across the room with his plate of food, but Lijah's already sent Jacob packing. He's booted him out and now stands firmly with his back to the room, arms wide, feet apart to block the doorway in case Jacob tries to return. Meanwhile, Abe slips past Lijah juggling three plates of food that he's taking home for later.

Aaron fumes. Lijah doesn't have the guts to vent his fury on him with everyone watching, which is why he's taking it out on Jacob instead. Rice sticks in Aaron's throat. His fury almost burns holes in Lijah's back. At that moment the single strip light flickers off, turning the room pitch-black.

The rising sound of grumbling and the scuttling for candles and matches force Aaron to step back, boiling with rage but still holding tight to the paper plate of messy food he'd like to have handed to Jacob.

When church candles lining the food table flare into life, the shadowy figures of Youssa and Hosi in the far corner are exposed. In that instance Aaron can see their true selves as ugly, lizardlike gargoyles. Everyone else, however, looks the same—just as they do in full light. *It would be great if they could see Hosi and Youssa like I do.* But they're all minding their own sad business.

With the candles for light, there's a softer, more party-like atmosphere, but Aaron's still standing there eating his rice and beans alone. Only the Mebaj brothers have smiled at him. Well, to be honest, it was more like a *serves you right, you idiot* smirk.

Aaron glances at Shareen refilling a plastic cup with water. The lotus flower in her henna-streaked hair looks like a used tissue. She turns her head toward him, a touch of guilt in her expression. Perhaps she's not sure whether to talk to him or not. Aaron has no desire to ever talk to *her* ever again. He turns his attention to Rachel, who's chatting to a crowd of scruffy girls beside the table. Even though she's part of the group there's something separate about her. A kind of nice humming feeling starts up inside as he looks at her. She's unlike anyone else in the room. It's almost as if there's an invisible light around her, something weird that maybe only he can feel. Until all the kids were about nine or ten, the girls and boys used to hang out together the whole time, but since then they've kept to their own sex. Aaron wishes he could go straight up to Rachel and her friends, but he can't.

Without making it too obvious, he sidles toward the group of girls, who are reaching for the bowl of saffron rice on the table. The rest of the room is empty compared to the crowd gathered eagerly round the food. The recently married Seham is wearing a smart blue galabeya and has probably sold her brown engagement dress to someone else. He's about to say hi to Seham and her hard-to-miss, huge teeth, when she looks past his shoulder and gasps as if she's seen a snake.

A black potbellied pig is cannoning down the room, snorting madly, rolling toward the food table. The choir girls scream. People scatter, spilling food as the pig's patchy snout swoops through dropped beans and rice with muffled thumps before twitching the table for the meat. In trying to stop him, someone pulls his short, curly tail, but the pig slams sideways into the table and the man loses his grip. People scramble to catch the church candles, which tumble to the floor, spluttering the room into darkness.

The women and children run for the door.

The older kids and men hang back, groping the wall while the pig forces the table over with a crash. Rice, meat, and beans go flying. Paper plates frisbee to the floor. Plastic cups and bottles crackle and crumple underfoot. Even the fake roses become part of the pig swill as Marris guzzles everything in his path. Finally two candles are relit and bearded men can be seen managing to grab the pig's warm, fleshy rear for a second before it charges off again, bullet-fast, snorting fearfully and being chased by several men and a mad kid waving a ribbon.

A wild stampede. It's one pig against the mob and the pig's winning. Aaron darts forward to join the crush, but he's no match for Marris. He backs off, envying the pig's ability to create such havoc. In a frenzy of yelling and thumping, the fleshy force bundles across the room and Aaron sprints toward it with the same surge of chaotic, scary energy he imagines the pig's feeling. He might as well try to catch a bomb. Aaron sticks a foot out, but the pig tramples it and skids, snorting and grunting, into the wall. Grabbed from every side, the pig vomits elastic goo, scumming up the floor. It's the perfect end and Aaron smiles. For once he's been let off the hook as the least-welcome guest, even if it was in a peculiar way.

An old woman with a stick stands there unmoved while everyone laughs. Her bony, bare feet drip with mustardy slop. The look on Shareen's face confirms what everyone's thinking: that this is the worst engagement party there's ever been in Mokattam. Not just because of this, but also because Daniel can't be bothered to leave his card game outside to see what damage the pig's doing. It's clear to everyone he doesn't care.

By the time the pig is forcefully pushed out of the door, the community room is a battlefield which looks even scarier by the light of only one candle. Marris has turned the quiet event into a war zone, which gets worse when Hassan, doing a hopeful jig, suddenly sparks the tape deck to life and a blast of pop music bounces from the stained walls. Bounces for less than a couple of minutes, because an angry bearded elder promptly switches it off.

"Another Shareen disaster," Rachel says, raising her eyebrows at Aaron as she peeps out from behind Farouk, the fat baker.

"Oh, I don't know. The pig had a great time."

They giggle for a second like children, then Rachel leaves the safety of Farouk's bulky back and joins Aaron. It's his high point of the party until Lijah, who's on the prowl, sneaks up on them. Aaron eyes his shadow on the filthy wall. Weirdly, it seems to have a strength that Lijah's body is missing. What's

136

real is his creepy shadow up above, while the limp creature in front of him looks weak.

"You've got some nerve," Lijah says, scowling.

"Yeah?" Aaron squares up to him, but only because Rachel's watching.

Lijah rolls his eyes at her. "Get out of the way. Where's that idiot kid who owns the pig?"

"Marris didn't do *you* any harm," Rachel pipes up. "He was only doing what pigs do."

"So who went and fetched it?" Scorning her, Lijah turns his attention back to Aaron—a much easier target than Rachel. "Where's that vile kid?"

"Why don't you see if your father's all right instead of wondering where Abe is?" Rachel says bravely.

Her words deflate Lijah for a moment, but he's still tempted to lash out. "Wipe that smile off your face," he threatens Aaron.

"No!"

Lijah starts forward, then abruptly changes his mind. Distracted by the whining sound behind him, he spies Shareen with a deathly pale face ripping the limp lotus flower from her hair and marching angrily to the door. They crane their necks to watch her go. That's it, the party's over, and it feels like a thousand years could go by before there's another one. It's especially bad because Sami's been filming the whole thing with his cell phone and Shareen knows he's going to show it to everyone.

"That kid's going to pay for this," Lijah says, stomping after Shareen as if it's up to him to save the day.

He's slowly followed by the remaining kids and families, who drift from the room, disappointed by the early finish.

"Who does he think he is?" Rachel says to Aaron.

"Someone important." Aaron sighs.

"What are you going to do?" Rachel asks.

"I don't know. Find somewhere to sleep, I guess."

"I reckon Father Peter won't mind if you sleep on one of the concrete pews," Rachel suggests.

The priest? Aaron suddenly remembers he asked to talk to him tomorrow. Well, that's not going to happen, which means he can't afford to bed down at the church in case he bumps into him in the morning. Aaron catches the white flashing of Rachel's almond eyes and realizes she's thinking the same thing.

"Might not be a good idea, then?" she says. Aaron remembers the stash of hidden perfume bottles.

"No." Aaron wishes he could explain. "Are you going to check on the ponies now?"

"Suppose so."

He knows it's on her way home and her three sisters have already left, along with her father, his brother, and their wives. "I'll walk you. Don't worry—no one will see you with me now that it's dark."

She nods and they're about to go when Jacob emerges next to them as they step outside. In the half-light his eyes are strangely huge.

"I was hiding round the back. Wasn't that a joke?"

No! No! Not now! Aaron squirms away from him. He could strangle Jacob as he slips between them, joining their stride past the card players, who are handing round bottles of beer. *Go away.*

Daniel clinks the coins in his fist and waves at them. He's won, but it's not enough. The cards are again shuffled and cut, bringing a hiss of pleasure to his wet lips.

Lifting her hair gently from her neck, Rachel mutters, "Shareen's in the lion's den."

"Aren't we all?" Aaron trembles with fear. That's exactly where he is—in the lion's den.

"Do you think we become stars when we die?" Jacob's determined to break into their chat as they move away from the darkening concrete units.

"Yes," Rachel and Aaron say at the same time.

They smile, but a sickening feeling that Jacob's going to ruin everything takes shape in Aaron, while his question stays written in the night sky forever. He glances up at a billion reasons to believe in something bigger than himself, then shrinks at the overpowering truth and secrets of the universe. He needs to find his destiny in Mokattam first.

"It's the same sky for everyone," Jacob says. "They can't wreck that."

"We're going to see the ponies." Aaron secretly half-winks. "Are you going home?"

"Nah. Not yet."

Flinging his head back, Jacob pauses to allow the blanket of twinkling lights in the sky to fall on him while Aaron gropes for an excuse to get rid of him.

"Maybe they'll take Cairo's trash to the moon one day," Rachel says.

Aaron fixes on Rachel. A ton of wordless emotions crowd him out. If she stayed here for the next half an hour, it would light up the night brighter than any star. Almost as if she can read what he's thinking, Rachel turns to go.

"Forget the ponies. I'm going home. See ya."

As she walks away, a dark mound at Aaron's feet suddenly comes alive with maggots.

Chapter Thirteen
Hope

Hope is all that's left over the next few days as Aaron lies on a patch of land behind the ramshackle pony yard, staring at the sky without seeing it. His eyes hurt from crying and the hours spent clawing through trash for stale food to eat are taking their toll. The old aches in his toe, knee, and elbow twinge slightly as he remembers Lijah pushing him off the cart.

His face is thin and drawn. He can't sleep from worrying about bumping into Father Peter and suffering the talk that's coming any day soon. He can't avoid him forever. The priest is bound to catch Aaron on his way to the wall.

The annoying sound of ponies stamping the scrubby earth wakes Aaron long before dawn and since he's been here, hiding out, Rachel's become cool and a bit strange. Yesterday she didn't say a word to him. She blushed, gave him some bread, and kept blinking at the empty trough and rubbing her arm, as if he made her skin itch. Then she turned and ran away, and her fluttering feet made his body throb. Each day it's getting harder and harder to survive; he's in trouble with the community, and now Rachel is increasingly distant. She pities him. He can feel it.

Perhaps someone's found out she's helping him. Aaron sighs. If the news gets around it will do untold harm to her reputation. The thought turns his stomach. Not only that but he's scoured the village hour after hour for somewhere else to stay and the only place on offer is one that's bringing him out in a sweat. What haunts his mind now isn't Lijah but images of being elbow-deep in leaking tubes of blood and dirty bandages.

For the last year, Noha, Jacob's mother, has been trying to persuade others to help Jacob collect the medical waste. She has put the idea to Aaron several times, but he's refused. Even with the torment of Lijah and Hosi, it's a job Aaron was too terrified to imagine and never in his wildest dreams expected to take up. Because girls and women aren't allowed on the carts, he knew, long ago, what Noha was angling at when she said, "Sometimes fortune plays games with us and brings us the things we want the least." Noha would prefer to go into the city with Jacob instead of staying at home.

"Did the ponies have a drink before they were tied to the carts this morning?" Rachel shouts, interrupting his thoughts.

"Yeah. Yeah." Aaron jumps up.

"You sure?" Only half believing him, she quickly unties the gate and goes to check. The water trough is as dry as a bone and the early sun is burning into the pits of the empty basin. "You didn't fill it, did you?"

"I did." He runs to help her. "But you know sometimes how thirsty they get."

"There's always a little water left. The ponies know to leave some for later. I would have done it myself if you hadn't promised." She frowns.

There's nothing Aaron can say. He lied. He let her down. She won't ask him again.

"I've got to . . . do stuff." Aaron nods. "I'll catch you later."

Guilt weighs down on him like a ton of bricks as he creeps away with a pounding heart. *You dumb fool. Why didn't you get up when the ponies were neighing? What was the point in lying? Why didn't you say you were too tired to wake up?*

Rachel watches him dip his hands into his torn jean pockets and straighten his back as if he doesn't care. It's obvious he does.

"Where are you going?" she calls.

"I . . . er . . ." Aaron stammers. "I need to stretch my legs."

"Did you know my dad's new wife's got cancer?" Rachel catches up with him.

"No," Aaron replies in surprise.

An overwhelming desire to put his arm round her hits him. He watches sunlight flicker over her lush eyelashes and clenches his palms with frustration. *Why is she telling me this?*

"Yeah. Fatima's only twenty-nine and it's spread to her lungs. She's going to die soon."

143

Staring at the ground, Rachel makes a diamond pattern in the dusty earth with her toes.

"I meant to water the ponies. It's just that . . ." Aaron starts.

"I know." Rachel forgives him with a kind glance. "Sometimes I've missed doing it because I was helping Fatima and stuff."

"I thought you . . ." Aaron stumbles. He can't ask her how she feels. "Fatima looked fine at Shareen's party."

"Yeah, but the effort took it out of her. She's been much worse since then. I can remember when Mom died last year, she went kind of gray. Her skin changed color. It was weird. Just like Fatima. Mom used to laugh about it, but Fatima doesn't laugh. Remember when my older brother died?"

Aaron nods.

Rachel continues, "He went gray too. When my sister died she still looked normal, but she's the only one."

Aaron's heart suddenly feels heavy in his chest. "You're not going to die," he mutters.

"One day I am." Rachel shrugs. "It's OK. I'm not scared. There won't be stinking mess and horrible diseases in heaven, will there?"

"There might be," Aaron says, looking into her sad eyes.

"No, there won't." She pauses, then asks, "Do you want me to find you something to eat?"

"I can do it." Aaron sees she's got enough to deal with. "Just don't get married," he blurts out.

"What?" His statement takes her completely by surprise.

"You know, your dad . . . He might need some help, after . . ."

"Aaron, I'm going to be a vet and look after animals, not get married to some old guy who wants a slave."

Aaron's stunned. She's never been out of Mokattam. "How are you going to do that? You need exams and loads of cash to be a vet."

"It's a secret, but this writer woman said that if you want something enough it will come to you. I heard her talking about it on Sami's TV. She said all your dreams can come true just by using the power of thought, so that's what I'm doing— thinking. Stop making that face, Aaron."

"Well, just don't get married." He's seriously worried about her now. "Maybe you should go back to school."

"Yeah, I might." Rachel gives him a look and a smile that makes Aaron feel sorry for her innocence. "But Mokattam only has a primary school." She sighs. "I'm going to find out about it anyway."

"You should."

Aaron doesn't want to trample on her dreams. His dream is to have a shop like Omar's, where people come from miles away to buy his perfume, which is distilled in the same way as it was at the time of the pharaohs. He wants to tell her, tell someone.

"You know Lijah's getting married?" she says at last.

"Who to?"

"Suzan! One of Shareen's friends."

"Suzan? Shovel Face? Are you sure? How is Lijah going to get married when there's no money to buy another pony and make a living?"

"They're getting married the day after Shareen," Rachel says. "Her family is helping Lijah, his brother, and his father."

"Maybe that's why he's marrying her. I hate weddings."

"Me too. But Lijah likes her." Rachel gives him a smile that says everything's mended between them and then, rubbing out the dusty diamond shapes with her heel, she turns for home.

Aaron's sad little hiding place doesn't feel so bad all of a sudden. At least he gets to see her every day and help with the ponies. She brings him bread when she can and there's a well with a tap right here and no Lijah to watch out for, so things could be far worse. Plus the only other option is giving him nightmares. Sadly, Aaron knows he'll have to face that option sooner rather than later. Rachel can't look after him forever. It's not fair on her—someone could easily discover what she's doing.

The longer he stays in Mokattam without a home or a family, the more likely he is to be accused of every crime in the village, including compromising her. When the flapping sound of Rachel's galabeya dies away, Aaron makes his decision.

———

A strange commotion is coming from a far corner of Mokattam. Judging by the rising level of the shouts, people are getting angry about something. Aaron rubs the dust from his face and stretches his stiff arms and legs. Without a mat to lie on, the ground is as unyielding as a bed of nails and Aaron's paying for it now. The rich smell of pony dung gets stronger as the sun rises in the sky.

When the next round of yells echoes in the distance, Aaron takes to his heels.

North of the pony yard is a steep path that divides into alleys. Aaron's eyes settle on a number of people standing in tight clusters, muttering, ears cocked to the shouts coming from the far end of the lane that leads to the biggest pig enclosure. Hurrying through the endless filth, Aaron hears angry voices interrupted by the sound of pigs bellowing like cattle. Their horrible howl is the sound of slaughter. Didn't someone say that pigs aren't responsible for spreading swine flu? Why is the government doing this?

When Aaron reaches the enclosure he nervously runs a hand through his matted hair at the sight of the fortress line of police and soldiers holding back the red-faced elders, who are arguing with them. At the same time they're trying to keep order among the shoving, yelling Zabbaleen behind the elders. Surely all the pigs aren't being killed off? What will happen to Cairo's food waste then? After running around the crowd for a minute, searching for a way in, Aaron gives a determined nudge and crashes through a throng of men and boys who are screaming at the murderers.

It takes only a second for the full horror to emerge. One glance at the carnage of bleeding, gasping pigs, stumbling to their deaths from knives that are working overtime, is enough for Aaron. He turns back, speechless and disoriented. By the time he reaches the pony yard, he's desperate to share the horror he just witnessed but there's no one to talk to. Not even a pony.

147

Jacob will be out now, collecting medical waste until after midday, and he can't tell Abe. He's only a kid and he'll be upset and scared for his mother's pig when he hears what they're doing. Aaron wishes he'd made the effort to catch a lift to the city with the Mebaj brothers, who left very early. Then he would have missed the slaughter.

He can't stay here. He'd like to, but he must go somewhere else. Get moving, instead of hanging around waiting for Rachel. As if she can make everything right. As if she can put him back together.

In slow motion Aaron sinks to the ground beside the fence. Resting his back on a hot, skinny metal pole, he fingers the dusty earth and looks at his filthy jeans and dirty feet. Instantly the energy he needs to get out of here and do something drains away. It's easier just to sit and do nothing. He used to think he was cleverer than most of the other kids. Clever enough to exist in Cairo on his own if he had to. Clever enough to get by living with a stepfamily he hated. Clever enough to see through tourists and hotel doormen and their stupid little lives. Clever enough to handle glass without cutting himself. And clever enough to understand some of what Omar said to his customers. Now he's come to this.

What he did was wrong. He knew that then. He knows it now. When it comes to feeling guilty he hates himself for stealing the perfumes but wishes he'd found a better hiding place and hadn't been caught. Only when it's time for the ponies to return to the yard does he shake off these horrors and make himself scarce. Then he wanders the alleys to the stalls and shops in the old part of the village, dodging the slime and shadows to find a clear wall to lean on until it's safe to go back.

Standing beside Ishaq, the icon seller's stall, opposite the electrical shop, Aaron watches Sami tinkering with a car radio, and frowns at the thought that Rachel might turn up. Then he sees someone moving quickly like her, coming toward him with her head down. But it's Mariah, Sami's sister, who's seventeen and already married with a baby. Now, dressed in black with a blue band round her head, she looks desperately poor and a lot more serious than she used to. He liked Mariah before he fell for Rachel. He still likes her. She's kind to everyone and easy to talk to. One of those grown-up girls who get on with things and never complain. She prays and fasts and does her best.

"You heard about the pigs?" Mariah asks her brother.

"Yes," Sami says, shielding the sun from his eyes with a greasy hand lined with purple veins. "A few hid them in their houses before they got to them. Abe's mother stuffed the pig's mouth with a cloth to keep him quiet." He laughs. "She forgot to cover his nose, though, and he started making a noise as if he knew his brothers were being killed. He escaped into the street."

"They won't catch him. And they won't look inside the houses for them," Mariah says. "They can't stand the filth.'"

"But if anyone hides a pig they'll be sent to jail," Sami reminds her.

"It's illegal now. We must get goats instead."

For a brief second Aaron looks at Sami and frowns then turns away, forgetting his problems and the slaughter of the pigs. Watching the sunlight dancing in Mariah's dark hair, he's transfixed by the tiny mole beneath her left eye. He used to love that mole. And as if she can hear what Aaron's thinking, Mariah glances at him leaning on the wall opposite and smiles.

Her smile lights Aaron up for a moment, until out of the corner of his eye he spots Jacob coming through the arch on his cart. Clonking and clanking along with bedposts, knives, scalpels, boxes, and plastic, he's swigging pink liquid from a small bottle and muttering to himself. A sudden fear wipes the effect of Mariah's smile from Aaron's face as his friend walks toward him.

"What's in that stuff?" Aaron asks.

"This?" Jacob stretches out a hand to shake the bottle at him. "Fruit cordial for coughs."

Making a click in the side of his cheek, he forces the pony to trot on, but Aaron scrambles up beside him, worried sick. They tussle for the bottle, but with two shakes Jacob empties the liquid on the street before flinging it at a wall, where it smashes and splinters.

"Stop it," Jacob says, and laughs, but Aaron can smell the strong chemicals on his breath and knows he's lying. There's a hint of steel in Jacob's eyes when he turns away. "It's only lemons and figs. Fruit," he says again.

More than a few times lately, Aaron's suspected that Jacob's on something but he's never caught him. Well, now he knows, and must pretend he doesn't. Today is the day when Aaron must do the thing he fears most and ask Jacob about becoming a medical-waster. He's thought long and hard about it, but he's decided this is the only work left for him in Mokattam. Even so, the sight of used bandages, syringes, and blood bags piled high on the cart is too much to take, and the smell of death and disease horrifies Aaron. Maybe he'll soon look for ways to feel better and start drinking cough medicine or whatever it is that Jacob's been gulping down. Aaron's eyes begin to water. He brushes away the tear rolling down his cheek at the thought that his glass-collecting days are over.

Doing his best not to burst out crying, Aaron swallows his tears, quickly drying his face with a dirty fist when he spots Abe racing toward them with news about their pig, his grubby ball held tightly under his arm.

"Marris went crazy this morning." Abe's voice is shaking slightly. "You look drunk, Jacob!" he adds.

"He does." Aaron narrows his eyes at Jacob, who seems shocked by Abe's comment.

"I'm not drunk!" he growls.

"Just drugged up," Aaron whispers, so Abe can't hear.

"They didn't catch him!" Abe grins. "They'll never catch our pig."

He throws the soccer ball at Aaron, who swings down from the cart to play. Eyes on the ball, Aaron chokes back the heat of the day, glad to have a reason to leave Jacob behind. Though he knows it won't be for long. The pony and cart clop past them and Jacob smiles as if nothing's happened. He's lying about what he's taking, but Aaron can't deal with him now or hang around kicking a ball with Abe for too long. He's starving hungry and needs to scour the lanes for food, as he's been doing for the last few days.

Starting in the nearest alley, he swings by the first houses, which are almost empty of people. Most are hard at work on the carts or talking about the devastation caused by the slaughter of the pigs. Sides of pork are still cheap to buy at the small butcher's and there's a good chance Rachel will bring him some later, but what about now? How can he fill his stomach when there's nothing but plastic cartons, flattened boxes, potato peelings, and a hotel brochure at his feet?

A demented, sour-faced old lady scratches her cheek and pushes a broken Game Boy in Aaron's face. He shakes his head, darting past her. Day and night she's here, peddling the useless thing, dressed in the same filthy galabeya, gray hair covering her face like a shaggy dog. On the opposite side of the lane a kid sucks on a ketchup packet, leaving dirty traces on his fingers and face. Aaron flinches, thinking it's blood at first—that he's been cut—then hurries past, head down when the kid waves the packet at him.

A memory flashes through Aaron's mind of Mahmud, a kid at school who won a scholarship to go to a private academy in Cairo. He's studying to be a doctor now and has never returned to Mokattam. He's the only kid who ever escaped the village alive, but Mahmud was a genius, the teacher said. Rachel's never going to become a vet and leave here. Aaron firmly sidesteps a heap of rotting food with the certainty he's not going to escape either. The feeling of hopelessness increases as he picks his way through the web of trash leading to his old home. Aaron can feel his stepfamily's presence before he sets eyes on them.

Lurking behind a mountain of bags, Aaron watches Hosi

swivel on his haunches in anger and throw his hands up.

"Without a pony there's no living. Now they're killing the pigs. Why go on?" He shakes his head. "I've worked every day for this—nothing."

Elbows on knees, crouched beside him and a group of men from the nearby slums, Lijah's sucking up to his elders every chance he gets. Listening to and nodding hard about the many obstacles they describe.

Hidden behind a plastic wall of rubbish, Aaron moves slightly to get a better view and the bags crackle.

An old man glances in his direction before saying, "Only a few pigs are left to eat all the food we collect and Cairo Corporation has a new fleet of rubbish trucks. The merchants are paying less and less for the trash we've sorted."

"Lord have mercy!" someone pleads.

"Yes, mercy!" Lijah echoes.

Lijah cheers up when he spots Suzan coming down the alley with a wide grin and a red tint to her roughly cut hair. Though she seems kind and friendly on the surface, Aaron's heard about her spiteful streak. With her long chin and caved-in cheeks, it's no wonder they call her Shovel Face behind her back. Why anyone would want to marry her is beyond him. But then Lijah is more like a vampire than a human being, so maybe they'll be very happy. Suzan works at the craft center with Daniel and, being one of Shareen's friends, Aaron guesses she's keen to follow her example and get married as soon as possible. That way, they can hang out together and compare notes.

Lijah stands up to greet her. They don't touch—just lock

eyes. Touching would break every rule in Cairo. Not even married people hold hands or kiss in the streets. Aaron stands up. He wants to swagger past them on the way to the church wall, show them he's doing fine without their help, but it's difficult with them gazing stupidly at each other in the middle of the lane. As he gets closer, Aaron decides to barge through them with his head held high.

Gazing straight ahead, Aaron strides past with a confident whistle. Hosi glances at him for a moment. A few of the men do the same, uninterested. Suzan's chin is longer than ever close-up, Aaron notes as he goes by. Then, passing a huddle of children sifting through mountains of congealed decay, Aaron catches his breath. Shareen's up ahead, leaning on bags, talking to Father Peter.

Aaron's stomach rumbles from fear as well as from lack of food.

He could go back, but then he'd have to see Lijah again, and if Shovel Face has gone he might decide to pick on him. Aaron hasn't got the strength for it. He looks ahead at the curving path and the limestone walls, which are just there in the distance. If he can only get past Shareen and the priest without being noticed.

Flicking hair from his forehead with a sudden burst of courage, Aaron surprises himself by the speed at which he takes off down the lane scooting past them in a flash. Though not fast enough to avoid the puzzled look on the priest's face, which proves that the missed talk hasn't been forgotten. Shareen shouts after him but he carries on running, heart pounding in his throat.

When he reaches the wide-open space in front of the church, Michael's settling a ladder against one of the high walls with a sharp click. Aaron would like to ask when the Jesus he's sculpting in the limestone will be finished, but instead he stands back to watch. Awed by each fine and tender mark the chisel makes, Aaron glances back down the walkway to make sure the priest isn't coming. He isn't, so, though hungry and pitted with fear, Aaron watches dust fall from the limestone as if something in the sharp edge of the figure of Jesus is drawing him to it. It takes a while before he can cut the connection to the emerging shape and look away.

Shielding his eyes from the sun, Aaron sees that the space in front of the church is empty apart from a black six-seater taxi van. Several local women lounge on the church steps, watching a tourist couple stare at the church with a look of amazement that asks how such indescribable beauty can exist this close to so much filth.

The Passion of Christ. The priest's words zip through Aaron's mind but he has no idea why. *What does that mean?* He turns away from Michael's ladder to walk over to the wall and to sit looking out at the tenements, ready to act when the perfect moment comes to dig out the earth. Which it does the second the tourists disappear into the taxi van with the clunk of a sliding door and the women on the church steps flap dust from themselves as they walk home to empty the carts.

Aaron's pleased he saw fit to leave a bottle here before he stuffed the rest in his jeans. If he hadn't he would have nothing now. Grit sticks in his nails as he claws his way through the earth to the small, rose-colored bottle. He should sell it but he can't. A hot meal isn't worth the only connection he has to his old life. What if he never sees Omar or the perfume shop again?

A small breeze touches Aaron as he whips the bottle from the hole to his pocket and rubs the earth from his hands. He feels better. Having the bottle feeds him with the energy he needs to do what he must do next. Breathing hard, he stamps the ground flat before heading for Jacob's tenement. Lighter on his feet now, and moving quickly, he stops only when he turns a corner and sees two fresh apricots, orange in the sun. It takes a moment for the sight to register. The apricots are somehow waiting for him in the middle of the lane, like a gift from heaven. Chewy and sweet, the flesh clings to his teeth and puts a spring in his step.

Feeling blessed, Aaron kicks a tin can in the air. Kicks it again and again until he reaches the point in the next alley where the bags block his path and he's forced to squeeze through the crackling plastic with arms held high. Out of habit, his eyes travel over the garbage, looking for leftover bread, not-so-old noodles, or half-eaten falafel that haven't been delivered to the remaining pigs.

The taste of apricots still fresh in his mouth, the smell of soiled diapers in his face, Aaron runs his fingers over the smooth bottle in his pocket until he reaches the towering tenements. So far he's found nothing else to eat and now the paths are divided by dark, filthy tunnels which morph into women and children picking through the garbage. The early shift is over and a raging tiredness fills their faces in the airless, midday heat.

It feels as if the sky is pressing down on Aaron as he pushes past a woman with a stove between her knees who is frying pancakes made from chickpea flour. There seems to be no way back as he hurries through a maze of filth to the cauldron where the medical-wasters live.

A few drug addicts huddle together in each alley. Aaron hurries past them and at last turns the corner to Jacob's tenement, then heads up the stairs. He sucks in his breath as he grazes an arm on something poking from a bag on the way up. Aaron grabs at the scratches on his skin, scared stiff they're needle marks. Turning back, wild-eyed and frightened, he focuses on a few copper wires, not needles, sticking out of the top of a bag. To calm himself he clasps the perfume bottle, pressing it to his nose like smelling salts. The scent of rose mixed with lotus and jasmine floods through him. Sniffing the stopper of the bottle again and again, he wallows in the ripple of peace it provides. Before he places the perfume back in his pocket, a new determination sets in: He'll try and talk to Jacob, then . . . get out. He won't stay here.

The calm determination stays with Aaron as he climbs the concrete steps to the second floor, where Jacob lives with his mother, Noha, and two sisters. When he reaches the top, he notices Fatima with the Filthy Mouth standing in the opposite doorway with a bundle under her arm.

Instantly, she swoops past him, flying down the stairs like a witch on a broomstick. The sight feels like an omen. A bad omen. Aaron shudders. He doesn't want to go in, even though the door is wide open.

Aaron's mouth waters at the smell of garlic and peppers

as he hesitates for a second before stepping slowly into the room. Heart beating wildly, he almost turns back at the sight of Jacob and his family, cross-legged on the floor, eating from tin plates and surrounded by bags of medical waste. The room is cleanly swept, Aaron notices, and the glassless windows are clear of cobwebs—like his home was when his mother was alive.

"Aaron?" Noha jumps up to greet him, as if she was expecting him. "Sit here. I was hoping you would come."

Chapter Fourteen
Fortune

Aaron's standing stock still. *Run for it. Go. Get away. Forget the chance of a proper meal. You know medical-wasting is the worst job in Mokattam.*

Now Aaron wishes he'd begged Hosi to take him back. Anything is better than this and he knows what will happen next.

Noha hands Aaron a plate of rice and oily brown lentils and a huge grin spreads across her wrinkled, kind face. For a moment the rich smell disguises the stink of plastic and old bandages coming from the bags, but it's already too late. Too late because he's accepted the food and he can read the payment she wants in her eyes.

Jacob's pretty sisters watch Aaron with interest. He's never been inside their two-and-a-half-room home before and they're surprised their mother has allowed a handsome boy to come this close now that they are twelve and thirteen years old, let alone that she's amazingly pleased to see him. While Jacob's always happy to see Aaron, he's more interested in eating just at this moment.

Casting off his fear, Aaron takes his place on the floor and hungrily digs into the first proper meal he's had since the engagement party. The delicious lentils are mixed with peppers and garlic and Aaron gobbles them up in record time. Noha looks at him carefully, aware that he's desperate and has no way of managing on his own. She doesn't speak until he's finished.

"Are you ready now, Aaron, to make up for your sins? For your stealing."

"I don't know," he answers sheepishly.

"I think you do," Noha says with a glint of triumph in her eyes. "Jacob, show—show."

At this, Jacob springs from the floor with a burst of energy, as if the "fruit cordial" argument hadn't happened, and leads the way to a tiny dark room, which is off the main room where his mother and sisters sleep beside the stove and sink. There's a basic bathroom to one side.

Jacob's half of the room has a yellow boxing glove that clearly serves as a pillow and a worn mat at one end. There's no need for him to point out where Aaron's meant to sleep. Beside the mat is an empty space just big enough for him to lie in. Beside that is a cardboard box with a bundle of clothes on top, a dirty white comb and a wax statue of Mary, Mother of God. Aaron picks it up for a second and smiles before putting it back.

"What made you come now?" Jacob asks.

"I got hungry," Aaron answers simply.

It seems fate that has propelled Aaron to this place and he starts to feel ill, wondering if he'll get out of here alive. A pang of regret for leaving the pony yard stabs him in the chest, until Jacob puts him straight.

"Shareen and her friends are gossiping about Rachel. You had to leave. She's got enough to deal with. That nice Fatima, her stepmom, is going to die in a few weeks."

"A few weeks?" Aaron shakes his head in disbelief. "I liked it there, Jacob—at the pony yard. The stars at night and the smell of ponies and the funny noises they make."

"And . . . Rachel?" Jacob grins. "Her too, eh? She's always down at Sami's, you know."

"Yeah." Aaron shrugs. "But it's OK, I think. I don't know. Rachel's different."

"Not that different. She's still a girl," Jacob says. "But not as pretty as Shareen."

"Don't be stupid." Aaron's shocked. "Shareen's not half as pretty as Rachel. You're joking, aren't you?"

"No." Jacob's glad to have made him smile. "But Rachel is a bit weird. Everyone knows that."

"She's not. Not really." Aaron touches the small bottle of perfume in his pocket and wonders whether he should try and sell it to Noha. She might have some money stashed away somewhere. The thought makes him smile as they re-enter the room and Noha looks up.

"I have a surprise." She unwraps a paper parcel on her lap to reveal a nest of pastries dipped in honey and stuffed with pistachios and walnuts. "Come. Come. Have. Have." She waves a hand at Aaron to show he's included.

With a pastry melting in his mouth, Aaron instantly joins the group of bewildered people in Mokattam who have no idea how Noha manages to look after her family so well on so little money when everyone else scrapes by on next to nothing. Two years ago, when the village was at starvation point due to another war with the merchants, Noha was one of the few people who appeared not to be suffering, food-wise at least. The rumour is that she has a magic way with money, but Aaron knows she has a magic way with Habi, the married greengrocer, more like. Jacob's never talked about it but eyes Habi with interest whenever he sees him—so he must know.

"Everyone's got their secrets," Aaron often heard his mother say. It's true, he thinks as he licks his lips and wipes his mouth with the back of his wrist. Jacob's younger sister, Salome, smiles at him sweetly from the middle of the floor, while the older one, Wadida, refuses to meet his gaze. She seems uncomfortable and wriggles and shifts in her dark galabeya, as if backing away from her own body.

She hates herself, Aaron thinks, and glances at the floor, wondering if she knows that she's got a really nice face. Then he realizes that Wadida is probably ashamed of her family. Or hates being a girl who will be of marriageable age in a couple of years' time and then palmed off, persuaded, sent away or even paid to marry the best available bet. Aaron can't help feeling sorry for her. She looks so miserable that, for a moment, he takes on her sadness as well—almost as if he's her. One thing Aaron's always been grateful for is that he wasn't born a girl. He's seen how the girls he knows are hoodwinked and fooled, often treated as servants by their husbands. How guys like Hosi and Daniel let them slave away while they play cards and talk about soccer.

Jacob distracts Aaron's train of thought by tugging at his elbow. "Visitors are coming to see the church today. We should check them out. They might give us something."

Aaron shakes his head. He has other ideas. "No. I want to go with Ahmet."

It's been several days since he last went into the city and he's pining for the noise, fumes and craziness of the streets, for Omar's shop and the excitement that only Cairo can bring. Suddenly he's desperate to get out of Mokattam.

Ahmet, the deaf metal worker, takes one afternoon off a week to ride his boss's pony and cart around the city because the doctor told him twenty years ago to give his ears a rest from the hammering and banging of the foundry and listen to different sounds. Ahmet took this to mean "listen to other loud sounds" and began haunting the noisiest parts of Cairo. He soon went deaf, but he keeps up the routine of riding the cart around the city with a happy grin and is always good for a lift.

"Right," Jacob says, nodding.

"Come with me!" Aaron suggests.

He stares at Jacob's open face. His friend looks normal, like his old self right now. It was stupid to worry about him. Maybe he was just hungry and the medicine bottle was all he had, Aaron tries to tell himself. He blocks out the lingering memory of pastries and lentils that proves otherwise.

Jacob shakes his head. He's exhausted. "You go."

Aaron nods at Jacob's mother. "Yes, I'll do it." Then he glances at young Salome, and tries to catch Wadida's eyes to give her a quick smile, but she squirms from his gaze. He shoots from the room. This could be his last afternoon of freedom for a long time and he's determined to make the most of it, knowing he'll be too tired tomorrow after working with Jacob to do much of anything else. But the sweet feeling of escape turns bitter the closer Aaron gets to the bottom of the stairs, where a woman is piling used bandages into a bag.

The smell of blood makes him gag. He grabs his stomach to hold back the need to vomit. How's he going to do this? He can't even bear to look. And if he survives the first day, there'll be another and another after that, until a vile disease brings him out in sores and finishes him off. He's not ready to give in to this, he realizes.

There's one last thing he can do to save his own skin—run to the perfume shop in the hope that Omar will take pity on him. Rescue him. Save him from a fate worse than death.

Soon Aaron arrives at the shops and stalls in the old part of the village. Glancing up the lane, he sees Ishaq, the icon seller, pulling down his shutter, closing up for his afternoon nap. The baker's shelves are empty. Only the butcher is hard at work with a meat cleaver by a wooden block that is loaded with chunks of pink flesh. At the small foundry where red-hot coals, high flames, and four smoky figures are pounding hot metal into a molten pulp there's a loud noise of tapping, knocking, and banging. The noises aren't too bad when one man slams his hammer down, but when all four do the same, the sound is deafening.

Aaron covers his ears.

"Where's Ahmet?" he asks the butcher, keeping his eyes firmly on his wide face and away from the meat he's cutting.

"He just left."

The butcher turns his head in the direction of the stone arch and Aaron takes off. He races past the laundry with its sudden alien whiff of soap, then Sami's electrical shop with a flickering TV in the window. Remembering Jacob's words, he slows down and peers inside to see if Rachel's there. A pulsing beat sounds from where Sami's perched in front of a radio beside Habi, the old greengrocer, who's smoking hard. There's no sign of Rachel.

Running under the arch, Aaron spots Ahmet in the distance and speeds up to catch him before the cart turns into the road. There's no point in shouting at the deaf man. Panting for breath, tensing his stomach, Aaron gallops alongside the cart. Ahmet finally spots him and slows down to let him on.

Aaron touches Ahmet's arm with gentle affection as he settles beside him on the scratchy bench. Several fig seeds are trapped between Ahmet's teeth. Aaron points to the seeds. *One there. Two there.* Ahmet nods and licks his lips. He doesn't find them. No matter. Aaron's here at last, on his way to the city. With sunshine skating across Aaron's shoulders, the pony ambles along the busy road, which is bursting with taxis and cars.

Ahmet grins with an animal energy that whips him up to steer the pony right in front of a blue truck.

"Don't be crazy!" Aaron cries, grabbing the reins.

The blue truck overtakes them in a cloud of exhaust fumes. Blasting horns and screeching brakes bring the traffic to a standstill. Aaron makes a fast clicking noise to get the pony out of the way of several stalled cars, but it lifts a hoof and stays where it is. Ahmet can't stop grinning as Aaron awkwardly pushes him aside. He wasn't expecting to be killed today, not when he's trying to escape another deadly fate. Afraid of what Ahmet might do next, Aaron gently tugs the reins and make soothing noises to the pony, which eventually lumbers on to a trot.

With one hand on the reins, Aaron reaches for the perfume in his pocket and it feels real—cool to the touch and safe. Everything else—the orange sun, the wide sky, the endless traffic—seems flimsy and made-up.

This weird sensation of unreality only leaves him when he turns the cart onto the familiar road leading to Omar's shop. The carved black door is open wide and Aaron glances in as he comes to halt a few feet away. Ahmet frowns, wondering why they've stopped, and Aaron reassures him by touching his arm briefly before handing over the reins and climbing down.

"Two minutes," Aaron mouths, holding up a couple of fingers.

It's only been five days since he was here but it feels like a long time ago and the window, with its pink, blue, and golden bottles, seems to glitter a welcome. Aaron stands, hands in pockets, wide-eyed at the new display. The noise of the streets fades to nothing as the reflections of the glass reach out from the mirrored shelves to a place deep inside his chest. He's lost in the sight of the smallest bottles placed between the ones with the bubbled, need-to-touch sides. The rose-glass perfumes are lined up together on the lowest shelf, while the bottles with tall blue necks and pointed stoppers have been carefully mixed in among the round ones with twisting golden spires.

He'd like to stay and work out the reasons for putting this one here, that one there, but he can just make out the dark shape of Omar behind the cash register. There's a chance he might look up and see Aaron gazing in. There's a chance he might feel sorry for him and offer to help. If only a miracle would take place right now and Omar could see he needed looking after and take him on. But then, if he's guessed who stole from him he'll just rush out and collar him again. *Can you be locked up for just looking? For just wanting?*

Aaron drops his eyes, remembering there's a bottle of stolen perfume right now in his pocket. He finds his way through the denim for the bottle. He's too nervous to stay— too sad to go. He suddenly becomes aware that he's not alone and turns swiftly to see Ahmet standing behind him, eyes glued to the window.

It's then that an earth-shattering blast rocks the city and a bolt of black smoke darkens the sky. A bomb. It's a bomb. Aaron knows it's a bomb. A second later cars slam to a stop. Speed to reverse. Taxis brake and screech, skidding and turning. Buses pull over to let passengers off. Police sirens wail. From the direction of the smoke, it's clear a bomb's exploded somewhere in the hotel district. Women pick up their children and flee. People scream, running for their lives.

But in a state of supreme ignorance, Ahmet rubs the

sides of his face and stares at the glittering bottles in the shop window. He hasn't heard the blast and is intoxicated by the colored glass. Then metal shutters cruelly unfurl, dropping to slice the window in two, but not before Omar spots Aaron out front. This clearly isn't the moment to deal with him and the black doors clunk shut. A key twists in the lock.

"Ahmet! Ahmet!"

Aaron tugs his arm, but the deaf man brushes him off, rooted to the spot. He can't look away, even though the window's shuttered tight. In the end, Aaron drags him backwards toward the pony, which is restlessly kicking back while trying to pull the reins from the lamp post. Staggering awkwardly, Ahmet's about to lose his temper until he wakes up to the incredible chaos around him. His eyes dart from cars and buses eager to go the wrong way down the street, to the ominously dark sky, to clouds of dust and dirt flying from the other side of the roundabout, while all around shops are clattering to a shut.

In a daze he climbs on the cart and lets Aaron guide the pony down the middle of the crazy street toward Mokattam. Looking back, Aaron sighs shakily. The main road's crammed with speeding police cars and ambulances. If they hadn't stopped to look in Omar's shop window they'd have followed the road to the roundabout, then gone on to the highway lined with posh hotels. They could be dead now.

Breathing heavily, sweating from head to toe, Aaron has a feeling that someone from among the Zabbaleen must have been caught in the blast. A hollow ache starts inside as he wipes flecks of black dirt from his forehead, racking his brains to recall which families are out on the second shift right now. Who's clearing the cafés and restaurants on the roads leading to the museum? Might they have avoided the explosion? There are hundreds doing that shift.

Ahmet's confused by the chaos as the cart dawdles its way through the traffic trying to leave the city. By the time the bedraggled pony wends his way into the silent cavern of Mokattam filth, Aaron's glad to be home for once. No bomb's ever gone off here.

The icon seller is asleep in his doorway. Insects have set up home on his feet. A small, half-naked boy crawls gingerly out from under the stall selling limes, bananas, and mangoes. Everyone else is at the end of the lane, arms folded, crowded around one of the few men in Mokattam who owns a cell phone.

Aaron thuds to a stop to listen to the breathless voice on the phone, which is held palm-out for everyone to hear.

"Yes, a hotel. I don't . . . Can't see. Yes, an explosion they think. It's Armageddon here. Blood everywhere. There's at least twenty dead. Even more injured. There's a mangled pony in the road between cars smashed with concrete. Glass everywhere. The police are moving everyone on. I can't quite see. Yes, the cart's on its side. Rubbish all over the place. Two, you say? The guy here says two on the cart are dead. One with a blue-and-white shirt. Can you hear?"

Simon. It's Simon. He has a blue-and-white shirt. Simon's dead. His brother, Mart, too. Aaron went to school with them. Simon's the same age as him, too cocky, but he's nice to Abe. Says he's going to get him a jellyfish on the Internet.

Abe adores Simon, like he does Aaron, as if he's an older brother. Since day one it's been, *Simon this, Simon that*. Aaron enjoys Abe waiting for him and following him around, but sometimes it's good to get rid of him and Simon was always happy to take over when Aaron got fed up. Abe'll miss him too. He's been blown up by some maniac while picking up trash. Aaron's stunned. It could have been him. Several adults are staring at Aaron and he doesn't know how to react. What can he do to show he's as shocked and sad as they are, when really the news has turned his heart to stone?

Strange as it feels, all Aaron can think as he climbs off the cart is, Shareen's wedding's supposed to be tomorrow. He feels sick and stunned—off balance as he heads away from the old village toward the tenements. Everyone's running the other way. Bad news travels fast in Mokattam. Already the smell of death is in the air and the bodies aren't even here yet. But they will be—Simon and his brother will be cremated within twenty-four hours.

Instead of turning down the lane that leads to the medical-wasters' tenements, Aaron races to the church. Suddenly in need of peace and something nice to look at, he walks beside the high, curving limestone walls with their pale frescoes of scenes from the Bible and looks up with envy. How does Michael know how to make those figures look so real? As he gets closer to the open walkway in front of the church he sees Michael talking to Mohammed, the guy whose daughter died of kidney disease last year. Aaron hesitates and lowers his head. Father Peter is up ahead, walking his way as if he has urgent business on his mind. He must have heard about

Simon. Surely he doesn't want to speak to Aaron about the bottles now?

Aaron turns his face to the wall to avoid being caught. Heart thumping, he can feel and hear the priest rush past in squeaky sandals. The skin on the back of Aaron's neck prickles with heat. But Father Peter has seen him and stops in his tracks and turns back.

"It's good to see you, Aaron," he calls.

"And you, Father," Aaron lies as he slowly turns to face him.

"How are you?" he asks.

"Fine." Aaron takes a deep breath and meets his pale, staring eyes.

"I have just one thing to say to you." Father Peter nods.

"Right." Aaron sighs, hoping it will really be just one thing.

"One day you will be judged for what you give, not for what you have."

With that, Father Peter looks past him, hitches up his black robe, and rushes on, his sandals squeaking more than ever.

The dreaded talk is over and Aaron's off the hook. But though he's relieved he got off lightly, the priest's words weigh him down as he looks around. At the front of the church, arranging a green knapsack of tools on his shoulder, Michael meets his glance with a look of understanding and half nods.

"Aaron," he calls.

"Yes?" Aaron gulps. *What now?*

With the sun lighting his face, Michael smiles. He looks

as if he has had an idea. "Yes, a moment please."

Aaron's jaw snaps tight with fear as he walks toward him. *I've got nothing to lose if he asks about the bottles. What do I care?*

"Why do you think you are here, alive, in Mokattam?" Michael says softly.

Aaron eyes him carefully. Apart from the dusty, knotted handkerchief on his head, Michael doesn't look suspicious—just curious—which makes the question sound strange. He seems to want a serious reply.

"Dunno." Aaron shifts from foot to foot.

"I believe we're here on earth to learn from our mistakes and become better people." Michael smiles again.

Aaron tries not to sigh. *Oh, no. The priest must have asked him to give me a talk. I should say I'm sorry for stealing the perfumes, but the words won't come out.*

"We're here to help each other."

Twisting the strap of the knapsack from his shoulder, Michael drops the tools on the floor with a clank.

"Really?"

Aaron didn't mean to say it out loud. All he was wondering was, what would Michael do if he asked him for help right now? Asked if he could go to his house and live with him? He'd take him home? Yeah, right!

"Yes, really. God wants us to be happy, Aaron."

At which Aaron laughs. How can someone as clever as Michael get things so wrong? When did God ever help him? Michael's stupid words make him angry, so angry he shoots his mouth off.

"Happy? Here? Simon and his brother are dead. His mom's not happy. Loads of people aren't happy. Shareen's not happy and it's her wedding tomorrow. I don't know anyone who's happy."

Michael looks thoughtful for a moment, then, "I'm happy," he says. As he picks up his tools to go, he looks Aaron in the eye and, as a parting shot, adds, "But maybe we can learn something from their deaths?"

Learn something? Yeah, that life stinks.

Just as he's about to speak, a soft padding noise interrupts Aaron's thoughts. Abe's running toward him, waving his arms like a baby.

Chapter Fifteen
Work

As if from a place he'd forgotten, Aaron puts an arm around Abe's skinny shoulders, hugging him awkwardly. The sudden heat of his friend's collapsing body makes Aaron's eyes well up. Quickly, he blinks the tears away and, embarrassed, sinks down beside Abe on to the low wall, with his arm like that for more than five minutes. For much longer than he wants—but it's hard to let go when Abe's crying and rubbing his face with his fist before starting all over again.

Aaron's trying to get Abe to calm down when he spots Shareen. Her eyes are painted so thickly with kohl, she looks as if she's wearing sunglasses. Standing with a group of older women, she puts her hands behind her back, then, for a second, stands on tiptoe. Her toenails are varnished bright red; tacky, not that nice plum color from before.

Aaron tries letting his arm slip down Abe's back, but the boy pulls in closer still. Now Shareen's staring at them. He doesn't want her looking. With damp eyes, Abe glances at her curious face and quickly buries his head in Aaron's gray T-shirt. Shareen walks over and pats Abe's head in a *poor thing* kind of way and her fake gesture drags a sharp claw across Aaron's stomach. She hardly knows Abe.

"Simon was nicer than his brother. Shame they both got blown up, though." Shareen shrugs.

Abe howls and bursts into tears again. Shareen glances at Aaron, eager to make him see she didn't mean to make Abe cry, but he turns away angrily. Shareen looks past him at the rows of tenements beyond the wall, staring hard, as if there's something to see, then glances back at the church. She seems ready to go, but something stops her from leaving. Turning around, Aaron can see this is a far better viewpoint from which to see what's going on than where she was before. With a little hum, she settles on the wall to the other side of Abe. Shifting slightly, Aaron pulls him away from her but, sitting on her hands, Shareen pretends not to notice and settles back to watch the comings and goings in front of the church.

Father Peter is flapping down the path to lead the prayers. It's obvious the deaths have already been confirmed. Someone shouts that a family who was out on the carts is bringing the bodies home, which means the church candles will be lit and left to burn all night until the sun comes up tomorrow. Incense will smother the smell of garbage until the brothers are cremated within twenty-four hours and sadness will drift over Mokattam until their deaths become another sorry fact of life for everyone here.

Eventually Abe wipes his eyes for the last time and joins in gazing at the crowd on the concrete pews of the church that is singing prayers to the darkening sky. The shadows lengthen before Shareen, without a backward glance, rushes off to greet her friends. The deaths haven't taken the spring from her step; she's almost skipping. By the sound of the giggles coming from her friends, she's chatting about her wedding tomorrow. She's the center of attention again, despite the grief all around her. Aaron guesses that means the celebrations will be going ahead regardless.

He stretches his arms and stands up. "Are you going home, Abe?" His voice sounds slightly forced—even to his own ears. "Your mom will be worried about you."

"Yeah, I'm going." Abe nods with big, dark, sorry eyes. "You can come too, but there's the pig and us in one room."

"Nah, I'm going to Jacob's." Aaron sighs and Abe gives him an alarmed look. "It'll be all right. Don't worry."
A piece of cellophane catches the early-evening breeze and floats above his head before fluttering to his feet. He glances at the dusty earth and another picture springs to mind: a delicious plate of oily yellow rice. He's resigned to being a medical-waster now, even if it kills him off.

Silence settles between the two boys before they smile and head off in different directions. A mosquito follows Aaron down the maze of alleys to the tenements. The annoying buzz forces him to blunder into the open doorway of Jacob's home as if he's drunk. Noha looks at him sharply before spotting the mosquito and capturing it with a single pinch. Flicking the squashed bug to the floor, she rubs away the blood on her fingers on the side of her black galabeya.

After Aaron gratefully finishes his plate of cold stuffed grape leaves, Noha blows out the candle at her feet and lies down between the garbage bags to sleep. By the time Aaron arranges his limbs in the tight space beside Jacob, who's flat out on the mat, Noha's already snoring.

Aaron's more than tired, but the stench of bandages keeps him awake. He reaches for the perfume bottle in his pocket and holds it to his nose. "Only girls like perfume," Shareen once said to annoy him. Well, what does she know? The sweet scent nearly persuades him to twist the stopper off for the first time and cover his face with the luscious oil, if only to send him into a deep sleep, but then Noha would smell it in the morning and question him before taking the bottle because she'll guess it was stolen. One day he'll open it, but for now pressing the rim of the bottle to his nose again is enough to give him wings. Wings to soar out of here, up into the sky like an eagle and along the banks of the Nile.

Jacob's on his feet at quarter to five but Aaron's in a state of sleep that takes more than a few tugs to bring him around. Try as Aaron might to snuggle back down, Jacob pulls him up by the elbow and gives him a beaker of warm hibiscus tea to drink. Clearly Jacob is excited not to be alone today; he smiles at Aaron as he gulps the tea down. Aaron's glad Jacob seems more awake than him and decides he hasn't had anything stronger than tea this morning.

They both duck into the shadows of the main room, where Noha's guarding the bags, and Aaron is even more surprised to be handed a warm flatbread along with a pile of folded bags as they head out of the door and into the early-morning light. The full force of hospital smells fades for a moment when Aaron buries his nose in the bread, which flours his mouth and fingers as he hurries down the concrete stairs with the faint clatter of pans in his ears.

Aaron doesn't have the nerve to ask Jacob exactly where they're going. It's a question he dreads knowing the answer to and at the same time his thoughts turn to Rachel, wondering if she'll be at the yard right now, looking for him and perhaps missing him. More than anything, he wishes Jacob's family kept their pony at her yard. At least then, like before, he'd have something nice to look forward to at the start of every day. But this yard is only two minutes' walk from Jacob's tenement and before long the flurry of pony petting and attaching it to the cart is over and they're on their way to the first hospital.

As they pass a stall a news vendor flaps open a newspaper with the headline "Another Hotel Bomb Blast! Names of Victims Inside!"

"Bet Simon's and Mart's names aren't there," Jacob says, staring dumbly ahead.

"Yeah," Aaron agrees.

"Let's not think about them today, eh?" A huge smile spreads over Jacob's face.

"OK."

Aaron leans back. The nice feeling of friendship that comes over him reminds him how awful it was to sit beside

Lijah each day. This ride is so different—peaceful and calm, despite the building traffic and noise of car horns. Even the thought of the pile of diseased waste that waits for them at the end of the journey doesn't seem so bad when Jacob grins like that.

Jacob lifts a hand to flatten his curly hair. Today's traffic is heading for the city faster than ever and with Aaron's help they can be home in less than five hours. Slogging around the city hospitals on your own is never fun, but now there's the unspoken worry between them that yesterday's bomb may not be the last.

"I saw Daniel yesterday evening," Jacob says. "He was behind the butcher's, talking to old Katerina. She was reading his cards and said the eight of swords means there could be conflict or misfortune if he doesn't seize an opportunity."

There's a long pause while Aaron takes this in. "What does that mean?"

"Dunno, but Daniel went yellow. He caught me listening and sent me away. He must be scared. I would be. Shareen threw a pot at him when he showed her the ring he'd bought."

Aaron can't help but laugh at that image.

"It's not funny, Aaron."

"Yeah, it is. I mean, he might think he will be able to control her, but nobody can control Shareen. He doesn't know what he's in for. He's going to get a shock."

"Well, let's go tonight and see what happens. Anyway, there'll be tons of food. The baker was up all night, Mom said."

Jacob tightens his hold on the reins and the dark, skinny

pony swishes his tail as he quickens to a fast trot.

Before long the traffic clears as they turn down the main road leading to the west of the city, where the wide avenues are lined by large houses with big satellite dishes and have nice cars parked outside. They pass a school, a mosque, and a sport's center. A feeling of ease seems to float over the area. There are trees at the edge of the pavement and patches of trimmed grass sparkle in the sunshine. Aaron's never been here before and can't help being amazed at how the cart glides over the flat, asphalted streets. Everything's so clean.

"Where's all the garbage?" he asks, wide-eyed.

"It's kept in black bins at the back." Jacob nods. "The Zabbaleen used to have this area, but now Cairo Corporation empties the bins in their trucks. If you live here you never think about trash. It disappears at night like magic."

Aaron finds this impossible to believe. "Really?"

"Yeah, honest. They say there's twice as much rubbish here because the rich buy what they want and then throw it away to make room for more things. Half the time things haven't even been unwrapped. I'm telling you, there are shoes that haven't been worn, olives left in jars, brand-new shirts, sunglasses even."

For a moment Aaron's baffled. He envies the people who get to clear the trash from this place. He wants their good stuff. Reaching into the left pocket of his jeans, he transfers the perfume bottle from there to the right pocket, where it feels safer. He wonders if Omar lives somewhere like this. Aaron wants to stop and look through the bins for himself, but instead they turn sharply down another tree-lined road leading to a mansion with a sign reading "The Sadat Hospital" painted in silver.

Halfway up the long path they turn sideways along a narrow dirt track that leads to a shabby wing of the main gray building. At the end of the track is the familiar smell of disinfectant and used bandages, together with a pungent whiff coming from a plume of smoke circling a high chimney. Soon the cart pulls swiftly inside a gap in a tall metal fence beside a yard crammed with bags of used bandages, grubby cloths, knives, beakers, scalpels, syringes.

"Ergh!" Aaron covers his nose.

"The incinerator's working, then." Jacob sighs. "But it must have been broken earlier, because there's plenty of stuff here. When it's operating twenty-four hours a day there's not much here and I have to do the sister hospital two miles away to make up the load. I hate that place."

Aaron eyes him cautiously. *He hates that place! What about this place?* First, it stinks to high heaven of death, then there are the leaking bags and boxes stacked against the peeling walls and filthy doors that thump and bang from whatever's happening inside. The plume of gray smoke choking the sky smells far worse close-up.

Jacob steers the cart along the wall to a small concrete area hidden from view to one side of the waste. It's this cover that allows the Zabbaleen to do their illegal job. Jacob climbs down, his eyes squarely on the white door near where the pony's parked. He pats the pony on the nose and says, "Stay!" Aaron follows Jacob quickly back to where the waste is stacked, aware that if they're caught collecting used and diseased plastic, metal, and glass, the hospital won't be blamed for what they're doing. The hospital managers rarely fulfil their legal duty of packing dangerous waste safely and paying special companies to take it away. They know the Zabbaleen will remove it for nothing so the blood bags, tubes, instruments, and test tubes are rarely packed correctly. And if the collectors are caught, the managers will say the Zabbaleen ripped the bags and boxes apart in their search for salable goods.

Today Jacob and Aaron have hit lucky. There's no one around and they work in total silence. A shiver of fear strikes Aaron's stomach. He's used to touching glass and these materials are new to him. He imitates Jacob's watchful eyes as he scans the sides of a huge white bag before kicking it over to check that nothing's leaking underneath.

Jacob handles the first bag carefully, pinching an exposed edge, any clear edge, with a finger and thumb to avoid getting his hands and arms cut by syringes, scalpels and knives that haven't been placed in the proper containers and are ready to stab at him like weapons. Aaron copies him, working hard to get rid of the bags as quickly as he can, as if they're unexploded missiles.

Once they've emptied the hospital bags they start on the stack of white boxes marked "Bio-Hazardous Waste." Only one box is tightly closed and taped; the rest have open lids and two are badly damaged and look as if they've been dropped from a window. Jacob is bending down to inspect one that's filled with half-used blood bags and medicines when a car engine sounds and putters to a stop in the distance.

Jacob straightens, holding his breath. Aaron gazes at the entrance and, listening hard, hears a car door open and then shut. Footsteps head in their direction. Low voices start up. Someone's coming.

Quick as a flash, Jacob grabs a box and runs to the cart, with Aaron close behind. As the voices get louder their fear grows. It sounds as if two men are having a heated row about the waste. Aaron flinches at the sight of Jacob's shaking body as they climb up. Jacob forces the pony back along the wall. Just before they reach the gap in the fence, Jacob pulls the pony close to the other side and, hidden from view, they listen to the conversation.

"If they catch us, say we're taking dead bodies to the crematorium and laugh," Jacob whispers to an increasingly nervous Aaron. "Look pleased."

"Pleased? With a cart full of dangerous medical waste that should be got rid of properly?" Aaron shakes his head.

"Shush!" Jacob warns. "Listen."

There's a shuffling sound as the first man raises his voice. "I'm telling you, don't let those Zabbaleen inside or you'll be fined and sent to jail. They're selling the medical tubes, blood bags, and intensive-care trays to Faisal, who's turning them into plastic knives, forks, and spoons for the restaurants. It must stop."

"They make plastic cutlery from the tubes and syringes? I don't believe you!" The second man may not be convinced, but Aaron is.

"Whoa . . ." Aaron mutters, shocked.

"Be quiet," Jacob mouths.

"The All Saints' Hospital is buying a new incinerator to cope with their waste. You must do the same here or pay the correct people to dispose of it. Those are your only choices," the first man warns.

"Ha," the second man laughs. "The manager of the All Saints' Hospital is a liar and a cheat. If you believe him you're the stupidest government inspector I've ever met. I'm busy. I'll walk back. You take a look at the waste if you want, but I'm done. Good-bye."

Things go quiet, then quick footsteps thud away.

Aaron wrings his hands, scared but ready to jump from the cart and run, while Jacob leans forward, grinning. They hear the metal fence shudder for a second, then a car door clicks open and slams shut.

"Phew!" Aaron sinks back on the cart.

"Don't worry," Jacob says, sighing. "That government inspector takes *baksheesh* from the hospital guy to ignore the stuff we collect. They're both crooks."

Aaron can't believe what Jacob has to go through each day. Not only does he have to clear syringes and dangerous medical waste, but he also has to avoid people like this, who will blame him for doing their dirty work.

"The new city rubbish trucks have picked six pilot areas to add to their clearing. How much do you bet they won't be doing the hospitals?" Jacob asks.

With complete understanding, Aaron shakes his head in disgust.

"What about Faisal? Does he really recycle this stuff into plastic knives and forks?"

"Probably. Who cares?" Jacob taps the reins and the pony clops toward the exit in the fence.

"I'm never touching plastic spoons again," Aaron says, and squirms.

"You'll be doing a lot worse than that soon." Jacob suddenly looks twice at him. "The guy who runs the incinerator here is one of the good ones. You wait and see how the Sulayman Hospital gets rid of their syringes and tubes."

Aaron frowns. "Can't wait."

Half an hour later they're staring at another tumbling mountain of ugly hospital debris in the yard. But this time the see-through hospital bags have been tipped out by drug addicts searching for medicines they can swallow or inject. Aaron does the only thing he can think of while straining to control his nausea. His stomach turns over as he grabs one of the bags from the cart, fluffs it open, bends the rim back over his hands to protect them, and using it like a shovel, scoops as much trash into it as he can.

Aaron watches Jacob for a moment. His friend is working slowly because he's searching the river that's falling into the bag and running down his arms and crashing to his feet—searching for the pill packets and medicine bottles the drug addicts have left behind. Aaron leans over him and, the second their eyes meet, Jacob speeds up. When Aaron turns to sling the bag on the cart, Jacob grabs a white packet he's had his eye on, squirreling it into his pocket.

With no need to clear another hospital today because the cart's full, they trot down the long dirt track to the main road, knowing they're more or less free now. Aaron's relieved it's over. Once they've emptied the cart of rubbish, Jacob's sisters and mother will sort the bags. The rest of the day belongs to them. They can eat and rest. His first day as a medical-waster has been scary, but at least he didn't get pricked by anything sharp. Maybe if he's careful he will survive this for a month or two, until something better comes along.

With the sunshine burning into his back, Aaron turns his thoughts to Shareen's wedding party later tonight.

"Shall we go to the wedding, then?"

"If it happens." Jacob nods. "Mom said Shareen's going to stay at the hairdresser's all day for threading her eyebrows and having her nails done. She won't make it, I bet."

"What about Daniel? Do you think he'll stay under the tap for longer than two minutes to wash his hair and feet?"

Jacob smiles and says, "Doubt it. He's worn that same galabeya all year. But Fatima with the Filthy Mouth says she saw him scrubbing his neck with a stone, so he must be keen."

"He'll need more than one stone to clean his neck!"

Aaron lets go of the bottle in his pocket when a dark-windowed white coach speeds past them with the words "Land of the Pharaohs" written in large letters on the side.

"Land of the Zabbaleen, it should say." Jacob laughs. "I've got some spray paint left . . ."

"How much?" Aaron asks.

"Enough for tonight."

Jacob waves a fly from the pony's back by flicking the reins and smiles at the mischief they can make later with a drop of red paint.

"Did you know there's a whole island of plastic

bottles in the sea near Japan?" Jacob says. "I saw it on Sami's TV."

Aaron hardly listens as Jacob expands on how the world's drowning in plastic. After the word *Sami*, the picture that springs to his mind is of Rachel, not plastic. Rachel wishing on a future with animals and trying to make it happen by dreaming and hoping, but never being able to do anything about it. She is already great with animals, but all that's open to her once her stepmother dies is a job caring for her father and younger sisters until someone like Sami gives her another list of tasks. Tasks to make his life, not hers, better.

The thought sparks a memory of the last hour he spent with his mother. Out of breath, clutching her stomach in pain, she told him not to fetch Hosi from a neighbor's house because there was nothing he could do to make her well again. "Do my share of the sorting, son, then sweep the floor for me," she whimpered, before collapsing for the last time.

He picked up her limp hand and felt the warmth of her skin. "Mom, Mom, don't leave me here," he pleaded. But he knew she'd gone and he stared at the tiny smile on her calm face with disbelief. Disbelief until her hand went cold. Then he ran outside, reeling from shock. In a daze, staring at the garbage, the dirty track, the woman opposite curled up in filth, her kid vomiting beside her, he wanted to punch the sun out. To scream, cry, yell, weep. Get rid of the poisonous pain rising in his gut, the guilt that he was somehow to blame for her sad end. Her sad life. The sadness he couldn't save her from. He should have rescued her. He should have helped her more. He should have shouted for someone, even though she told him not to.

Then he came face to face with Lijah.

"Mom's dead."

"So what?" Lijah said.

The cart suddenly stalls.

"You OK?" Jacob asks, catching the desperate look on Aaron's face.

"Yeah. Yeah." Aaron smiles wearily. "Just thinking."

The main road is crippled by traffic. A thick gray smog blocks the tenements from view and, when the car horns start blaring, a feeling of suffocation stirs Aaron to action. He jumps down, eager to get away.

"Where are you going?" Jacob calls, but he's off.

Aaron runs down the middle of the road, darting between buses and coaches, squeezing through backed-up taxis and cars. A man in a red truck leans out of the window to stare angrily. His fierce eyes follow Aaron to the pavement, where he disappears down a narrow road leading to Mokattam.

Ten minutes later Aaron wanders under the stone arch of the village, where a red paper banner hangs between two pillars. The names Shareen and Daniel are intertwined with painted hearts and a white balloon at either side. The smell of fried onions and spices in freshly made *kushari* fills his nose as he rushes past the small food stores. The fat laundry man is ironing a black jacket on a huge board in the street. He sprays water from the bubble in his bulging cheeks to smooth the hard cotton every few seconds.

"Daniel's?" Aaron shouts.

The laundry man pauses to stare at Aaron, remembers

what he's done, and turns away.

"Is that Daniel's?" Aaron points at the jacket and nods.

Without looking at him, the man says, "This borrowed suit is threadbare. I told him to buy a new one but nah, nah."

By the time Aaron reaches Sami's secondhand electrical shop he's feeling moody and angry at the laundry man's reluctance to answer his question. But his face relaxes when he spots Sami in a yellow T-shirt at the counter, which is crammed with old-fashioned radios. He's rewiring a plug with a sharp fingernail and cursing the short wires. Rachel's nowhere to be seen, which pleases Aaron.

Switching his attention to the path ahead, he quickly avoids a group of women busy scrubbing stains from their rags with screwed-up balls of paper. The carts haven't returned yet and their soft voices rise and fall like birdsong as he scoots past, hands in pockets. The recent deaths have darkened their smiles.

Then he sees—almost bumps into—Shareen, who's sitting on her haunches, caressing a pair of silver slippers in her lap. She hasn't been done up yet. Her hair's still a tangled mess.

"Hey! Hey!" she shouts as Aaron races past. But Shareen's a lost cause. If he can save Rachel from Sami instead, that would make him happy.

Rushing on through the alleys, Aaron soon turns the corner that leads to the yard. There's the rumble of a train in the distance and he pauses to listen. Whenever he hears that sound he recalls Jacob saying that 150 years ago, ten thousand mummies were dug up from the necropolis and most were sold to the railway for fuel. It's hard to believe they ran the trains on mummified corpses. But they had so many. Some people say there are too many Zabbaleen.

Maybe they'll get rid of us too, Aaron thinks grimly. *Sell us for fuel.*

Chapter Sixteen
Rachel

Aaron can hear *swish-swishing* sounds before he gets to the yard.

"Rachel?"

She's there beside the trough, washing a metal bucket in the water. Silver arrows of light skate across her arms. Her dark hair gleams. She looks so lovely, a sudden attack of nerves stops him from speaking. He'd convinced himself she wouldn't be here. It feels tougher attempting to talk to Rachel than it does to suddenly admit to himself that he's a medical-waster.

Rachel lifts her head and curls her lips. "Look," she says. "I got bitten by a snake."

She stretches out an arm and a whiff of jasmine fills the air. Aaron leans in to examine the blotchy patch of skin below her elbow and the smell becomes stronger.

"Nice perfume," he says.

"No. It's special soap." Rachel swings the bucket from the trough and places it at her feet. Drops of water darken the earth in spreading patterns. "Fatima's been saving it for when I get married, but she says she won't last until then. Are you going tonight?"

"Married?" The word almost chokes Aaron. It feels as if the pyramids have just collapsed. "When are you getting married?"

Why did I say that? Don't tell me!

But, as she splashes her arm with gritty water, softly patting the red mark where she was bitten, she says, "Who said I was getting married? You're not listening." Rachel raises her eyes to heaven. "It wasn't much of a snake. I was sitting on my hands over there, watching the ponies, and felt this nip, then it slithered off fast as anything. I knew it wasn't bad before the nurse from the clinic worked it out, because when I saw the bite I said to myself, nothing can hurt you unless you let it, and it didn't. It's a kind of magic I've got going with God. You know?"

"I guess," Aaron mutters, without really understanding. She's talking, but not particularly to him, and there's a lovely dreaminess in her eyes that he's never seen before.

"What, Aaron?" she asks.

"I was . . . thinking about glass." Aaron flushes.

"Glass?" She sighs. "On this show on TV it said girls should say what's on their mind as boys are going backwards because they have the same chromosomes they've had since the times of the pharaohs. While we have two big XX ones which are growing, you have an X and a Y and anyone can

192

see a Y is just an X with a bit missing. I said that. Not the TV. Anyway your Y is shrinking. It's just a stump now. Our Xs are growing. They share information, but your Y is useless. It doesn't share. It's just a tiny lump."

A lump? Nice!

For the first time, Aaron realizes Rachel's more interested in watching TV these days than looking after the ponies and he knows why.

"What does Sami think about this stuff?"

"He says don't believe everything you see on TV."

A heartfelt smile spreads across her face. A smile that tells Aaron she's impressed by Sami, who swears at plugs and sits on a stool all day. Plus he walks on the hems of his jeans.

It's a truth Aaron doesn't want to see. A tight cluster of sweat breaks out on his forehead, while miles and miles of emptiness open out in front of his eyes. His brain throbs into a pulp. He'd been feeling sorry for her, while all along she's been feeling sorry for him—for being born a boy and now for being an orphan medical-waster.

All Aaron can do is walk away. Heart in his mouth, he takes a deep breath. If he can hold his temper until he gets to the edge of the yard, he can run to the church, to the low wall, and slam his fist on a brick—stamp the ground, kick something hard to take the sting of jealousy away. He scrabbles for the bottle in his dusty pocket and, just as he reaches the path, he hears Rachel shout.

"Fatima . . . died last night. You're the first person I've told."

Aaron turns slowly to look at her standing there like a

beautiful, sad-eyed statue, trapped in perfect sunshine. So still and lovely. Instantly, he understands why she didn't tell him about Fatima before. She couldn't. It wasn't real until she said it. He knows that feeling and he wants to run back and hold her, but that's the last thing he can do. He must say something, as long as it isn't stupid. Isn't like Lijah's horrible *So what? Go. Go on. Go. Move.*

Aaron shifts slightly. There's quarry dust on his toes. He clenches a fist. She'll remember this moment for the rest of her life. The first time she's told someone Fatima is dead and he's staring at his feet. Frozen to the spot.

Don't be like Lijah. She'll remember what you say.

Aaron stumbles toward her, arms trembling. Boys aren't supposed to touch girls, but his hands reach roughly for her shoulders and she grabs them as if they're life rafts. Pressing them to her eyes, she smothers his palms in tears which sting his skin like prickly pears.

Aaron whispers to her wet lashes, "I'll look after you. If you want . . ."

"That's mad," she sniffs. "What with?"

"I couldn't think of anything else to say," he murmurs, embarrassed.

"I know," Rachel sobs. She uses his hard, dirty hands as tissues to dry her face, then drops them. "They're scratchy."

"It goes with the job." Aaron shrugs. Their eyes meet. "Sorry about Fatima."

They're both silent for a moment. *Now the only friends I've got with a mother are Abe and Jacob*, he thinks to himself.

"What's it like?" Rachel tries to sound normal. "Someone

194

said you're doing . . . medical-wasting."

Aaron has trouble thinking with Rachel standing this close, and it feels as if she's talking to someone else. He's not a medical-waster, is he?

"Awful."

The answer forces his thoughts away from the fantastic sensation of Rachel beside him, so close, to the alarming face of Noha with her wrinkled neck, sorting through syringes. Noha, pinching mosquitoes out of the air above his head. What was natural now feels unnatural.

Rachel picks up on the sudden change in him. "It's not up to anyone to make me feel better," she says, stubbornly folding her arms.

And Aaron's back to square one. Back to the beginning. Teetering between owning up and running away. Her look tells him she's thinking he's a . . . half chromo thing who isn't quite right. Who isn't Sami either, with his safe job fixing radios. The longer they stand there, the wider the gap between them grows.

He's somehow messed up, even though she's smiling sweetly between her tears.

"Do you think you can have what you want if you just want it enough?" she says.

"Maybe." Aaron sighs.

"I prayed for Fatima to live, but she didn't."

"She might have wanted to die," Aaron offers.

"You mean what Fatima wanted was more important than what I wanted?"

"It was her life, wasn't it?" He forces himself to smile.

"How about what God wanted, then?" she asks.

A jumble of answers crash around Aaron's brain before he says, "Maybe God hasn't made up his mind yet. I mean, look at all the garbage in the world. He hasn't figured that one out, has he?"

Why is Rachel starting things up between them again? His answer's not good enough and her lips begin to quiver.

"I want to know. I want someone to tell me why she died."

There's a roar behind her soft words that she can't let go of and Aaron feels as if *his* mother just died. Died again. Leaving the same question on his lips that Rachel's asking. He doesn't know how to make her feel better and the comforting smell of her, the sound of her voice, the flashes of light in her dark eyes, make him shrink like a shadow into the dust.

"The Holy Family came this way once." Rachel gazes at the clear blue sky with troubled eyes. "They were in Cairo. They must have seen the pyramids."

"I bet there weren't any bags of rubbish here then," Aaron says, and Rachel laughs.

Her laugh destroys the dark feeling inside him and the sunshine comes home to them both. A picture of the Holy Family here in Mokattam is hard to get rid of once it has sprung to life and it's not until the sound of a pony and cart tumbles down the lane toward them that Rachel remembers Fatima and her face fills with sorrow again.

Jamal comes round the corner on his cart. It's his sister, Suzan, who's going to marry Lijah, and Aaron feels a stab of guilt for what the whole family is about to receive. He wonders

196

whether Lijah will treat his brother-in-law like his stepbrother.

"Hiya."

The atmosphere lightens when Jamal jumps down to give them some strange news.

"There's this thing in the paper about a woman who saw Mary, Mother of God, going into the Imperial Hotel. Honest." He throws the crumpled newspaper at them.

"That's stupid," Rachel says, as Aaron catches the flyaway page before it lands in the dirt and her words stab him through the heart. *It's true. It's true.* He wants to yell but doesn't have the nerve.

Opening it up, Aaron flattens the paper with the side of his palm by resting it on his knee. Underneath the headline is a picture of a smiling middle-aged woman in a green headscarf who's described as thirty-four and living in Heliopolis with her surveyor husband and three kids.

She looks normal enough.

"Read it out loud," Rachel says as she helps Jamal offload the cart and gently leads the pony to the trough. Even though most Zabbaleen children learn to read at six years old, she's too shy to show off in front of the boys. "Go on, Aaron."

He smiles, happy to do what he's told.

" 'On Thursday morning at nine thirty I was coming back from Aunty's house—she's deaf and I do what I can for her. I was hurrying to cross the highway to get to work. It was murder, the traffic was—' Hang on . . ."

The pony makes a snuffling sound, as if eager to hear the rest, and Aaron skips the next bit to stutter over the next sentence.

"'I thought I was . . . was . . . er, imagining . . . imagining things, but no, I'm telling you, I'm not like that. Look at me, I'm an ordinary married woman and I saw the ghostly figure of the Virgin Mary in front of the Imperial Hotel opposite me. But it wasn't a ghost. I almost fainted at the sight of her. I nudged the woman next to me and she saw it too. We aren't Christians. We don't pay attention like them—we're Muslims—but we know her. She was there. When we got to the hotel she was gone. We went inside but, bah, nobody saw her. We told the reception girl, but she had her nose so high in the air she couldn't even see her desk.'"

"What did I say?" Jamal quickly nods. "She went to the priest and the church sent people down there with cameras. They saw nothing. Now everyone's crowding the hotel. The police have set up a cordon to keep them away. It's all over Cairo."

"Really? Wow," Rachel pipes up.

A strange sensation spreads through Aaron at the thought that it could have been his picture in the paper. Now he knows he didn't imagine Mary. She came to him. She did.

"You've gone gray," Jamal says.

"Nah, I was just . . ." But Aaron can't explain. He can't tell them he saw Mary too. They wouldn't believe him. He turns to Rachel. "Does Sami let you on his computer?"

"Of course."

"He won't let me touch it," Jamal says sadly. "But sometimes he doesn't mind if I look over his shoulder, as long as I don't lean in too close."

"I wish Mary would come to me."

Rachel turns away with a funny skip, so funny that even the ponies prick up their ears at her. It's almost as if she can feel Aaron staring and is swinging her arms because she knows he likes her.

Rachel is deep in thought as she heads away from her family who is outside the coffin-maker's house to pay the bill after Fatima's cremation. "Don't look back when I'm gone," Fatima told her before she died. "And stay away from Sami." That was a bit rich, coming from her, because her own mother had tried everything in her power to keep her away from Rachel's father, who is the nicest man in Mokattam. All these things are on Rachel's mind as she rushes through the alleys, shyly waving at everyone and sidestepping trash bags and leaking filth to get to the secondhand electrical shop at the other side of the village.

As soon as the sun goes down the wedding procession will start at the church and Shareen has given Rachel the highly prized job of chief bridesmaid, even though she hardly knows her and her best friend went crazy. Mind you, Shareen was desperate to borrow the silver slippers Fatima wore on her wedding day and had kept wrapped in old tissue paper ever since. Fatima told her she could borrow them if she gave Rachel the honored role of bridesmaid. Surely with one eye on the eligible men who would see her. But still Shareen's invitation was nice. It's something to look forward to after the sadness of Fatima's cremation this morning.

When Rachel arrives at the shop, Sami's on the street,

chewing gum, hanging back from a group of angry men who are threatening Faisal, the rich, beefy merchant, who's standing in front of his truck, lazily batting flies from his neck. Rachel pauses beside the fruit stall to listen and Habi, the greengrocer, hands her a small stalk of black grapes to eat.

"*Shukran*," she thanks him.

The sweet grapes melt in her mouth as Rachel lowers her head to hear what one of the men is saying.

"Don't give me that story. You're making a good living while we're getting poorer every day."

There's a long silence. The atmosphere becomes tense. Faisal fumbles for a handkerchief to avoid answering. Beads of sweat form on his lined forehead. A younger man pulls a knife from a pocket, hiding it behind his back.

Shocked, Rachel turns away. Habi tries to wave her inside Sami's shop, but at that moment Lijah comes speeding under the arch on a rickety motorbike. He swerves, skidding around the truck, and almost splutters into the fruit stall. At the last minute he snaps the handlebars up and the engine grinds to a halt. Habi pulls Rachel out of the way as Lijah stands up, his gangly legs on either side of the bike to stop it from toppling over.

"Come on now. What can I do?" the merchant says to himself, grateful for the sudden distraction as he climbs into the truck.

"Where did you get that bike?" Sami asks Lijah, baffled.

Rachel stares at him. Sami hasn't once glanced her way. Without him noticing, she slips into the safety of the doorway of his shop and folds her arms to wait for him.

"Someone gave it to me to pay back a debt." Lijah laughs as the men gather round to examine the wreck, nodding and holding their chins while pretending to recognize the make and design. "I'm going to sell it and buy a pony."

Before too long the merchant escapes in a stink of exhaust fumes and the lane fills with more men. Rachel stands waiting in the doorway of Sami's shop for someone, anyone, to say hi and ask how Fatima's cremation went. Last night Simon and Mart were put to rest and everyone was there.

"Who will it be tomorrow?" Rachel wonders aloud to the column of ants marching along the edge of Habi's stall toward the pomegranates.

She's about to run home when she spots Aaron, Jamal, and Jacob coming down the path.

"Hey," Jacob shouts, waving the newspaper. "There's a list of all the names of the tourists who died in the bombing, even the doorman and the taxi driver, but Simon and Mart aren't here. Why not?"

"Let me see." A long-faced elder grabs the paper from Jacob angrily, without looking at him. Then stares at Aaron. He hasn't been forgiven for stealing, even though everyone knows he's been reduced to working as a medical-waster.

"And a lady saw the Mother of God in front of the Imperial Hotel." Aaron tries to be friendly, but the elder screws up his eyes.

Scanning the list of the people who died in the bombing with a grubby finger, the elder dismisses the vision-of-Mary story with a grunt. But the longer he reads down the list of names, the more he frowns. And the more he frowns, the angrier he grows, until finally he says, "Forgotten in life and forgotten in death!"

Aaron gazes at Rachel, who's chewing a knuckle and trying to be invisible in Sami's peeling doorway. She looks crushed and beaten.

As the newspaper is passed from man to man, the list of the dead is more interesting than the description of Mary at the Imperial Hotel. More interesting to everyone except Aaron, whose eyes are fixed on Rachel.

He once overheard Omar say that love is a cauldron of flames that drive sane men crazy. Aaron didn't know what he meant at the time, but he sort of understands it now. Sympathy, hope, desire, need: so many emotions tangle up inside him that he can hardly breathe. He can't go over there. Not with everyone watching. All he can do is give Rachel a kind look and send her a silent promise to take care of her.

A rough piece of plastic sheeting falls from a heap of bags and a child drags it across the dust with a galloping sound. Feeling pinned down by the force of Aaron's burning eyes, Rachel peeps out from the shadow to watch, wishing he would stop going out of his way to embarrass her. Everyone can see him gawping at her with that lovesick look. A heaviness inside tells her to walk away, but there are people everywhere. If she steps out of the doorway they'll know she's been hiding there all along and Sami will know she's been waiting for him. And then what?

Her chance to escape doesn't come until Lijah sparks the motorbike to life. The wheels wobble, then screech off to an intake of surprise from everyone that the battered old reject can move so fast. Everyone but Aaron looks on, while his eyes face in the other direction, chasing Rachel's quick shape as she sprints from the doorway, ducks behind the fruit stall and runs down the winding lane.

As the last puffs of exhaust fumes die away, Aaron's heart follows Rachel while his body stays put, feeling heavier and heavier the farther she disappears from his sight.

Chapter Seventeen
Bad News

Undecided whether to go to the pony yard in case Rachel's heading there or to pass by her home, Aaron slouches against a shop wall, sheltering himself from the sun for a while until Jacob interrupts his yearning.

"Let's see what's happening at the church, yeah?"

Aaron half nods. The moment's gone. She's gone. He'll have to wait for the next chance to come. He has no choice but to follow Jacob past the shops and stalls and down the winding alleys to the long path that leads to the church.

Aaron's happy to go with Jacob, who still seems his usual self, thank heaven. Things are easy between them as they walk side by side, but something Rachel said earlier is troubling Aaron.

"Did you know that boys are going backwards?"

"Like that film?" Jacob asks.

"What film?"

Aaron shakes his head as they leave the bags of garbage behind and amble toward the open walkway beside the high limestone wall.

Jacob pauses to scratch his wild hair. "I'm not sure what it was called now."

"Me neither . . . hmm. Hey! What's Noha doing here?"

Aaron has never seen Jacob's mom anywhere near the church. She doesn't believe in Jesus. Now she's beside the high wall, looking agitated, next to Sahira, the tallest, thinnest woman in Mokattam. As they approach they can hear Sahira muttering the latest news from behind a hand covering her mouth.

"The best doctor in Bab el Louk—he was there—he said that was it. He did. They won't. No. Not coming home."

"Who's not coming home?"

Jacob has excellent hearing and his question startles Sahira into dropping her hand.

Warning him off, Noha points a finger at him and says, "Shush. Go away, Jacob. And you, Sahira, you shouldn't have been listening. Don't say a word to anyone."

Whatever they're talking about looks serious enough for Sahira to make the sign of the cross twice on her chest and beg Jesus for help with a whisper and raised eyes, even though Noha's giving her actions a snarly look.

"Someone else died?" Aaron guesses.

"Be quiet!" Thumping the air with a fist, Noha's face is sliced by so many lines it looks as if it will split into a hundred pieces if she gets any angrier. "They said to keep it until later."

"Trying to get information from her is like trying to get blood from a stone," Jacob whispers. He nudges Aaron as they walk away. "You're right, though, and they can't say anything because Simon and his brother and poor Fatima have recently died and anyone else now will be another bad omen for Shareen tonight."

But rumors spread faster than quarry dust in Mokattam and news of the latest tragedy has already fallen on most people's ears as they sort the garbage and gather up the food slop to take to the pigs that are now hidden illegally in homes all over the village.

It seems that Merry, the teenage daughter of Said and Esther, medical-wasters, died of hepatitis during the night. The deacon is going to announce it soon but everyone already knows and her cremation is taking place later today.

When Shareen hears the news, she's furious and stomps upstairs to the small room she shares with her father and kicks her faded mat. This is a terrible omen. When she glances at the pillowcase printed with a picture of a curvy belly dancer, she almost freaks out. The last time she lay down to sleep, she was free. Tomorrow she'll wake up as horrible Daniel's wife.

As a special treat for breakfast, Shareen's father paid someone to bring a McFalafel back from Cairo's McDonald's. The spicy smell of the fast-food treat still hangs in the air as Shareen stares at the pointy silver slippers that look like Cleopatra's canoes on her dainty little feet. Why did she beg

Fatima to give her these stupid shoes?

It's not easy to imagine a happy wedding when everything is falling apart.

Most of the day has been spent being waxed and plucked; her hair is set and curled but dropping out in the afternoon heat. Her make up is melting. The red lipstick is a shade too dark. Mostly polished and shiny, several nails have chipped since they were varnished an hour ago, and where's Rachel, her bridesmaid? Her stepmother's cremation took place this morning. She should be here by now to help and spoil her. Shareen doesn't even like Rachel, who's drippy and never listens when she tells her what to do. Plus she likes boring Sami, with the sagging shoulders and silly grin, who watches *Candid Camera* on TV or sits in front of that crummy computer all day long.

This is not how Shareen imagined her wedding day. She wipes sweat from her face with the damp sleeve of her gray galabeya. Where are the gold shoes she dreamed of? The white silk dress and red ribbons to braid in her hair? Where's the excitement she hoped to feel? Her handsome husband from a Hollywood film?

Her eyes linger for a moment on the cheap dress with a threadbare hem that's hanging from the curtain that divides the room in two. It's a faded cream color, the waist is too low, and the material is crumpling in the afternoon heat. Shareen borrowed the dress from Marlina, a woman with eight sons, who wore it more than ten years ago. Why did she allow Daniel to talk Marlina into giving the old thing to her? Knowing Marlina went on to have so many sons after wearing that dress scares the life out of Shareen, who guesses that's exactly the reason Daniel wants her to wear it.

She catches sight of her face in the mottled mirror and pats a sudden outbreak of sweat away with the back of her hand. The more she puts off getting dressed, the hotter she becomes. The silver slippers slide from her feet as she moves a few steps to swing the dress from the curtain. Where is Rachel?

It's not supposed to be like this.

The surprising stutter of a motorbike engine sounds outside the glassless window. Shareen slips across the floor to look out, taken aback to see Lijah sitting on a rusting bike, revving the engine to wake up.

"Take it away," Hosi yells. "Help the neighbors. Sort your share of their rubbish before you go riding around on that thing, otherwise they'll give us no rice."

Lijah snarls. "I won it at cards. I'm keeping it for a couple of days, then I'll sell it and buy a pony."

"You're getting married. You can't pay for gasoline," Hosi says, red-faced.

But Lijah sparks the engine to life and pretends to run his father over. Hosi jumps out of the way and trips, forcing Youssa to stumble up from the middle of a pile of bags where he's been sleeping, to help his father to his feet.

At the same time Rachel comes racing around the corner to Shareen's. She stops dead, shocked to come across Lijah cranking up the yowling motorbike engine while squeezing the brakes and tempting Hosi and Youssa to take him on. It's no use. All Hosi and Youssa can do is flap the air in front of their noses to get rid of the gasoline fumes.

When Lijah senses Rachel a few feet away, hanging back, he laughs at the flicker of fear in her little smile and twists the bike around to face her. Challenging her to try and get past, he stands upright to shift the spinning wheel in the air and pumps up the power until the rickety exhaust pipe makes a coughing sound.

Rachel flinches. Then freezes and turns pale.

Help appears to come when a bag of stinking garbage is flung from an upstairs hovel. Lijah turns to elbow it out of the way as the handlebars shoot from under him and he somersaults off. The wheels whirr, thud, and bounce before the bike springs toward Rachel, rolling over her legs, then careening into a pile of bags.

Someone screams.

A child runs to look. A man with knotty skin races over to Rachel's twisted, whimpering body. Two yelling women wave their angry arms at Lijah, while a man grabs the reeling bike from the ground and turns off the engine. Mouth open, Shareen dashes out as fast as she can in her slippy silver slippers and the bad omen she's been dreading stares back with the clearest of warnings not to marry Daniel. In a stunned rage, she gazes at Rachel lying there for only a second before fainting clean away.

———————

At the church, women are hurrying up and down the aisles arranging the flowers for Shareen's wedding. They're racing to complete the task so they can get to the farthest side of the village in time for Merry's cremation.

Meanwhile, outside, Aaron and Jacob are sitting on the wall and squinting at the pigeons on the tenement roofs until they blur into the distance. Jacob should go to Merry's cremation—she was from a medical-wasting family, like him—but it will be stuffed with ululating women crying their hearts out and anyway neither of them have the energy to move. It's too hot and making an effort on an empty stomach strikes them as foolish. Just waiting for the wedding is enough to be going on with. It's better to sit here until then and slowly make their way afterward to the area where the feast will take place.

The koftas, roast chicken, and special sweet biscuits are very much on their minds when they see Michael the artist running toward Father Peter, who's talking to one of the women before heading to the back of the church to check that his robes will be ready in time for the wedding ceremony.

Aaron's vaguely surprised by his quick little steps.

"Maybe Shareen's called the wedding off?" Jacob leans forward to listen. But he can't hear.

Jacob stretches out on the wall and Aaron lies back. Their feet almost touch as the sun circles the church. With the sound of pigeons cooing in their ears, it's an hour before anything distracts them from their silent, lazy rest. Then, eventually, they become aware of a distant procession lurching toward them along the walkway.

Aaron jerks up to rub sleep from his eyes and blink at the dark sky. Jacob springs alive with excitement at the thought of food, but instead of happy sounds coming closer to the church, he hears the distant noise of wailing starting up on the other side of the village.

"Merry's cremation should be over by now, shouldn't it?" Aaron's confused.

Jacob agrees by frowning long and hard. Something isn't quite right. Weddings are often delayed in Mokattam but never funerals. And the wedding is obviously going ahead, because lights are glowing in the open-air church and the pews are filling up.

A moment later a distant shadow morphs into the shape of Daniel striding toward the church in his secondhand black suit and crisp white shirt, his face as hard as stone. He is surrounded by his brothers and sons and they all quickly take their place at the front. A few minutes later Daniel's cousins race down the aisles in freshly laundered galabeyas, apologizing for being late.

"Why so late?" Jacob knows those cousins. "They're never late."

Aaron shrugs. "No, never."

A woman in a billowing black galabeya with a funny walk is next up the lane, soon followed by Shareen, who is holding her father's arm.

"She looks happy!" Jacob grins.

"Yeah, right!"

Aaron's shocked by the grim determination on Shareen's face as she tries her best to look gorgeous while staggering along in an outsize pair of silver slippers. Her cream dress hangs from her shoulders like a sack, but the saddest thing of all is the state of her hair, which is pushed back by a skimpy red band that shows off her frown.

"Where's Rachel?" Aaron guesses she's fallen out with Shareen in the short space of time it's taken them to get ready.

"She looks too good in her bridesmaid's dress," Jacob says with a knowing look. "That's why ugly Salema's holding the candle."

"Weird that the pig isn't here either!" Aaron fires back, in case Jacob thinks he's disappointed not to see Rachel.
His distraction works and they laugh. Together, they shift along on their bottoms to the far edge of the wall, where they can see the action better. "

"He who loves his own wife loves himself," the priest reads.

Aaron leans in to hear the sentence that his mother hated . . .

"Wives!"

Here it comes . . .

"Wives, submit to your husbands, as to the Lord."

"Submit! Hah!" His mother's contempt rings out crystal clear in his mind. "You submit. You do it. You, husbands. Don't be one of those men, Aaron. Let your wife breathe and she will stay beside you and share your smiles. Don't check up on her. Trust her. She's living her life, that's all."

Which reminds him. Rachel—where is she?

Aaron longs to see her. Some of Rachel's cousins and uncles are there in the church, sitting side by side. Obviously it's too upsetting for her father and younger sisters to come to Shareen's wedding after the cremation this morning, but Rachel—where is she? Even if she's no longer the bridesmaid,

Shareen wouldn't want to lose face by not having her here at all. But perhaps Rachel has gone to Merry's cremation instead? But Rachel hardly knows Merry.

Then it occurs to Aaron that Lijah, Hosi, and Youssa are missing too. Strange.

A piercing headache tells Aaron he needs water, but he can't leave the wall yet. The ceremony isn't over. The community room won't open until the bride and groom arrive. In a haze he watches the anointing of Shareen and Daniel and listens to the prayer for the crowns as the priest places them on their heads.

"Lord have mercy," the priest intones.

The congregation joins in and a bird flies overhead. The flapping shadow makes Aaron restless. Underneath the restlessness is a reminder of his failure. His failure to win Rachel's heart.

The wedding procession forms, with the choir singing and children clapping. As Shareen leaves the altar, arm in arm with Daniel, to walk up the aisle, the smile on her face changes second by second with a broad beam here, a short grin there and a fleeting downturned mouth when she spots a prettier hairdo than her own. Daniel seems glad the ceremony is over and tries to hurry Shareen out of the church.

Walking slowly toward the community room, the bride and groom, with their families and friends close behind, head off into the night like a procession of bobbing boats on a dark sea. Abe and a group of kids follow them for a bit but, knowing it's rude to dash in front of the happy pair, soon give up walking at that slow pace and run around instead. Abe comes back to pass the time with Aaron and Jacob on the wall.

"I thought that was going to go on forever." Abe jumps on the wall to kick an imaginary ball at the moon. "Shame about Rachel."

"What?" Aaron and Jacob say at the same time.

"Rachel, you know?" Abe stops kicking and stares at their shocked, wide eyes, realizing they don't know. "She's in the hospital. Her leg's crushed. Lijah lost control of his bike and it crashed into her. They said she might die, but she's alive. I think she's alive. She might not be."

"What hospital?" Aaron leaps to his feet as if possessed by demons. "Which one?" he shouts.

"Um . . ." Abe racks his brains for the name. "She got in there for free because that hospital doctor was here at the clinic when it happened. It's the one near the American University."

"The Eastern First National." Jacob knows it well.

"Lend me the pony and cart," Aaron begs him.

"No, the pony can't go out. Not again. Anyway, the hospital won't let you in. Don't be crazy," Jacob says. "It's too late."

"Why do you want to go?" Abe's confused and Aaron can't answer.

It's impossible to believe that Rachel's in the hospital—dead maybe. All through the stupid wedding Rachel was in trouble and he didn't know. How can he get there? Each breath he takes is an effort as pain floods his body. He must see her.

Aaron turns to run but Jacob grabs his arm. Abe grabs the other arm as Aaron struggles and moans like a wild animal. Together they twist him to the wall and push him down.

Chapter Eighteen
Silent Prayers

"Tomorrow, first thing. We'll go there. Whatever you want," Jacob promises.

Every cell in Aaron's body collapses as his mind soars through the city, skimming main roads, minarets, domes, shiny hotels to get to the hospital. At the same time he silently prays to Mary, the Queen of Heaven, to save Rachel. To keep her safe. To let him see her again. His fingers clasp the bottle of perfume in his pocket, while he swears that if she will let Rachel live, he'll look after her forever.

"I'll find out more for you," Abe says, and scuttles off. Meanwhile, a whirl of emotions passes between Aaron and Jacob. Aaron's ashamed to have revealed his true feelings for Rachel to his friend.

"She'll be fine!" Jacob holds Aaron's arm tight in case he decides to run.

A lonely glittering sky meets the dark, dusty earth as, one by one, the church lights are dimmed. Soon the priest and deacon emerge from behind the altar in their ordinary black robes to join the festivities and the silence of the night feels like something too hard to live through. Bruised and battered by the desperate longing to see Abe come back with a smile on his face, Aaron hovers between heaven and hell.

"She likes animals," he mutters, as if Mary will save Rachel for that reason alone.

"Yeah, I know," Jacob murmurs.

The distant throb of music tells them that Shareen's wedding party has started.

Slowly, Jacob asks, "Want to wander over there, Aaron?"

"You go," Aaron says, sighing.

"Nah, it's all right."

Jacob lets go of his arm at the very moment Abe's footsteps come padding up the path. The second he appears, Aaron jumps from the wall and rushes to meet him, with Jacob close behind.

Abe waves his arms, gasping for breath. "She's not dead. She's not dead. Everyone said prayers for her."

"Tell us!" Clutching Abe's shoulders to shake the news from him, Aaron can barely wait.

"There was a Dr. Sameer visiting the clinic when the bike ran over her. He's got his own charity to help poor people like us for free." Abe pauses to nod and push hair from his wild eyes. "She was lucky he came immediately and got her to his hospital. She won't have to pay, but her leg's bad. They're all saying God's on her side."

"Let's go and see her now." Aaron's eager to leave.

"No way!" Jacob pulls a face. "There's no point—they won't let you in. I'm going to fill up at the party. Coming, Abe?"

"Yeah, course. Hey, Aaron, come on." Abe tilts his head to tempt him. "There's a stack of honey sweets. Fatima with the Filthy Mouth says Shareen's been singing like a strangled crow. You missed seeing Lijah drunk, drowning his sorrows. Everyone knows the bike accident was his fault for fooling around. He's gone home because Shovel Face is flirting with Youssa."

Jacob frowns at Aaron's crestfallen face. "When's Rachel coming home?" he asks on his behalf.

"I dunno. They gave her morphine." Abe's enjoying his role as important messenger and adds, "She's got to have an operation tomorrow. She might die then, you don't know." Jacob shoots him a look. "Well, you don't know, Jacob. Stop looking at me like that."

"Who says we track down Lijah and make him feel bad about Rachel?" Jacob says, hoping this will shake Aaron out of his stupor.

"I want to see her," Aaron starts again. "I'll go on my own."

"Forget it. She'll be asleep. And the hospital's miles away." Jacob slips his arm through his. "Don't be stupid. Let's get some food. We'll go tomorrow."

Aaron grabs his arm desperately. "We will? Honest?"

"Yes!" Jacob nods firmly, giving Aaron hope for the first

time that things will turn out all right.

The three boys start walking toward the sound of the party. Deep down, Jacob thinks it would be better not to go for a few days, until Rachel's recovered from the operation, but Aaron is so desperate to visit her he had to say yes. Tomorrow he'll try and make him see sense. The Eastern First National Hospital isn't on their route and the detour through the center of town after working all morning will be a pain, but what else could he say?

A harsh, crunching drumbeat and sharp tooting noise drift from the music deck as they turn the last bend of the dark alley leading to the concrete shed where the festivities are taking place. The smell of koftas and roast chicken fills their noses as the tension of having to enter the room increases for Aaron. He gives a final shiver when he reaches the open door and sends a quick, simple prayer to the framed picture of Mary hanging from the wall. *Please make this all right and look after Rachel for me.*

A few people look Aaron up and down like before, but most are so used to ignoring him they carry on chatting and eating as if he's invisible. Abe scoots off to chat to a boy his age and Jacob hangs back to make sure Aaron's OK.

Daniel marks the place in the center of the room where the groom is greeted by newcomers, who bow and nod as they pass on their congratulations. Surrounded by male cousins, Daniel looks as if his fight with the devil's over and he's won, while Shareen, who's leaning on the wall next to her father, has lost her purpose and gazes at Aaron as if he's changed into someone she's never seen before.

Walking toward him with a demure smile, Shareen's suddenly glad that Rachel's out of the way, but angry that she's stumbling slightly in these stupid silver slippers. If only the dress fit her better she'd feel more attractive, but it's too late to worry about that now.

Aaron's fills his plate with rice and chicken, then searches for a quiet corner to eat in. He turns around and bumps straight into Shareen, who's looking at him oddly.

"OK?" he says, trying to get past her to join Jacob and Abe who are eating hungrily while leaning on the wall near the door, but Fatima with the Filthy Mouth steps in front of Shareen and bares her huge, wonky teeth, grinning to let him know she's watching him. Her sudden curiosity in him stops Aaron in his tracks. Then Shareen pushes her out of the way.

"Aaron," Shareen says, sighing. "I'm . . . married. Can you believe it?"

"Yeah. Sure."

Aaron lifts the well-stacked plate over his head to shift past her and Fatima with the Filthy Mouth, but Shareen's determined to stop him leaving.

"You didn't congratulate me. You weren't at the church. Aren't you going to say something?"

"Um, good luck. Oh, and er . . . got any news on Rachel?"

Aaron's eager question results in a look of pure venom appearing on Shareen's face. It's her wedding party and he's asking about Rachel? Fatima with the Filthy Mouth starts cackling her head off, which distracts Shareen from spitting out the nasty comment that was on the tip of her tongue and allows Aaron to get away without excusing himself.

Confused by her sudden interest in him, Aaron glances at Daniel and fears for the worst if he hears anything. It's bad enough having Lijah on his back. He doesn't want another enemy, especially for the reason that he can't stand Shareen. She seems to think he's forgiven her for reporting his stolen bottles to the priest and ruining his life. Well, she'll soon learn the truth.

Gazing around the room while he leans against the door beside Jacob, Aaron swallows food as fast as possible so he can leave this awful party. His eyes land on Suzan, Lijah's fiancée. It looks like she's having a heartfelt chat with Youssa, who looks sober for once. From where Aaron's standing, he can just hear Suzan lecturing him about booze. Youssa's so ashamed he daren't pick up the half-empty beer bottle that's positioned safely between his bare feet. It's no wonder Lijah went home angry. Suzan's a nag and they're not even married yet.

It's the kind of party where the old people are smiling and talking nonstop, and the little kids are climbing under the table and pulling the grown-ups' clothes. The teenagers are bored out of their skulls and would rather be watching TV, talking about football or, better still, crowded round Sami's computer.

But it's slightly better than the engagement party because there's more food and no crazy pig running wild. Jacob soon brings them each a plastic glass overflowing with melon juice. Aaron drops the paper plate on the floor before reaching for the drink. The second Jacob nods at the door, suggesting they leave, the music blares out louder, battering the room. They step outside into the pure Mokattam night. Aaron gazes at the halo of smog hovering over the distant city lights and wonders if Rachel is asleep or awake.

Aaron doesn't see the stacks of garbage as he carefully winds his way to the tenements, head down, eyes half closed and Jacob whistling behind him. The pungent smells drift over him while his mind forms a picture of a hospital bed with Rachel curled up in pain. The tube in her arm, which hangs from a blood bag on a metal stand, is like one of many he's touched while out with Jacob this morning. He can see the rich red color trickling down it. Tomorrow there'll be more blood bags and, when he feels the leathery plastic between his fingers, he'll think of her.

"What is love anyway?" Aaron asks before he can stop himself.

But Jacob doesn't tease him. Instead, whistling while he thinks, his friend suddenly stops and says, "It's when you feel sick inside and you can't think straight because you've turned into a snake."

"A snake?" Aaron's baffled. "Why a snake?"

"Snakes get stuck in mud and can't get out. Like people in love. Yeah." Jacob's pleased with his answer. "You've had it then."

"Stuck in mud? That's stupid, Jacob." He decides to change the topic. "What happened to the spray paint?"

"You don't think I've forgotten, do you?" Jacob looks smug all of a sudden. "Follow me!"

Drunk on the effects of the still, bright night, food, and melon juice, he darts into the side alley where Daniel lives. Jacob longs to make a name for himself as something more than Noha's son who's a medical-waster. He's not good-looking like Aaron or sweet like Abe. The only gift he has is not being seen at night when he sprays messages around the village. He started off small, doing small ankhs and scarabs, but now he sprays words and sometimes whole sentences.

Dark and gloomy, the concrete hovels resemble entrances to underground caves where visitors have urinated on the rubbish. Quick as a flash, Jacob reaches for a plastic bag that's closest to Daniel's tiny home. Behind it is a small can of red paint he hid earlier. He waves it in the air and a cloud of flies swarm to sniff the silver can. Jacob laughs when Aaron starts head-butting them.

"Ready?"

Jacob strains to see Aaron's face as they creep up Daniel's stairs but it's too dark. Two seconds later, they peer through the shadows at the thin mattress on the floor, which is covered by a striped sheet with a red, folded blanket at the end and, side by side, two blue embroidered pillows. Someone has sprinkled lotus petals on the pillows and the smell is sickly sweet. There's a church-sized candle on the floor and a print of the Ten Commandments stuck to the wall. A deathly quiet adds to the atmosphere of disbelief as they imagine Daniel and Shareen lying there together.

Aaron starts to feel restless. It doesn't seem right, standing here and thinking what he's thinking.

"Hurry up," he hisses.

Wondering what message to leave, Jacob hesitates for a second before flipping the lid from the spray can and misting the air with a burst of red paint. He moves quickly, holding the can tight, his skinny body leaping after the letters he paints across the floor. In the silence, the spraying sounds like whispering—until Aaron groans.

"You can't write that!"

"Why not?" Jacob pauses to admire his work.

LOVE IS GOOD FOR THE SOUL.

"Where did you get that from?" Aaron's never heard such a stupid thing.

"I overheard Habi talking to his friend last week."

Jacob's anxious to get out of here before the so-called happy couple return. Without another word they sneak into the night. Jacob slips the paint can back into its hiding place until he needs it again.

It's late. Rachel's almond eyes flash through Aaron's mind. A large cloud covers the murky moon as they make their way through the darkness and Aaron comes to the conclusion that Jacob's never been in love. This feeling inside—this bewildering, overpowering warmth that rises up whenever he thinks of Rachel—is so normal to him now that he wonders how he ever lived without it.

Chapter Nineteen
Rubies

Wearing the same threadbare clothes as yesterday, Aaron twists on the wooden board of the cart to find a comfortable spot to sit as they wend their way through the traffic on the main highway. Already this morning, they've cleared two hospitals of waste, and the drifting smell of disinfectant and warm plastic mixed with car fumes is getting to him. Then there are the flies that keep buzzing around his face.

Every day for the last week, Jacob has patiently forced the pony to go another three miles across the city to the hospital where Rachel is. Every day, he's tied the pony to the thorn tree beside the entrance to the car park so that Aaron can jump off and race inside. Every day, within five minutes, Aaron returns, having been refused permission to get in the lift or climb the stairs to the wards by the woman on the reception desk. Every day, Aaron insists on trying again, even though Jacob's running out of patience.

"This is the last time," Jacob warns as the cart stops beside the thorn tree. "I'm not kidding!"

"I'll see her today. I will. Just you wait."

Deep inside, Aaron can't help believing that he really will see Rachel. From the rumors circulating in Mokattam, Rachel is doing well. She's had the operation on her left leg and two steel plates have been inserted for her bones to grow along, and the doctors have been incredible and haven't stolen her liver. As long as she doesn't get ill, especially with a virus like swine flu, she should be home in a month.

Swine flu! Aaron worries and worries about swine flu. Now he's growing angry with the families who are hiding pigs in their homes in Mokattam. He's tempted to report Abe's mom and the rest of them to the authorities in order to save Rachel from getting the disease when she eventually comes home. These things are on his mind as he pats his hair and straightens his shoulders to walk through the plain doors of the modern hospital.

A pregnant woman in a navy headscarf briefly looks Aaron up and down when he steps aside for her to enter first. Three children scurry after her and Aaron quickens his pace as the *rat-a-tat* door shuts behind him. He follows them, pretending to be part of the family as they hurry for the elevator.

The stairs are at the far side of the foyer so not worth running for. Out of the corner of his eye, Aaron can see the receptionist talking to a man in baggy jeans with long hair who's nervous about something. As bad as it would be to get caught now, Aaron knows he can get to the elevator before the receptionist has time to come around her desk to stop him. Luckily, she's busy and for once doesn't notice Aaron as the elevator door clacks open and then shut.

Aaron doesn't know what to do. He's never been holed up in an elevator before. He's only seen elevator doors open and close when peeping into hotel foyers. Yesterday, someone said that Rachel was on the tenth floor, but the buttons on the wall here don't look capable of sending the elevator that far on their own. There's no steering wheel or engine or anything inside the metal box. When the woman asks him where he's going, Aaron blurts out, "To see my friend."

The woman presses the button for the third floor and the elevator shoots into action. Shocked by the sudden movement, which makes his hair stand on end, and knowing he might as well have the word *Zabbaleen* stamped across his forehead, Aaron doubts the woman believes he has a friend in this hospital.

When the elevator reaches the third floor and the woman and children give Aaron a final once-over before getting out, he sighs with relief that the corridor is empty of people. He presses the button for the tenth floor, feeling strangely powerful when the elevator shoots upward. It feels so good, he's half tempted to go back down and come up again. He'd like to play around here, but the idea of seeing Rachel eclipses the excitement of riding in the lift.

"Room nineteen, the tenth floor," Aaron mutters to

himself as the elevator rattles to a stop. He eagerly brushes past two men in white coats and braces himself for being caught and thrown out as he creeps down the hallway, searching for the correct room.

The sound of pattering feet echoes down the wide corridor. The familiar smell of disinfectant is mixed with polish and fly spray. Weirdly, no one seems interested in him as doctors, nurses, and workers pushing trolleys hurry on by and Aaron starts to sweat the closer he gets to Rachel's room. At last he slows down. He's nearly there, but what's he going to say?

A young man shuffles past on crutches, leaving a whiff of strong aftershave behind. Gazing at the number 19 as if it's the start of a terrifying ordeal, Aaron feels his knees almost give way. When a burst of crying from a baby in a nearby room closes in on him, the smell, noise, and feel of damp linoleum under his feet turn the number 19 into a giddy blur. Kicking against the instinct to run, Aaron barges through the door like a wild animal and, hand on the perfume bottle in his pocket, and swings round to face Rachel, who is asleep in bed.

In the heavenly afternoon light, her coppery hair gleams and the blue sheet and creamy pillow are like a wide sky with a perfect cloud. The cage that has been placed under the sheet to protect Rachel's leg makes her look like a floating angel. She's so lovely it almost hurts him to look. Aaron stamps the picture in his mind and seals it tight.

But what's the crumpled piece of paper clasped in her hand?

He peers at a crinkled, serrated edge of glossy white

paper that looks as if it's been cut from a magazine. It's a picture of something. He's tempted to twist it from her but doesn't want to wake her up, she's sleeping so deeply. If the clacking noise from the corridor would only stop, he could listen to the gentle pattern of her breathing. With nothing in the room but a glass of water on the bedside table to distract him from her peaceful face, Aaron stares and stares until a band of smog outside the window smothers the sun and the light in the room changes from creamy white to a dusty yellow.

By the time Aaron creeps from the room forty minutes have passed.

Jacob isn't happy. Sitting under the thorn tree, watching cars come and go with sick kids and women clutching their swollen bellies, is testing his patience. Hospitals scare him. He pulls a white packet of out-of-date pills from his shirt pocket and swallows three.

Lolling around in the still heat doesn't feel so bad, though he's coming to the rapid conclusion that Aaron's the most selfish person he's ever met. In fact, there are lots of reasons why Aaron's getting on his nerves. First, he eats too much. Even Noha's been complaining about the amount of rice he puts away each day. Then, Aaron ignores Wadida, his sister, who clearly likes him. Fatima with the Filthy Mouth says he's got the devil in him. "Just look in his eyes."

Since she said that, Jacob's been watching Aaron closely. Shareen told him that Aaron prefers to be on his own because he doesn't trust anyone, and who knows why he keeps asking for a lift to the perfume shop. Since Aaron's come to live with him, Jacob's been feeling more and more hemmed in.

When at last Aaron appears from the hospital, Jacob's had enough. "Where have you been?"

"I was watching over Rachel," Aaron says, and smiles.

Jacob isn't keen on that self-satisfied smile.

"She getting better?"

"I dunno."

Aaron climbs up and that's it. He doesn't say another word. There's a strange look on his face as he stares at the traffic—lost in his own world. His silence not only leaves Jacob dangling but widens the gap between them. That's it. Jacob's had enough. Ferrying Aaron back and forth is finished. The sooner he moves out of his home the better.

Over the last few days, when the cart enters Mokattam through the stone arch that leads to the tunnel of shops and stalls, Shareen has darted out of the shadows of the laundry and forced Jacob to stop. Today's no different.

"Hiya," she yells, glad to see them.

"What is it now?" Jacob sighs.

Each time he's been ready for her to mention the message he left on the floor on her wedding night. But every day she makes a different excuse for preventing them from going home.

Shuffling to the side of the cart, Shareen glares at Aaron, desperate for his attention. There's a hint of jealousy on her face when she asks, "How's Rachel doing?"

"What?" Aaron eyes Jacob with suspicion. He hasn't told anyone they've been going to the hospital, so it must be down to him that Shareen knows.

Curling the sleeve of her navy galabeya between her fingers, Shareen sniffs. "Don't pretend." A whiff of used bandages from the cart and the drowning smell of decaying garbage force her to cover her nose for a second. From the glimpse of her short fingernails and red knuckles, Aaron guesses she's been scrubbing clothes or sorting garbage. Something her father never made her do. Clearly her days of learning to weave and make cards are over now that she's Daniel's wife.

"Well?"

Determined not to let them pass without getting an answer, Shareen plants herself in front of them and, when Jacob tries to steer round her, she buries her nose in the pony's neck, nuzzling him as if her life depends on it. Her over-the-top affection forces a woman with tangled gray hair to stop picking up cigarette butts and stand and watch. It's hard to stay back when Shareen's making such a fuss of the skinny pony.

With a sack of oranges on his shoulder, Habi stumbles past, eyeing her strange behavior, then pauses to smile at Jacob.

Jacob ignores him, even though he's a close friend of his mother.

"How's Rachel doing?" Shareen barks at Aaron again.

Aaron nods. "Tell you at the wall later."

Shocked, Habi drops the sack of oranges and widens his eyes. Jacob catches the surprise on his face and nudges Aaron.

"You idiot!" he says under his breath. "She's married. You can't just arrange to meet her like that."

Startled by the hiss of anger in Jacob's words, Aaron frowns. He's been acting weird lately but has never called him an idiot before. The pony lifts a knee and walks on as Jacob snaps the reins.

"I'm not staying married," Shareen yells at the top of her voice as Habi shakes his head.

"That girl's nothing but trouble," Jacob finishes.

With each *clip-clop* of the pony, the calm of Mokattam soon replaces the madness of Cairo. When at last they pull up to unload the cart outside the tenement, Aaron bites his thumb to try and remove a splinter under his nail. His hands are covered in scratches but only the splinter bothers him as they tip syringes, bandages, empty blood bags, tubes, beakers, unmarked bottles, plastic gloves, and torn gowns onto the path for sorting. It feels as if the gods are rolling the sun into his eyes as Aaron catches sight of something bright and sparkling in the blurry heap beneath his feet.

Jacob folds and slaps the last plastic bag flat. He's about to fetch his mother and sisters to sort the waste when Aaron startles him by picking something delicate out of the hospital debris.

"Hey! Hey!" Aaron cries, holding a pink stone necklace to the sky. It shimmers in the sunlight.

"Rubies?" Awestruck, Jacob touches the glittering stones and thin gold chain. "Where did you find it?"

Aaron eyes the mound of medical waste at his feet and visions of the hospitals they've cleared shoot through his mind. They both stare hard at a broken clipboard, empty soap dispenser, soiled bandages and tissues, trying to work out where and how this expensive necklace was lost.

"Give it to the priest," Jacob says.

"No way," Aaron shouts. "Are you crazy?"

"You are if you think you can keep it. Everyone knows you're a thief!"

Jacob's words are like a knife to Aaron's stomach. "I don't take anything from the Zabbaleen."

"It could be worth a lot of money. You should give it back," Jacob says.

"You're mad. What about the perfumes? You didn't say anything then."

"I knew you wouldn't listen. That's why," Jacob sighs.

Aaron slips the necklace in his pocket. It hits the glass perfume bottle with a tinkling that he dares Jacob to notice. Heart racing, he's furious that Jacob's staring at him in that superior way. He found the necklace. He'll decide what to do with it, not Jacob.

Confusion adds to Aaron's trembling as he wanders to the doorway of the tenement, desperate for food, but Jacob runs at him and slams him against the wall. Aaron gasps, doubling up with shock that Jacob is prepared to hurt him to get what he wants. Struggling and twisting to prevent him from plucking the necklace from his pocket, he slaps Jacob's elbow from his neck. There's something laughable in the grunts they make, pushing and kneeing each other like five-year-olds, until Aaron accepts Jacob's desperation is real and lifts the sparkling rubies from his pocket and hands them to him.

From the look of surprise on his face, Jacob reacts as if he's been given a fist of maggots. Sweat rolls into his thick eyebrows as he gently takes the necklace and races up the concrete stairs to tell his mother and sisters.

Aaron draws a deep breath and sighs, listening for voices to echo down the stairwell, while an empty shell of loneliness opens inside him. What's about to happen next sinks in slowly like a cold, painful death and all the time, for comfort, his hand clenches the glass bottle in his dusty pocket. Suffering and grieving are what his life is about, but this is different. How can Jacob be so nasty? Aaron could have sold the necklace and rescued Rachel. They could have run away to a village in Upper Egypt and built a house. They could have been happy.

Then footsteps sound at the top of the stairs.

Blue-patterned scarf on her head, Fatima with the Filthy Mouth *pit-patters* toward him. Her galabeya floats out behind like a storm cloud. When she sees Aaron leaning on the wall, a quick sideways glance says she knows something's wrong. Suddenly fascinated, she pauses and folds her arms, and a whiff of saffron smothers Aaron. She's been cooking and the strong smell makes his stomach lurch.

They eye each other for a second until she scratches her lined chin.

"You never visit your mother's grave. Not even on Easter Sunday," she says accusingly.

As Aaron glares back at her guilty, the truth of what she's saying turns to anger and then frustration, but something stops him from retaliating. How can he explain to her that visiting his mother's grave will make her death real again? Something he tries hard to ignore for fear of losing control of himself. Instead he feels pity. They might live in the same world, but Fatima's is a far uglier one even than his. Stuck here with nothing but pictures of Jesus and Mary to keep her company, she's kept going by the weekly gift of milk, rice, and vegetables from the church. He can't help feeling sorry for her, even though the new pull of just telling Fatima where to go is a strong one. Instead he shrugs, then tilts his head to the footsteps hurrying down the stairs.

By the time Noha crashes down the stairs, followed by Jacob, Fatima has gone and Aaron has resigned himself to sleeping with the ponies again and foraging for scraps of food. One glare from Noha's disappointed face is enough for Aaron to regret showing Jacob the pink stones that are now tinkling in her thrusting, open palm.

"I spit on you," she says.

Aaron had hung around, hoping she'd feed him first. Furious with her, Jacob, and himself, he flies into the lane. Speeding past the unsorted bandages and syringes with Noha's angry voice in his ear.

"Go on, run. You coward."

The midafternoon sun blinds Aaron for a second as he pauses at the side of the tenement to listen. He gazes at a dirty boy in brightly colored rags who is picking through heaps of gauze and plastic tubing with bare hands, searching for drugs to sell. A whiff of dung awakes Aaron to the plight of the pony, which has wandered off after waiting for Jacob to remove the cart and is nosing the dry potholes and furrows in the path for water.

It occurs to Aaron that some battles aren't worth fighting. It's easier to just think that life is like this. If only it was that easy. If only he could stop the shouting in his head. Shouting that tells him he's useless and stupid and will spend the rest of his life on his own. Behind him is the rapid sound of Noha's footsteps going back upstairs. He can feel Jacob's shadow, still and silent, somehow watching him, which forces Aaron to get moving.

Darting between stacks of medical waste, he runs down the dark path between the tenements, careful not to tread on anything sharp, wondering if he and Jacob will ever be friends again. They fell out once before, several years ago, when Jacob accused Aaron of stealing two Egyptian pounds from the church collection box. On that occasion, Aaron had fiercely defended himself, while fingering the stolen coins in his pocket. Sometimes it's easier to lie. Sometimes it's easier to push difficult feelings down and pretend you don't care what happens next. The necklace will end up in the priest's hands and be given to the police first, and then, when no one claims it, given back and sold for cash to support the church. This thought sparks Aaron's fury, making him want to yell from the top of the highest hill. Noha doesn't even go to church. Neither does Jacob.

Their honesty is dishonest.

Right now, the hollow feeling in his chest and the gnawing in his stomach are caused not just by lack of food but also by the thought of Jacob digging into a plate of lentils and rice while he hunts for a slice of bread. It's enough to drive him crazy.

Heading for the pony yard, with a cloudless blue sky above and the sight and stench of waste all around him, Aaron's lost in thought when he turns the last corner leading to the yard and comes face to face with Shareen. Not her . . . Not now. She looks as wild as he feels. Moody. Mad. Her eyes are red with tears and bad temper.

"Aaron! Aaron!" she cries, falling on him and flinging her arms round his neck with passion.

Her soft, warm—no, hot skin smothers him with a sweet smell of rose petals. And is that jasmine on the twist of hair tickling his nose? Yes, jasmine. Smooth skin and silky hair rub his face. Lips brush his ear and then she kisses him. He should pull away, but it's nice. He could pretend she's Rachel . . . He should stop her.

They're in the middle of the path. Too close to the corner. Any minute now kids will be coming this way, going home from school. It feels crazy to hold her like this . . .

Her lips crush his ear and there's a cart rumbling toward them. Only a few feet away.

Aaron comes to his senses just in time, shouting, "STOPITYOU'LLGETMEKILLED!"

He untangles himself at the very moment Lijah turns the corner. Instantly, Lijah comes to the correct conclusion about what's been happening and makes a sucking noise in the side of his cheek to force the pony to stop. Then he laughs at himself, shaking his head as if he should have known all along that something was going on between them.

He's got a new pony, Aaron thinks dumbly, wondering where from.

"What a lovely couple you make!"
Lijah is smirking as he jumps down from the cart. It rattles and

shakes, like his face, which changes from pleasure at catching them out to a clear need for violence. Only he's not interested in Aaron. His bubbling, hard eyes are firmly fixed on Shareen.

"You whore!"

"Shut up!" Aaron shouts, trying to push past his threatening body. Nothing is more frightening than Lijah in a temper and, like a brick wall, his stepbrother stands firm and hard.

"Wait!" Shareen tugs Aaron's shoulder, pulling him back. "I'm coming with you."

"Hadn't you better tell your husband where you're going first?" Lijah sneers, then lunges at her with both hands.

Aaron elbows him in the side as Shareen yells and tries to duck out of the way. With popping eyes, Lijah grabs her wrist with one hand and Aaron's hair with the other, then drags their screaming, struggling bodies past the pony and cart to a stretch of path where there's more space.

He swiftly knocks them together like rag dolls, bashing Aaron's nose until it bleeds, and they stumble and trip. Dazed and reeling, Shareen plunges her teeth into Lijah's hand for a second and Aaron pounds him with his fists, but it's too late. With an effortless kick from Lijah, Shareen crashes backwards on the dusty earth, bringing Aaron down with her. The world goes dark for him while she catches her breath, stumbles to her feet, and rockets away, heart pounding, scared to death Lijah's coming after her. A few quick checks behind convinces her that Aaron has disappeared in the other direction.

Hands in his pockets, Lijah watches her go. The shifting light of the afternoon sun casts a shadow from the cart, hiding

Aaron's body from view. Torn between chasing Shareen and getting out of here before someone comes, Lijah glances in the direction of Aaron and a deep jealousy sweeps over him.

Chapter Twenty
Help

The sound of singing from a child coming home from school saves Aaron from further cruelty. While Lijah jumps on the cart, wheeling it to the end of the path, nine-year-old Rafi, with a blue shoulder-bag swinging from his arm, wanders in a haze of heat toward the figure slumped on the lane. Rafi approaches cautiously while watching the disappearing pony and cart. He thinks the body with blood leaking from the mouth and the clopping pony are linked in some way, though he can't think why the person on the cart would leave the injured man here.

At first sight the man looks dead.

All afternoon Rafi's been desperate to get home, but now

he isn't sure what to do. His innocent eyes stare at the flies buzzing around the man's mouth. Rafi's never seen anyone hurt like this before. Mokattam is a peaceful place.

Down on the ground, Aaron blinks. Some kid's staring at him. He should open his eyes. On the other hand, the blackness at the back of his mind is so warm and welcoming, he rolls, drifts, and sinks—yearning to give up and just die.

Rafi wipes his nose, drops his bag and bends over the figure. Perhaps he's not dead after all? He twitched just then. Rafi touches his face. The skin's still warm. Something tells Rafi to fetch someone, but this path leads back to the pony yard and beyond that to the school and main road. His home is a ten-minute walk in the opposite direction. He's early today because the other kids needed to change their books at the library van on the other side of the village, then head home from there. Because he's top of the class, the teacher gave Rafi his book this morning.

Rafi's tempted to try to help the man, but he doesn't know how to and all he wants is to show his book to his dad. Plus he's hungry, so he swings the blue bag on his shoulder and walks off, and by the time he reaches home, he's forgotten about the sleeping man with the bloody nose.

———————

Shareen arrives home before Daniel and has time to push her face and hands under the tap and wipe dust and dirt from her face. Breathlessly excited by the kiss and the fight—by everything—she examines her arms and legs for scratches and bruises and sees she's gotten off lightly, all things considered.

Later, when she empties the last of the rice from the brown paper bag into the pot of boiling water on the stove, the only thing she feels is a profound, overwhelming sensation of pleasure. Pleasure at the memory of her arms on Aaron's warm neck. The feel of his strong muscles against her body is somehow more real than the rough, wooden spoon in her hand with which she is jabbing at beads of rice on the bottom of the pot. Jabbing at them to hurry them up. With her fired-up face veiled in steam and pointed up to the cracked concrete ceiling, Shareen dreams of Aaron—and her.

Him and her. Kissing. A new fantasy. A new escape.

With the faint echo of children playing outside, Shareen builds a wall in her mind to keep her husband out. A cloud of flies drift across the room and in that moment, as she waggles the spoon at them, she decides it would be fun to make Aaron fall in love with her. And no one need know.

He doesn't love her yet. But he will. He will.

"It's always the woman who makes that decision," her mother once told her.

Soon Daniel will be back after spending the day carving walking sticks for tourists in the craft center. Coming home to mock his wife while she hands him rice and beans to eat. Until then, Shareen conjures up ways of making herself irresistible to Aaron. Her eyes fall on the fading red words sprayed on the floor. Day after day she's been trying to scrub them away. No matter how much Daniel complains, she's not going to get down on her hands and knees again. From now on, she'll spend her evenings rubbing coconut oil into her rough hands, curling her hair with strips of cotton, painting her eyes with kohl, and practicing being gorgeous. And if Lijah tells Daniel he saw her kissing Aaron, she'll laugh and call him a liar, then report him to the priest for trying to wreck her happy marriage as well as her good reputation.

No other footsteps turn into the empty path leading to the pony yard until the last flickers of daylight fade to darkness. Since Aaron is within range of a million insects and rats, it's not long before something nips his ankle. He jerks his leg and slowly becomes aware of the pains in his head, arm, and shoulder, and soon the old ache in his knee starts up. As the path fills with shadows, the taste of blood hits the back of his throat, forcing him to gag.

Aaron tries to wipe the taste away, smearing blood from his nose across his face with the back of a hand. The sound of quick footsteps catches him off guard for a moment and he half-sits. The humid night turns in on itself to power up the smell of rotting garbage. The stench is sickening. When Aaron glances sideways, he sees Michael hurrying toward him. As always, the old patterned handkerchief is tied in knots on his head. His jeans and shirt are crusted with dust. He looks no different from normal, except the expression on his face isn't polite and calm but deeply troubled by the sight of Aaron lying there with a bloody nose.

Michael doesn't ask what happened. Only a handful of words leave his tight lips as he helps Aaron struggle to his feet: "There are two ways to deal with an enemy—outwit them or join them."

"Join Lijah?" Aaron murmurs, gasping from the effort to straighten up.

Giddy with pain, his mind wanders back to Shareen flinging herself at him, then Lijah banging their heads together. A few wobbling steps later, Aaron manages to steady himself and, anxious to prove he's all right, places a hand on Michael's shoulder to make it easier for him to lead the way to the yard. All the while a fierce anger fires him up, while dizziness drains his face of color. Anger at Shareen for throwing herself at him. Anger at Lijah for finding them. Regret for being stupid enough to try to protect her. But the worst of these festering hatreds is the guilt he feels for enjoying kissing Shareen, a married woman, while thinking of Rachel.

He screwed up and he despises himself for it.

The clear night shelters them in a velvety blue light as they walk. When they reach the end of the path and turn to cross the pony yard, the sharp outline of the beautiful ponies catches Aaron's eye. Their profiles look like sculptures on the distant hills. Michael nods at the appreciation he sees in Aaron's expression. Like him, he smiles at the sight of the ponies.

Michael has often seen Aaron watching him work and has been aware of him sauntering back and forth while he's up the ladder carving. Usually a child's interest in his sculpting and painting dies away by the time they're twelve. But not with Aaron. His interest has grown. They've never spoken about it, but Michael senses the time has come for him to help this orphan boy. Didn't God arrange it this way?

When they reach the old white car parked at the edge of

the village, Michael clicks opens the passenger door for Aaron and waits until he's comfortably settled before climbing into the driver's seat and turning over the engine. The mosquitoes are out in force, messing the windscreen, as Michael drives along the track to join the busy road. Being in a car for the first time sparks a strange, tickling nervousness in Aaron's stomach.

Where are they going? Aaron's eyes fix on the fuel gauge, flapping glove box, empty McDonald's carton at his feet. A sudden bump on the track and screech of the wheels makes him grab the edge of the seat. Even the taste of blood in his mouth and the unexpected sight of his swollen face in the side mirror can't prevent the feeling that this is a fantasy come true.

So this is what it feels like to speed along the highway . . . How Aaron wishes someone he knows could see him.

They overtake a blue car with ease. The driver honks the horn. A donkey laden with sacks of bananas stops to relieve himself. Michael puts up his hands for a second and Aaron freezes, thinking the car will crash now he's let go of the steering wheel, but they suddenly turn right and the donkey is lost in a jam of blasting vehicles. Aaron's aches and pains are almost forgotten in the enjoyment of zooming past taxis and buses instead of slowly plodding behind them in a cart. The pleasure he feels when they sail past a massive truck is beyond thrilling.

"I want to show you something," Michael says.

But the thrills recede when, a few miles north of the city,

after passing several mosques, new apartment blocks, and a racecourse, they turn down a highway. Ten minutes later they join a wide, flat road that seems to lead to nothing but dark hillocks of barren land, inhabited by mosquitoes, tiny insects, and scurrying rats.

The bumps in the road keep shifting the focus of the car lights from one patch of scrub to another. There's nothing to see beyond the odd clump of grass. Aaron's confused and wants to ask where they're going. But the question becomes unnecessary when a familiar smell sinks in and the car stutters to a stop on an incline. The car's swooping lights beam over a chasm of waste bursting from a pit so wide and disgusting that Aaron gasps. Like massive eagles lunging at their prey, swarms of flies hover over the garbage and shudder.

"Cairo produces more than six hundred tons of garbage a day," Michael says. "This is one of the Corporation's dumps. By law they only have to recycle twenty per cent. The rest is burned."

Aaron's never seen anything like it. Everywhere there are mountains of food that could have been fed to the pigs. Plenty of paper, cardboard, and clothes that could have been recycled, plus oceans of plastic bags. His eyes pick out hundreds of broken bottles, mirrors, vases, and pieces of shattered glass that have been thoughtlessly tossed aside.

"The Zabbaleen collect three-quarters of the city's rubbish and recycle more than eighty percent," Michael says as he stares at the scene with the same horror as Aaron. Beneath the horror is the thought that without the Zabbaleen this pit would need to be twice the size.

For the first time, the usefulness of his work comes home to Aaron with a hammer-like force. He's been told many times that they provide a service for the city, but after seeing this crawling sewer of filth, he can barely take in just how badly the city needs them. The Zabbaleen would never allow a place like this to exist.

"Why don't they recycle it?" Aaron asks.

"All over the world the problems with rubbish are the same. A lot is taken to recycling plants, but that involves labor, time and money to transport. The more stuff people throw out, the more waste ends up in pits like this and our planet teeters on the edge of destruction. Only when we stop wanting things will our lives change."

Aaron feels a slight sense of guilt, because there are loads of things he wants: a computer, a TV, clothes, gym shoes. But when they leave and Michael reverses the car, the headlights sweeping from the pit to the scrubland again as they rumble back down the road, his guilt's soon forgotten. Only the stupidity of so much unwanted stuff fills his mind.

Soon, opening out like the start of a movie, the twinkling lights of the city reappear and streets lined with modern bungalows and houses—many decorated with Muslim motifs—come into view. Eventually, they pull into parking bays by a large square lined with shops on the ground floor of old five-story buildings with big windows. To Aaron's surprise, there's rubbish and piles of rotting food on the street here too. The Corporation's workers—men in green uniforms—toss leaking bags onto trucks tumbling with garbage but they ignore the stinking food. The place smells bad, though not as awful as Mokattam or the pit.

"Since they decided to kill the pigs the food waste in Cairo is out of control. The Zabbaleen won't pick it up from the streets any more." Michael shakes his head.

The square is busy with people buying vegetables, leather goods, and coffee. The streetlights make bright ribbons of the red, green, and pale-blue canopies over the shops and charcoal smoke drifts from a nut roaster on the pavement.

Michael switches off the engine and says, "The square was built for the Europeans who lived here." The keys rattle as he explains. "My father spoke only French to my mother. She spoke only English to him. They spoke Egyptian to everyone else."

Aaron raises his eyes in wonder at Michael as they get out of the car. He's never heard of such a strange way of communicating.

"They're both dead now." There's a sudden sadness in Michael's voice as he leads the way to a door beside a shop selling garlic and onions, tomatoes and dried tamarinds, then up to a first-floor apartment. A tiny apartment with one bedroom, a kitchen-cum-sitting room, and a white-tiled bathroom.

The apartment is cluttered with things like knotted branches, feathers, and odd stones. There are drawings of the Holy Family on the walls and Aaron realizes that this is Michael's home. Aaron's in awe that he's sharing it with him, and in return he would like to tell him about the face he saw on the glass doors of the Imperial Hotel—the picture of the Virgin Mary that made him feel special. But he can't, because he might tell Father Peter. Aaron doesn't want to be pushed to the front row of the church every saint's day and special service for the rest of his life.

"You can stay here," says Michael.

Chapter Twenty-one
Back to Normal

Over the next few days, Aaron becomes used to sleeping on the brown sofa, elbow falling to the wooden floor while he listens to the annoying sound of motorbikes revving up all night in the square. He becomes used to eating at a pull-out table, having a bath and being looked after. Bit by bit, he begins to enjoy living in a home without garbage, glass, used syringes and plastic tubes. The kind of home he'd only glimpsed through windows.

Slowly he gets to know Inga, Michael's Danish wife, who's also an artist. She's different.

"This is nice," she says, handing back the perfume bottle she found in Aaron's pocket before throwing his jeans away and presenting him with new ones made from thick navy denim.

Michael's different too. He still doesn't say much, but Aaron's come to the conclusion that when he looks distant and distracted, he's actually watching and listening to everything around him. Every morning he asks if Aaron wants to come and help him carve the walls in Mokattam and when Aaron shakes his head Inga laughs.

"OK," Michael says, smiling, and off he goes.

By the way he says OK, Aaron can tell Michael knew he wasn't going to come.

"Good," Inga says, her mouth full of food. "He can sit for me again while I paint his portrait."

Sitting for Inga is deathly boring and her paintings are strange. She adds what she calls symbols to her pictures that look to Aaron like circles with squiggles and upside-down triangles, but at least it gives him time to think.

Aaron remembers Omar telling his assistant not to be afraid of change, of bad events, death, grief of any kind, because pain, like chaos, is a way of rearranging the elements so that life can start again in a different way. At the time he thought Omar was just being Omar. But now Aaron understands what he meant and his frustration falls away when he realizes that, if Jacob hadn't taken the necklace from him, he wouldn't have run away. Then Shareen wouldn't have kissed him, Lijah wouldn't have hit him, and Michael wouldn't have found him and brought him home. But most revealing of all, he wouldn't have seen how important the Zabbaleen are to the running of Cairo. His city.

In the afternoons, Aaron wanders round the square, sidestepping cars and squeezing past shoppers to rescue the oranges that roll into the gutter from the greengrocer's shop. Often he sits on the steps of the building, watching people go by and breathing in the smell of leather from the purses, belts, and sandals on the nearby stall while ignoring the stench of rotting food piling up on the pavements and doorways. All the time imagining and hoping that Rachel is missing him. He'd like to go to the hospital to see her, but it's a long way from here—too far to walk, and he doesn't have any money. Instead, Aaron stares out at the cars and people until he can't stand the clouds of flies any longer.

Tonight, when the lights from the street cars stop flashing around the walls and the lamps go out, Aaron sighs deeper than he's done all day. Glad to be alone. Glad to flop out and not have to talk to Inga or eat with her and Michael. Kind though they are, Aaron finds it hard to be himself when they're around. Now he can drop the effort of listening and trying to be helpful, when really there's nothing they want except for him to rest and get strong.

Resting is tiring for Aaron. He's never felt this exhausted in his life. He takes the perfume bottle from the pocket of his new jeans and holds it to his nose. The faint whiff of rose mixed with lotus and jasmine reminds him of Rachel. Everything reminds him of her these days. The feel of the glass in his hand brings back the touch of her silky skin when she took his rough hands in hers to wipe away her tears. He didn't know skin could feel that soft. It makes him wonder what it would be like to kiss her. It makes him wonder where feelings come from and whether Michael feels that way about Inga. After everything that's happened, all Aaron cares about is Rachel.

Two motorbikes rev up in the square, bringing Aaron back to the small flat to remind him that this isn't his home. Mokattam is peaceful at night, unlike the square, which comes alive at two in the morning. There's no longer a reason to stay now that his cut lip and swollen eye have healed. It feels strangely dead—this bright, clean apartment where nothing happens. He thought he'd like it when he first came and he's surprised by the feeling of suffocation that living with people you don't know can bring.

There's no air here. No one ever comes.

Now that he's back to normal, he can't help wondering how Michael and Inga don't go crazy living here on their own without any outdoor space and family or neighbors to share their lives with. They have nice cups, a clean floor, and a fridge full of food, and most of the Zabbaleen don't have these things. But Mokattam is heaving with the lives of thousands of people who are all in the same boat, and even though they're struggling to survive, there are dramas, gossip, and challenges that make living in this little box feel as dull and lonely as a desert cave.

How many people would come to Inga's funeral if she died? Aaron might be an orphan who's not very popular at the moment, but the Mokattam church would be packed to the rafters if he died. And then it hits him that he has only to work hard, show respect to the elders, and help his neighbors, and they will forgive him. Not stealing and not bearing grudges are equally important in their close-knit community. He can show he's sorry. That's all he has to do.

Aaron thinks about all the people he's known since the

day he was born. People he understands because they're like him. He misses sitting on the low wall and gazing at the night sky, surrounded by a world he recognizes. He wants to know what happened to the necklace and what Jacob's been up to this past week. As for Shareen, she's dangerous and he'll tell her to leave him alone. And then there's Lijah. He's probably married now. And Rachel. Rachel. Where is she?

At breakfast the following morning, Michael seems to know what he's thinking and mentions a way out.

"Mokattam is a world of its own," he says. "That's difficult to give up."

"I was thinking I might . . ." Aaron starts.

"Go home?" Michael gazes at the pull-out table with sharp little eyes. "You'll know when the time's right to leave." With that, he gets up, fetches his knapsack from the bedroom floor, nods quickly, and goes.

The thing about Michael is that although he does these amazing frescoes and carvings, if Aaron asks him how he learned to do them or where the ideas come from, he just says, "You can access all knowledge if you're willing to tune into it."

Aaron's not sure what he means. Sometimes he sees a resemblance between Michael and Omar. Both men baffle and fascinate him. They give him a strange confidence, leaving him with the feeling that he can recover from anything. Suddenly realizing this changes Aaron.

The next day, sitting on the hard brown sofa while Inga sketches him, Aaron says, "I have to go."

"Well, I've finished. For now." Inga drops her pencil. "I

have to paint two dogs this afternoon to make money. What Michael gets from the church just covers rent, so, yes, go. Have good day! No? Do some fun."

Do some fun? Her odd Egyptian phrases and accent make Aaron laugh. The formal greetings, inquiries after his health, smiles, and long good-byes that are part of life are things she's never learned. Michael is a quiet Egyptian, while the mad, foreign Inga is loud. She flaps her hands and squeals even when pouring a glass of water.

Aaron accepts a few coins from her and, wearing a yellow T-shirt and new jeans, he leaves. The smell of sandalwood soap from his own skin surprises him as he reaches the street. But the sweet scent is soon overpowered by the familiar stench of rotting waste. A man swears at a pile of loose garbage that has been dumped beside the door of the building.

He nods briefly to Aaron. "Look at this filth. We pay for this rubbish to be collected!"

Aaron takes no notice as he heads out of the square, where three shopkeepers are collecting cigarette cartons, newspapers, and food remains that the men from the Corporation have left behind. Aaron calculates there's enough trash here to fill five bags. The Zabbaleen would have done a much better job. Suddenly feeling proud of who he is and what he does, he straightens his back and holds his head high.

Ten minutes later Aaron jumps off a bus heading to the museum. When two girls giggle at the sight of him running toward a road that's closed to traffic, Aaron stops to glance at them.

The local teenagers are obviously on a trip to the museum

and he hears one of the bubbly girls saying, "He's so fit!"

"Like a Greek god!"

"Egyptian, you mean."

"Apollo? Was he Greek, then?"

"You're thinking of Adonis . . ."

It takes a moment for Aaron to realize they're discussing him. Their words make him wonder if Rachel might think he's fit too. He catches sight of himself in a shop window and is startled to see he looks nothing like a Zabbaleen. There's not a speck of dust on his skin, hair or clothes. In a weird transformation, his time at Michael's has turned him from a filthy kid into a handsome man with shiny hair, bright skin, and only the faintest trace of a cut lip and black eye.

Gazing around him at passing shoppers filling their baskets with fruit and flowers, Aaron sees the road to the hospital and university is crowded with policemen. He slips down a side street to avoid the crush of people waiting to cross at the lights. It's then that he realizes that something out of the ordinary is happening in the city. A new one-way system has been invented to force traffic away from the center and there are police everywhere directing cars in the wrong direction. But he knows Cairo like the back of his hand and slips down an alley where cheap restaurants and cafés pretend to sell real Egyptian food to backpacking tourists.

It takes an hour and a half to cover a distance that should have taken twenty minutes, so many roads are barred by men with sniffer dogs. When Aaron finally walks down the road leading to the hospital, he's covered in sweat and is shocked to the core when a beggar at the gate holds out a hand for a coin.

The beggar bows eagerly, but Aaron knows for sure he's richer than him by the gold tooth he reveals when he grins.

In a flurry of excitement at being mistaken for someone worth begging from, Aaron rushes past the man, into the hospital, and up in the elevator, as if he's used to making this journey every day. For all he knows Rachel could be back home in Mokattam by now, but a burning feeling inside tells him she's still here. Still here.

Aaron pinches himself to calm down from the speedy, breathless way he arrives at her slightly open door.

A sound of light coughing comes from inside the room. He pauses to listen and holds his breath in case she can hear him standing there—being stupid. Wiping his clammy hands on the side of his jeans, he feels as if he's about to fall off a raft, crash on a rock, and drown.

Aaron gently touches the door, which remains firmly in its place. He tries again. Nothing happens. Then he spots a wooden wedge jammed firmly underneath the door, keeping it ajar to allow air to travel freely from the window to the dank corridor.

He can make a big entrance by kicking the wedge out of the way or pitching himself through the narrow space. Either way, he'll surprise Rachel, which he doesn't want to do. That leaves only one option. He raps his knuckles on the door.

"Rachel . . ."

The slight coughing noise stops.

"It's me, Aaron."

There's a rustling sound.

"I wanted to see you, Rachel."

Formalities over, Aaron breathes deeply and, clutching the door, pushes sideways into the room, where his jaw drops. A pale, middle-aged Western woman is sitting on the bed in a blue gown. Beyond her, dead flies dot the dirty window and a hazy sky blots out the sun. The beautiful light from last time is gone and this cold, hard vision shows up the threadbare sheet on the bed and the gray, bumpy linoleum on the floor.

"Sorry. I was looking for . . . someone," Aaron says.

The woman smiles, answering in fluent Arabic. "I know what you mean, love! That's what we're all doing, eh? Some find it easier than others, don't they?"

Frustrated and sad, Aaron nods and backs out of the room, sneaking down the corridor to peer into every room he passes. Rooms that reveal several beds with desperately sick patients attached to blood bags, many of whom are being washed and fed by members of their families.

Where's Rachel?

Confusion takes over when he reaches the lift and begins to wonder how Rachel got a room of her own here. Someone said a doctor from this hospital was visiting the health clinic in Mokattam when she was run over. In that case someone at the Mokattam clinic must know where she's been taken. He must go home and find out.

The sticky heat and hazy sky add to Aaron's despair as he reaches the hospital gates. A roar of dust from a passing truck points the way to the center of town. As he trundles down the busy road, his knee begins to ache at the thought of all that walking down the hot, shimmering, noisy road that stretches out forever in front of him.

He regrets not going to the perfume shop first, before heading to the hospital.

At the mercy of his own misery at not seeing Rachel, Aaron remembers another dream he had about his mother. A dream where she came to him on the night she died. In that dream, he saw her smiling, standing in the lane facing him, surrounded by a golden light. When he woke up in the morning he ran into the lane expecting to see her. He was shocked when she wasn't there. Only a child with a runny nose returned his gaze. Then he remembered his mother was dead and the joy of seeing her in the dream made it feel as if she'd died twice. He'd lost her again and the effect was a splintering of reality. A devastating howl in every cell of his body. Even now that feeling makes him recoil from himself.

The pain of her death runs away with him until he reaches the third road so far that's barred from pedestrians and traffic with police and dogs.

"What's going on?" someone asks.

"The American president, Barack Obama, is coming to the university to give a speech," the police officer answers.

"Really? What time?" Beaming wildly, the onlooker can't hide her excitement. "Is he coming this way? When? When?"

The police officer shrugs. Aaron doesn't wait to hear the answer. What's an American president's speech got to do with him? His life isn't going to change because of that. What's the use in him coming to Cairo? What's the use in speeches? The Egyptian president didn't do anything for the Zabbaleen, so why should the American one be any different? Politicians make no sense to him.

Sometime later, when he reaches the entrance to the underpass beneath another barricaded road, Aaron touches the familiar bottle in his pocket. The smooth glass feels like a warm hand. Something real to hold on to. Because of the closed road, the peeling ochre-painted tunnel is swarming with people and neither side wants to give way, bumping into one another, mingling scents of sweat, tobacco, perfume, and the odd sharp smell of mint tea. Squeezing the glass bottle, Aaron elbows past a man carrying bread on his head. Then a large family.

Two police in navy garb, guns held high, force Aaron to slow down until he reaches the exit to the street and, without thinking, pushes through the crowd. As he steps into the blast of sunshine, gasoline fumes and rushing people, a young, dainty woman in a green galabeya brushes past him. It's Shareen.

Stunned, Aaron races down the pavement to the traffic lights to catch up with her, but a moment later he sees her getting into a gray car to sit beside an older man with a bushy beard. The car shoots off in a puff of exhaust, leaving him standing there, bewildered. Shareen had golden sandals on her dainty feet. A silver chain on her wrist. Where did she get them from? Who was that man? Where's Daniel?

Still amazed, Aaron hurries toward Omar's perfume shop, bracing himself for answers he doesn't want to hear when he gets back to Mokattam. He hopes that Shareen will be home by then and that there's an innocent reason for her being out alone in Cairo with a man who clearly isn't a Zabbaleen. Maybe it wasn't her after all.

On he races past windows packed with patterned galabeyas, shawls, and scarves, then stalls selling painted papyrus and King Tut souvenirs. But Aaron senses something isn't quite right before he reaches the shop. He suddenly stops in his tracks. What he sees fills him with panic and disbelief.

With the constant sound of traffic behind him, Aaron gazes at the empty, sun-speckled shop windows and the hummocks of dust on the smudged glass shelves and then the huge, dark, closed doors with a half-alive fly buzzing by a sign which reads "Closed for Remodeling."

Grabbing the window, Aaron presses his face to the glass and peers inside at a rolling expanse of space. Empty but for a stained red carpet, a strip of metal on the floor, and what looks like the corner of an oil lamp on the far wall.

Distraught, he swallows back hot tears. The window mists from his breathing. He wipes the glass with the back of his hand and the full force of the emptiness of the room hurts his eyes and freezes his mind. Turning to slump against the window, his shoulders make a grinding noise on the glass that he can feel in his stomach. Not now. He needed this.

Aaron blunders to the alley in search of glass. Anything that can feed his desire for beauty. Squinting away from the sun, the first thing he notices is that the side window is partly open. Below is a cardboard box and the firm shape proves it's packed with rejected bottles. With the swish of cars in his ear, Aaron fills his pockets with as many small bottles as possible. Pale bottles without stoppers. A slender pink one with a twisted rim. A miniature blue bottle decorated with a broken leaf. And cheap, plain, oddly shaped bottles that rub together like marbles and land on the rose-colored bottle of perfume that he's kept forever in his pocket. All of them rolling and clunking as he runs.

Soon he's part of the pack. Part of the streets, the people, traffic, noise, heat. The madness of the city. A glass collector again.

Chapter Twenty-two
A New Beginning

"What happened to you? You look different. Older," Luke Mebaj says.

"Dunno. Dunno," Aaron gasps as he climbs on the cart.

Slumped in the back, an overpowering weakness takes over and all Aaron can do is clutch his chest, close his eyes, and be thankful he caught up with the Mebaj cart after putting his life at risk by leaping in front of a bus and racing across the street.

Soon—the second he can speak—he'll ask them the question that's on the tip of his tongue. Right now the stem of a bottle is digging into his thigh. Aaron twists around, rubs the spot, and rearranges the empty reject bottles in his pockets until the full and perfect bottle that he's carefully hung on to slips into the corner of the denim, protected from harm.

Joseph Mebaj glances at Aaron before clicking the reins, then says, "Something up?"

"Nah!" Aaron mutters.

He's used to Michael and Inga not saying much, so he shuts down and lets the question drift. It feels strange to be on a cart again, surrounded by bags of oozing trash. He gazes at the traffic like someone who belongs in a wide, empty desert, not this stinking heap of junk. The cars, buses, and taxis are crowded with people whose faces reflect his and behind their eyes is the same yearning for something better, something good. Something more meaningful than getting through the day swinging from crisis to crisis and then sorting out the debris.

Aaron's mind travels back to Omar's shop and the customers who went there to buy more than perfumes. More than a pretty bottle with luscious scents. Some went to buy oils to heal their souls, to bring back a feeling of connection to their bodies in the hope it would turn their lives around.

"He brought my missing soul back to me!" Aaron once heard a customer say.

"Omar is an ancient shaman!" his assistant would boast. "He's as mysterious as this city."

Who knows when the shop will open again? Aaron can't quite believe it is closed. His mind turns to the city's extraordinary past; to the fact that Mary, Joseph, and Jesus passed this way once. Did they stop in front of the pyramids of Giza and wonder if they were used as star maps and a means to communicate with other life forms, as Omar said?

Or did they believe they were a way to help the pharaohs to the afterlife, as they were taught in school?

"Nothing can satisfy our minds like the kinds of journeys we are capable of when we use our imaginations. Only then can we discover the truth," Omar also said.

As the cart slows to a snail's pace, the sun blinks fiercely at Aaron from behind the shopping complex. He holds up an arm to blot it out, then ducks behind the nearest bag, which cracks like a whip. Stuck there with the smell of rotting fish and an old water pipe in his face, it dawns on Aaron that he can revisit the shop whenever he wants.

All he has to do is use his imagination.

Now when Aaron remembers the shop, he sees it through his mother's eyes. He almost smiles her smile as the huge wooden doors judder open. Sprinkled with sunshine, the bottles glimmer on the shelves and the interior glints like a sultana's boudoir with rich velvet cushions and brass lamps. Soon soft, padding footsteps cross the polished floor to greet the woman with a rag held to her weeping eyes. Omar takes her hand, Aaron's mother's hand, and tells her not to worry.

Not to cry.

Then Omar leads her to the corner to sit down and says she doesn't have to pay him. He's happy to give her his time. Whether she's a Zabbaleen or not is nothing to him. He asks about her life. About her son. About her pains. He listens. He offers her kindness and good wishes. Then he lifts a stick from a black ceramic vase and soaks it in Rose of the Nile perfume, offering it to her with the promise that the scent will bring her the peace she seeks.

The cart suddenly jerks. The water pipe smacks Aaron on the head as the traffic comes to a stop, forcing his mind to snap back to the busy Cairo street. He throws the pipe at a passing truck at the very moment a fighter plane screams across the sky. As the vapor trail fades, Aaron's heart softens. Softens when he remembers the peaceful expression on his mother's face when it was all over. The half-smile. The tilted head.

Aaron lowers his eyes. He wishes he could fly over the streets, over the nearby bazaar and tall buildings. Over the citadel to the slums of Mokattam and a time when everything felt possible. A time before she died.

As the cart follows the curve in the road leading to the entrance to the village, Aaron grasps a smooth knot of wood on the side of the cart, realizing he is suddenly nervous to be back. The nearer they come to the high arch, the louder the tapping and thudding ring out from the foundry. The moment they leave the arch and dusty pillars behind, he flinches, burying his nose in his hands, and when the brothers halt the pony to deliver a broken TV to Sami, Aaron swings his legs over the side and leaps off. He glances briefly at the stool beside the counter but Rachel's not there.

The sun sinks and the dark cavelike shops and stalls crawl with half-human shapes.

He'd forgotten how badly Mokattam smells. As he weaves through the endless trash lining the walls of the shops and stalls, Ishaq, the icon seller, gives him a welcoming nod. Habi flings an orange at Aaron with an understanding smile and, though no one asks what happened, it seems everyone knows he's been staying at Michael's and that he's sorry. Each step brings another nod, a silent message to say, *So you're back?* It may not be the greatest of welcomes, but at least they know who he is, unlike the people who live in Michael's apartment building. They give Aaron the courage to stand on top of a mound of garbage bags and steady himself before cupping his mouth in his hands.

"SORRRRRY!" he yells.

The Mebaj brothers turn round and laugh. Everyone in the lane laughs. Their attention puts a spring in Aaron's step as he hurries toward his stepfamily's home. But the spring in his step dies suddenly when he sees Jacob up ahead with a bunch of men who are counting out white pills in the palms of their hands. Empty brown medicine bottles lie at their feet.

"Jacob!" Aaron shouts as he gets closer. "Why aren't you out on the cart?"

"Hey, Aaron." Jacob looks scared. "I—yeah . . ." There's no hint of a smile on his red, swollen face and sunken eyes.

"His cousin's taken over until he gets better," one of the men says.

"I've got that skin disease." Jacob holds out his bony arms, which are bleeding from where he's been scratching an ugly rash. Then he lifts up his T-shirt to show a stomach marked with the same blistering scabs. "It's driving me crazy."

By the patches of limestone dust on his ears, nose and hands, Aaron sees that living in Mokattam is adding to Jacob's problems and the terrible state he's in.

"What did they say at the clinic?"

"They gave me some cream, but I've used it all up.

I should get some more," Jacob mombles, tripping slightly. One of his friends catches him. "If we'd kept that necklace I could have sold it and afforded the best doctor."

His new friend places an arm around his sagging shoulder.

"What did you do with it?" Aaron asks. It seems to him that Jacob needs more than money or a skin doctor now.

"Noha gave it to the priest," his friend answers for him.

The quick response is an excuse for them all to nod in a self-righteous way—as if they would have given it to the priest too. All the while covering up their real problem, which isn't what they might have done with the necklace, but something more ordinary—drugs.

Aaron's sure that Jacob is lying. He hasn't been to the clinic. Aaron doesn't bother to look back as he walks away disappointed, sad and full of suspicion that Noha will try to persuade him to help the cousin collect medical waste. If Aaron wants to eat that might be his only option. The thought makes him shudder. Makes him want to run for his life.

When he reaches the last alley he hears the familiar sound of Abe thudding a ball against a concrete wall. Before the boy sees him Aaron shouts, "Hiya."

"Where you been?" Abe cries, clapping the ball to his chest and admiring Aaron's new jeans.

"Nowhere much." Aaron grins. "Anything happened?"

"Nah. Nothing."

"Nothing?" Aaron sighs. "You sure?" He eyes Abe closely before asking, "What about Rachel?"

"Oh, her? She's back home."

Suddenly understanding what he's getting at, Abe smiles. Aaron wants to hear Mokattam news, not what *he's* been doing.

"Rachel's leg was in a fat cast. Her knee still bends funny. Lijah married Shovel Face and Shareen disappeared."

Rachel's here. Aaron grins to himself.

"I saw Shareen getting into a car in Cairo," he says out loud.

"She ran away just after you left," Abe says. "Daniel went crazy looking for her and everyone's been praying for her to come back. Nobody knows why she went."

"Where's the wheelbarrow?"

"Old man Mebaj bought it," Abe tells him.

"Oh, right." Aaron nods.

"Why do you think she left?" Abe asks, curious for his opinion.

Aaron thinks for a moment. He understands exactly why Shareen left.

"She married an old man. It wasn't her dream," he explains. "That's why she went."

"Yeah, but she didn't have to," Abe says.

"Her father *made* her marry Daniel. Anyway, she may have escaped Mokattam but not old men. She got into a car with one."

"Maybe he's rich?"

Abe's about to mention the merchant's latest stupid price offering, the argument with the council about their new fleet of trucks, and the trouble his mom's having hiding her pig, when the sound of a high-pitched wailing interrupts them.

269

It's coming from the next lane, where Aaron's old home is. They take to their heels, stumbling over bags, with a thousand possible disasters flashing through their minds.

A crushed white plastic bottle rolls over Aaron's feet as he slows down to approach a dozen men and women in front of his stepfamily's open room, which is dripping with trash and food slop. From a nearby home the Christian radio station is echoing a recent speech of Pope Shenouda III. Out of fear, Aaron hangs back while Abe rushes in. His first thought is that Lijah's beaten someone up, probably his new wife, and he'd rather not look at the result.

Stepping backwards, Aaron tries to avoid being noticed, but a cranky man with a solid jaw commands him to come closer with a wave of his arm. Aaron hesitates and Abe pushes back through the group to join his friend. Slightly apprehensive that Aaron's going to react badly to what he's just seen, Abe grabs his hand, squeezing it tightly.

"Get off." Aaron's embarrassed by his affection.

Abe laughs, then pulls a sad face. "Hosi had a heart attack."

"Is that all?" Aaron was expecting something worse.

"No, he's dead now!" Abe says. "He's still warm but he's dead."

"I heard you."

Aaron doesn't feel anything much except relief. He shivers for a second before realizing he'll never have to listen to his snoring again. He'll never again have to look at Hosi's ugly, gnarled hands. Now there's no one over him and he's glad to see the back of him. Aaron knows it's wrong to feel what he feels, but he can't help it. His life has just changed for the better.

In a strange way, Hosi's death also means that Lijah is suddenly irrelevant. Youssa the drunk is head of the family now and no one can know how that will work out. Even so, neither stepbrother can demand the kind of respect from Aaron that Hosi could as an elderly stepfather. A whole layer of judgement has fallen away and it feels good. Very good. As if his death has given birth to a new life for Aaron.

A new beginning.

The family is going to need his help more than ever now and he won't have to return to medical-waste clearing again. He can go back to collecting glass like he wants. But even that pleasant thought doesn't help him take the twenty steps needed to see Hosi's dead body on the dirty ground.

A light rain begins to fall as Aaron hightails it back down the alley before Lijah or someone else insists he pay the proper respects to his stepfather. The damaged perfume bottles clink, hum, and vibrate in his pockets as he runs toward the pony yard, enjoying the fantasy that Rachel will be there waiting for him. Abe doesn't try to follow him. He knows well enough that when Aaron's in the mood to take off, he's also in the mood to be on his own.

Firing on all cylinders, Aaron turns the corner to the yard and stops abruptly at the shock of seeing three scraggy ponies nosing the bare, dark earth and no water in the trough. Littered with dirty cigarette cartons, lighters, and used tissues, the place is disgusting. He'd convinced himself Rachel would be here, but now he's glad she isn't.

His gaze wanders to the disappearing hills in the cloudy darkness and the smell of pony flesh mixes with the stink of dung. The memory of the beautiful, velvety night the last time he was here with Michael briefly returns and a tiny smile crosses his face as he picks up the rubbish and adds it to the pile in the lane before filling the trough with water from the hose.

Having time to himself makes him feel free. He'd rather be here, out in the open, than cooped up on Michael's sofa, listening to the sound of motorbikes revving up in the square. Michael and Inga have cared for him so kindly, he's grateful, but being part of the shadows feels familiar and safe. But what about the empty reject bottles he took from the alley beside the shop this morning? Where can he hide them? Does he need to hide them? The straggles of hay behind the shelter aren't big enough to disguise a box of matches, let alone all this glass. Why not throw them away? Or try and sell them to Faisal. He won't care where they've come from. But then people are always watching Faisal. They'll see Aaron trying to offload the bottles and get angry with him for stealing. It's clear they're only good for melting down. But to Aaron they're windows to look at the world through and something to call his own. His bottles. His glass.

Deep in thought, Aaron moves behind the ramshackle shelter and shivers. The blackness feels like a demon that's about to pounce. Aaron pauses to glance at three wheel spindles beside the wire fence and for a moment thinks they're vicious snakes. He wants to strangle them even though he knows they're not real. The real snakes are weaving in and out of his mind, not the creepy fence.

Hosi's last words come back to him: "You've cost me my reputation. Stay away from my family. You don't think about anyone but yourself."

The sudden echo of a distant barking dog brings Aaron back to his body with a jolt. The world around him returns: the rickety shelter, the wheel spindles, the straggles of hay, and the wide, dark sky.

Wandering to the front of the yard, Aaron watches the ponies nuzzling each other while sniffing the air. He sits cross-legged on the hard earth with the sound of rustling and pony snorts in his ears. Carefully, he inches lumps of earth out with his fingernails and soon a small mound forms beside his knee. When the hole is big enough, he lines the clinking rejects up one by one to examine the stems and bases for defects, as he's always done. All except the one perfect bottle. The veil of night disguises their beauty, making them just bottles, not things capable of holding, transforming and reflecting light.

In a few deft movements, Aaron buries them quickly, patting the ground with his hands and then stamping the uneven bits with his feet. It's done. He eyes the ponies for a second before climbing over the fence to mingle with them, breathing in the smell of their skin. With both hands, Aaron rubs the gray one's bristly neck, then, when tiredness sweeps in, lies down beside the biggest pony to sleep, arm across his rising and falling stomach. Throughout the night, Aaron jerks awake several times, looks around, remembers where he is, and goes straight back to sleep.

The moment the sun comes up, Aaron's on his feet. For

more than an hour he stands waiting, watching the dusty lane for Rachel while the ponies pummel his back with their noses to remind him they want food and water. Eventually Aaron fills the trough and gathers up the hay scattered behind the shelter.

Wiping his hands on his sides, he glances at the ground where the bottles are hidden. He kicks dust over the dark earth to disguise it, then takes off. He can't just turn up at Rachel's house. It would lead to questions being asked and her father jumping to conclusions. Instead, he darts down the alleys with a mad energy that doesn't fade until he gets to his stepfamily's home.

Hosi's funeral took place a few hours after he died and Aaron didn't hear about it until it was over. Although he's glad he missed it, something he can't quite put his finger on brings him to a sudden stop. Hopeful but slightly hopeless, Aaron hides in a patch of shade at the end of the alley, staring past the waking families and piles of bags at a shamefaced Lijah, who's apologizing to his wife.

"Sorry. How many times do you want me to say it? Sorry I forgot to tell you about the meeting."

"You didn't want me to come!" Suzan sniffs.

"I didn't think you'd want to!" Lijah smiles. "Look, there's Aaron."

Look, there's Aaron?

A chill runs down Aaron's spine but he creeps forward toward the opening in the house. Seconds later Lijah gives him a friendly cuff around the ear. Aaron flinches. Lijah's face is inches away and the sudden closeness feels weird, because it's not scary.

"We kept a place for you." Lijah points to a miserable spot on the floor between the rubbish bags where he can sleep next to Youssa. "I knew you'd be back. We've got the upstairs room now." Lijah nods. "Some of the kids have been on the cart to help collect the glass, but they've cut themselves so many times it's not worth it. And the house next door is empty now that Shareen's gone and her father moved in with his sister. I told Youssa to take it but he likes being here."

"You're back, then?" Suzan interrupts.

Aaron shrugs. It looks like he is. When Youssa slopes over with a grin and welcomes him by handing him the ball of rice he's about to eat, a powerful feeling of defeat settles on Aaron.

"You know, Aaron can pick up glass faster than anyone in Mokattam, Suzan, and he never cuts himself," Lijah boasts.

Aaron blinks with shock, but the neighbors watch the scene with huge smiles. They can see by the way he stands that Aaron has changed. He's a man now and they know him. They knew his mother. His long-dead father. They're part of his past. His history. Aaron can feel their acceptance of him in their quiet faces and it feels good.

Suddenly the merchant's truck rumbles toward them and the women disappear like magic so the men can take care of business.

Seven elders scurry from the side alleys to confront Faisal and form a ring around the battered white vehicle with an enthusiastic look on their faces. *This time we're going to win.* The elders are followed by two foreign men in dark trousers and white shirts who aren't part of the community; they do a winding gesture with their hands to force Faisal to lower his window. Everyone is paying attention now.

A blast of air conditioning fans the watching men's faces before the merchant switches it off. Unprepared for this confrontation, the jowly, middle-aged crook narrows his eyes. Standing slightly back beside a mountain of bags, Aaron watches Lijah hurry Suzan upstairs.

A local man who's hard of hearing shouts to the man beside him, "The foreign men are from a charity that is trying to build recycling factories in Mokattam."

Aaron looks at the foreigners and their fine black shoes and listens to their polite threat. One man speaks while the other translates his words into Egyptian.

"These people are doing all the work but are being squeezed out of a living by the low prices you're paying for the trash. Our charity's raising funds to allow the Zabbaleen to make goods from the plastic, metal, and glass they collect. Soon you'll be out of business."

"That's what you think." Faisal laughs.

Charity workers have visited Mokattam many times with good intentions. The craft workshops and school have grown out of Egyptian as well as foreign aid, but no one has ever mentioned doing the merchants out of business. Aaron moves closer to listen as a ripple of excitement passes through the crowd.

"You think the price I get for this stuff stays the same? The companies who buy the recycled material lower their prices every day. The more factories there are, the less everyone will earn from the goods we make."

Faisal reaches forward to wind up the window but the charity worker rests an elbow on the filthy glass, forcing him to lean back.

"You can afford to pay more," the charity worker says, nodding. "And you know it. All they're asking for is a share of your profits."

For the first time in Aaron's life he wonders what it would be like to be paid a fair amount for the garbage he collects and recycles.

"That's all workers ever ask for, less work and more money," Faisal complains.

"We'll build recycling factories in Mokattam," the man says, and Aaron's heart flickers with hope. If they have their own factories here, they can sell the recycled material for five times what the merchant's paying. "We'll build them—one day. I promise," he adds.

The merchant's eyes glaze over. He isn't troubled by the warning. Instead, he looks bored. "Good luck!" is all he says.

Aaron wishes the charity man hadn't added "one day." Now it's obvious to everyone that they don't have the money to build the factories. They might never have the money. The crowd slowly breaks away. The charity man was trying to help, but nothing has changed.

With that sad thought in his mind, Aaron picks a path toward the pony yard. Once back collecting glass, he'll be here every morning and hopefully Rachel will be too. The one person Aaron wasn't expecting to see when he reaches the end of the last alley is Michael.

"I've been waiting," he says, his warm eyes smiling. "What are you doing?"

"Now?" Aaron hesitates. "I have to stay here now. I can't go back to your apartment again, but thanks for everything you did for me." Michael's expression of acceptance and understanding throws him for a second, then he says, "I'm going to the pony yard."

Chapter Twenty-three
Creation

Every day before work, Aaron races to the yard, hoping to run into Rachel. She's never there. Someone said she's scared to leave the house after the accident and won't be at the pony yard for another few weeks, so he waters the ponies for her and looks after the place as best as he can.

Life feels so different now, and he commands a respect from his stepbrothers that he can barely comprehend. After returning from collecting glass in the city with a strangely calm Lijah, Aaron's welcomed by Suzan, who hands him a rag to wipe his hands on. Soon a plate of food is pushed in front of him and they eat silently before sorting the garbage. Their hovel has become a place of peace, order, and routine. Everyone says that's because there's a woman in the family again. Even Youssa's happy to do what he's told, emptying the buckets and fetching the bread from the baker, which he never did before.

The sound of neighbors chatting wakes Aaron the next morning. He turns over on the floor in the open room and breathes in a smell of dead flowers drifting from the nearest rubbish bag. He stretches his arms and blinks at Youssa, curled up in a ball next to him, then watches as Suzan and Lijah hurry down the concrete steps ready for a brand-new day. When Lijah tries to hoick wax from his ear with a finger, Suzan shakes her head and, when he grins, smacks his hand.

Lijah seems to like being bossed about. Suzan's given him a reason to behave and his eyes don't leave her side as she kicks Youssa and Aaron to get up. She's desperate to fling their mats in the alley so she can sweep her beloved floor. There's hardly any sticky slop here anymore, or any noises coming from the two-room hovel next door, which is still empty.

Quick as a flash, Aaron's on his feet and off through the alleys to fetch the pony. He picks up a discarded computer cable in his way and throws it at the sky. It whizzes to life for a moment before landing on the top of a garbage heap.

The last person he's expecting to bump into is Rachel.

Aaron pinches himself at the sight of her standing with her back to him. Her bare foot isn't in a cast and, by the looseness of her galabeya, neither is her leg. She's filling the water trough with the leaking green hose. Struck by the amazement of seeing her, Aaron forgets who he is—where he is.

Time stops. The world stops. His heart stops.

The flood of sunshine on her coppery hair makes him feel in and out of his body. At first she doesn't see him because she's humming along to the trickling water, but then she senses someone watching and turns round sharply.

"Aaron?" She drops the hose and limps a few steps.

"I wanted to see you. I was looking for you," he blurts out.

She smiles and all awareness of the trough, hose, yard, ponies, sunshine—everything but her smile—fades from Aaron's eyes. He sees nothing but her. Her heart-shaped face, perfect mouth and long neck.

"You looked after the ponies," Rachel says, and grins. "In hospital I had a dream you came to see me. When I woke up I couldn't open my eyes or move. I tried to say something but nothing came out. It was so weird."

The vision from the hospital of her half-submerged body floating in clouds flashes through Aaron's mind. "Once I dreamed I saw my mother in heaven," he said. "I knew she was dead but we just talked like she was alive."

Rachel nods. "That happened to me with Fatima. Only she was with all these people who were smiling, like they were expecting me. Do you think you know when you're dead?"

"I hope I don't," Aaron says. "Did you hear Lijah's married now?"

"Yeah, to Suzan." She looks serious for a moment. "I'm getting married."

Aaron freezes. "Why?"

"Because if I die it's better to have a husband around to bury you. It's more romantic than your father," she says.

Aaron's heart sinks. All of a sudden it feels as if an angry, yelling mob is charging through his body. He can hardly breathe, let alone look at her.

Her eyelashes flicker as if she's teasing him, but he knows she isn't.

A pony whinnies suddenly, as if to remind Aaron to attach the cart and hurry back to collect Lijah. He glances at the spot where the reject perfume bottles are buried and the earth blazes as if it's on fire. In a daze, he fixes his eyes on the pony, determined to walk past Rachel without looking sad, roll out the cart, and get going.

Rachel shakes hair around her shoulders as he works and fidgets, watching his every move.

"Jacob told me you like me," she says at last. "Do you?"

"What?" Aaron starts, his cheeks flushing hot.

Thanks, Jacob.

He's not going to answer that. Now, when she marries Sami, everyone will stare at Aaron to see how he's taking it. A jarring ache in his chest makes him tremble as he brings the cart to the track, swiftly attaches it to the pony, and loops the reins over its neck. As he's about to climb up, he becomes aware of an intense sensation that Rachel's close by. Full sunlight on her glittering face—she's only an inch away. The soul of her eyes sink into him and the silence overpowers them both until she eventually blinks.

"I was thinking of marrying . . . *you*," she says softly.

Every emotion explodes in Aaron.

"You . . . were?"

Happiness, shock, and disbelief rise in a dangerous current that speeds through his body. At last it slowly dawns on him that she actually likes him.

"I was thinking . . . hoping . . . the same!" he gulps. "What about Sami? I thought you . . ."

The pony nudges Aaron's back impatiently. Eternity is a long time and that's how long Rachel's smile seems to last before she replies.

"Nah. He's ten years older than me. You and me are the same age—nearly. We understand each other. Don't we?"

Aaron nods. There's fire in his belly. A feeling he can't control. There's the small chance of a kiss hovering on Rachel's lips and he wants to tell her about the empty house that's next door to Lijah's, but the sound of footsteps forces them to glance at the track, where someone's hurrying to collect his cart.

"I better go," Aaron says.

Rachel squeezes their secret into his hand as he tugs the reins. With an indescribable feeling of liberation, bliss, joy, peace, perfect everything, Aaron stares dumbly ahead as he rides the cart at a gentle pace to collect Lijah. However it happened—it happened. Rachel is his. But then . . . the worrying thought occurs to him that if Rachel discovers the buried perfume bottles she might change her mind. What if it rains and the bottles are revealed? Aaron pushes the picture out of his mind. It's too terrifying to think about.

An hour later Aaron and Lijah approach the first alley

in Cairo and, from the way Aaron leaps off the cart to begin work, Lijah notices a new, charged electricity in him. No longer prepared to haul the rest of the gluey filth home before separating the glass, he does two jobs at the same time, flinging glass into one bag and food slop, rags, plastic, cans, and packets into the other as fast as he can.

Instead of taking the pony around the roundabout twice and then returning to fetch him, Lijah leans forward on the hard wooden bench to watch Aaron pick out sharp pieces of broken glass as if they're feathers. Tossing them into the bag as if he's on a mission to create a tinkling, crashing, musical racket. For the first time Lijah realizes how expert Aaron is at fishing out cracked vases, mirrors, wine glasses, beer, and soda bottles. Watching him reminds Lijah of something he'd forgotten: how he always hated Aaron and his mother for the loving bond they had. The way she looked at him. The memory stirs sympathy for Aaron. Stirs sympathy for himself and his own mother, who died when he was nine, and a surprising flicker of shame lodges in him for the way he's treated his stepbrother.

By the time Aaron's on the cart, with traffic beeping and echoing around him, he's out of breath.

"Here," Lijah says—the first word he's spoken all morning.

In his hand is a plastic bottle of iced water. Aaron spots the street hawker with his cool bag nearby and with complete shock takes the much-needed drink from Lijah's clammy hand.

"Thanks."

Swiftly Aaron bites off the blue lid and glugs the icy water, which bubbles in his throat, forcing him to slow down while he gazes at the calm face of the stepbrother he once dreamed of poisoning. It's the first act of kindness that Lijah's ever shown him, but by the look of him it won't be the last. Then Lijah mutters something so surprising, Aaron almost drops the bottle.

"The first love is the greatest love of all."

It sounds as if Lijah's talking to himself. Aaron doesn't want to chance his luck by saying the wrong thing, so all he does is smile and nod as if Lijah's right. Maybe the priest had a word with him after he lost control of the bike and nearly killed Rachel. Or perhaps he's so in love with Suzan, she's all he thinks about. Either way, it's good news for Aaron, though he knows Lijah might be different tomorrow.

Aaron swigs the last of the water and throws the bottle at the bags behind him. With a flash of inspiration he decides to leave the reject perfume bottles hidden in their burial chamber. No amount of rain and mud will uncover them, he stacked them too deep. From now on, he'll try hard to tell the truth and never steal again.

A bright moon blinks when, later that day, crazy in love, Aaron sits back to watch the sky sprinkled with stars. He gazes at Rachel and it seems as if the whole world is smiling. Now he knows, sometimes the person you love loves you back. For now that huge, warm feeling is enough to give him the courage to face whatever comes next.

A magnetic sensation draws Aaron's hand to his pocket. His fingers clasp the final perfume bottle, the one he's kept back that's been his secret medicine—the remedy to all his problems.

"I meant to give this back to the shop," he says.

Rachel takes the rose-colored bottle and immediately twists the stopper off to sniff before dabbing her wrists and neck.

"Let's smell it." Abe is suddenly beside them.

Rachel hands him the perfume bottle, then digs in her pocket for the crumpled picture she tore from a magazine in the hospital.

"I've got something for you, Abe," she says.

Abe pulls a face at the sickly smell and passes the bottle to Aaron, before rubbing the creases from the magazine page with his knuckles. "Wow! It's a see-through moon jellyfish!"

He wanders off, eyes down, while Aaron holds the glass up to catch the real moon above.

"Look," Aaron says. "You can see things differently whenever you want."

Rachel squints through the glass and a door opens to her imagination, which changes the blurry moon to a bird with a thousand pearly wings.

Chapter Twenty-four
Gifts

After the wedding, Farah, an elderly neighbor, gave the first gift: a wooden food box with two shiny metal hinges and a lid sprayed by Jacob with a red heart. Shareen's old home now belongs to Aaron and Rachel and the stepfamily's rubbish bags fill the open downstairs room. Upstairs, the mats, the green dividing curtain, the pillowcase with the curvy belly dancer, and the poster of the Cairo International Stadium have disappeared. Instead, the food box takes pride of place next to the sink. Along with a new gray mat, striped mattress, cotton sheets, and fluffy pillows, for which Rachel's father somehow managed to pay.

All day long people came with arms full of gifts. Harun, the laundry man, arrived with a cotton tablecloth with lace edges. Next Fatima with the Filthy Mouth rushed in with a bag of hibiscus tea that she could ill afford to give away.

Leya, Rachel's aunt, brought dried tamarinds, salt, and sugar. Father Peter blessed the house and Noha gave them a box of pistachio nuts. Michael and Inga brought a blue glass vase and placed it on the ledge of the glassless window.

"To catch your sunlit dreams every morning and hold them there forever," Michael said.

Habi, the greengrocer, filled the food box with bananas, oranges, pomegranates, mangoes, and lemons—enough to feed the whole of Mokattam. Sami gave them a second-hand broom. Abe and his mother handed over a thick bundle of cinnamon sticks and the Mebaj brothers gave them two brand-new matching saucepans with lids. Ahmet offered them a car magazine he'd loved and kept for many years, which they refused to take. People Aaron and Rachel hardly know turned up with nuts, flour, and butter.

Youssa, Lijah, and Suzan greeted everyone and behaved like the family Aaron had always hoped for, but one person— Mahir, Shareen's father—failed to appear at the wedding and no one has seen him for quite a while.

By the time dusk dawns on the sixteenth day of their married life, Aaron decides to visit Mahir. But he must take him a gift after all this time.

Aaron opens the food box and screws up his face with disappointment to see that most of their wedding presents have gone. They eat their meals with his stepfamily and have shared everything with them and their close neighbors. All that's left is a bag of sugar and half a packet of dried tamarinds. Aaron knows Rachel won't mind if he takes them. No one has a sweeter, kinder nature than her.

Tucking them under his arm, Aaron races down the stairs and he's off along the alley, jumping over rotting food and leaking bags, all the while shaking away the remembered smell of medical waste as he makes for the tenement where Mahir now lives with his sister. But the person in the doorway isn't old man Mahir. It's Jacob and he's fiddling with a white spray can that has lost its squirter.

"Hey, friend." Jacob slaps him on the back and flashes his big yellow teeth.

"How's it going?" Aaron asks, glad to see the whites of Jacob's eyes are clear today. He looks well for a change.

"I've gone back to medical-wasting." Jacob glances at the can for a second. "But Mom only lets me sit on the cart now. I'm not allowed to collect or touch any of the stuff. Karim my cousin does it and watches me all the time. They seem to think I'm into drugs or something. You should tell them, Aaron. I'd never do that."

Aaron doesn't want to get into this. "By the looks of it, your skin's cleared up."

"Yeah, I'm fine." Jacob's eyes light up. "Do you know anyone who might want to marry me?"

Aaron grins. This feels more like the old Jacob. "What about Constance, Shareen's old friend?"

"She's nice, but I think she likes Malik. He's much better-looking than me. Did I tell you Constance said her dad saw Shareen with a man nearly as old as Daniel, selling knockoffs near the museum?"

"Really?"

"Yeah. Anyway, do you think I stand a chance with Constance?" Jacob looks hopefully at him.

"Only if you look after yourself," Aaron says firmly.

Jacob stares at him, knowing what he says is true.

"Fancy sitting on the wall?" he asks.

"I'm going to see Shareen's dad. I'll see you later." Aaron smiles warmly. "You're still my best friend."

With that, he heads up the stairs to Mahir's sister's home feeling about a million years older than Jacob.

The door to number twelve is wide open. There's the usual smell of decaying food and rotting garbage from the rubbish bags that fill every inch of the room, apart from the cooking area and small space left in the middle for sitting. Scrawny Mahir is on the floor, cutting lengths of twine with a blunt knife from a ball in his lap. At first he doesn't notice Aaron, but then he turns around sharply.

Aaron nervously greets the old man by smiling and nodding several times before approaching him slowly with the bag of sugar in one hand and half a packet of dried tamarinds in the other.

"It's good to see you, Mahir. I hope you are well."

"Put them there." Mahir gestures to the sink, which is crammed with damp washing.

Aaron looks around for somewhere safe to put the food and spots the metal box underneath the clothes hanging over the sink. There's so much rice and flour in there that he has trouble closing the lid. He wipes his forehead with a wrist, worried that rats will slip through the tiny gap he's left.

Quickly, he rearranges a flour bag until it's flat enough to allow him to slam the lid down, all the while feeling slightly angry with himself. He should have kept the sugar and dried tamarinds, because this family clearly has tons of food to last until the merchant comes in a few days' time, while his family has nothing left. On the other hand it's important to show respect by bringing a small gift when you visit an older member of the community.

Mahir sniffs and bores into the ball of twine with the blunt knife, a pained expression on his face. Aaron doesn't know what to do now. Mahir clearly has nothing to say to him. Not even a thank-you. Well, at least he tried. He's about to leave when Mahir drops the knife and looks him up and down.

"Don't have children. They bring you nothing but misery."

His dark eyes reveal a sadness that stabs Aaron through the heart. What can he say to that?

"I got a message from her," Mahir says, pulling a piece of lined yellow paper from his pocket. He carefully unfolds each crumpled square before reading it out in a cracked, chesty voice: "I'm never coming back. I hate Mokattam. I hate you for making me marry Daniel. I hate him. Hate him. Hate him. Make sure you tell him."

"She doesn't mean it," Aaron tries. "She wrote it when she was angry. You know how she is when she loses her temper. She yells, but then she forgets all about it. Shareen's like that. You know she is. She hasn't changed. Anyway, she only hates you for making her marry Daniel. Nothing else."

Mahir sniffs and his eyes brighten for a second.

"I hadn't thought of it like that. It's true there are some fires that not even marriage can put out, son."

Son? Mahir called him son.

Like a son, Aaron makes his way to the door with Mahir's eyes still on him. The throbbing warmth of that word stays with Aaron as he makes his way down the filthy tenement stairs and into the lane. Jacob has gone. Another day is almost over and he has lovely Rachel to go home to.

Calm, peaceful Rachel. Shareen is out there somewhere and Aaron hopes she's happy, because he is, and in a way he has Shareen to thank for that.

―――――――――

How Aaron feels is full-up, sitting with his back to the rubbish bags in the downstairs room with his feet in the lane.

"What are you thinking?" Rachel asks.

"I'm just remembering how lucky I am." Aaron turns to smile at her.

"Me too," she says.

"We like it here, don't we?" he says.

"We do!" Rachel giggles. "I really like saying 'we this'— 'we that' . . ."

At that moment, Ishaq, the icon seller, and Sulayman, the metal worker, walk past and nod to them with huge smiles. Ishaq's wife, Parvin, is becoming a close friend of Rachel's. Then Hafeez, a neighbor, coughs long and hard and waves as he tosses burned coffee from a tin mug into the lane.

They watch the brown liquid trickle between a squashed cigarette carton and a moth-eaten green lampshade.

These are his people.

Finally, a feeling of absolute, overwhelming, complete love that Aaron never thought he'd feel is amazingly, truly, and wildly his.

Author's Note

After being sent an article about the Zabbaleen—a community of mostly Coptic Christians living in Cairo who collect and recycle eighty percent of the city's trash—I decided to visit the city.

My sister happily agreed to come with me, and I hired a translator to take us to Mokattam, the abandoned-quarry home of the Zabbaleen. The translator kindly brought us black galabeyas to wear as a mark of respect and to help us gain better access to this fairly closed community. I loved wearing the galabeya. Until then, I had no idea how comfortable and freeing the flowing black dress was, and, from the quiet acknowledgements of the local people we passed, how thrilling it would feel to be accepted by them.

The surprises continued when the sheer horror of living among thousands of tons of stinking, decaying garbage sank in, as did the poverty, hard work, and continual threat of disease that accompany the Zabbaleen's every breath. I tried to feel my way into their lives while noting the surroundings and it was both a shocking and a liberating experience, because this despised and hidden society does more to help their world than most people realize. But where was the story I hoped to write?

An elder met us at the magical, stunning church of St. Sama'an—a pristine oasis surrounded by filth. He kindly answered my endless questions and, later on, as I stood beside the nearby low wall and looked out over hundreds and hundreds of roofless tenements, I picked this as the location for my story, even though the main character didn't yet exist in my mind.

It's a common sight to see the Zabbaleen going about their business in the streets of Cairo, but Aaron sprang to life only after I noticed a boy of about fifteen, his hair, face, hands, and old sweatshirt and jeans covered with quarry dust, coming down the middle of four lanes of beeping cars, buses, and taxis in a pony cart piled with trash. What struck me about this particular Zabbaleen teenager was that despite the manic traffic crashing past, he wore a look of complete bliss on his round face that I'll never forget. He was absolutely still inside, in a way that's rare to witness these days, and it was this luminous peace that inspired the creation of Aaron and his love of glass.

The Zabbaleen are under extreme pressure from problems caused by misapprehension about the spread of swine flu, the expansion of Cairo's fleet of rubbish trucks, and the fact that they are beholden to unscrupulous merchants who make a killing out of the glass, metal, rags, and paper that they recycle.

I set *The Glass Collector* around the time President Obama made his first presidential speech on the Middle East in Cairo, June 2009. The title of his speech was "A New Beginning," and the irony of those words was something I wanted to explore by providing a glimpse of Aaron's life as a waste-collector. The Egyptian dictator, Hosni Mubarrak, had been in power since 1981, and all sections of Egyptian society had suffered under his rule. The Arab Spring revolution ousted him in February 2011, just two weeks before *The Glass Collector* was released in England.

The revolution brought Muslims and Coptic Christians together in Tahrir Square to demonstrate against the abuse and corruption of Mubarak's presidency. Sadly, in the months that have followed, there have been a few violent divisions between the two communities and the situation remains volatile.

Despite the pressures and tensions, there exists a vibrant, united, and useful society among the Zabbaleen people, and many in the West could learn a great deal from them.